CORRUPT EDUCATOR

THE SYNDICATE ACADEMY

BIANCA COLE

CONTENTS

1. Oak — 1
2. Eva — 11
3. Oak — 23
4. Eva — 35
5. Oak — 47
6. Eva — 61
7. Oak — 73
8. Eva — 85
9. Oak — 97
10. Eva — 107
11. Oak — 121
12. Eva — 131
13. Oak — 139
14. Eva — 149
15. Oak — 159
16. Eva — 169
17. Oak — 179
18. Eva — 189
19. Oak — 199
20. Eva — 209
21. Oak — 219
22. Eva — 231
23. Oak — 243
24. Eva — 257
25. Oak — 269
26. Eva — 277
27. Oak — 287
28. Eva — 299

29. Oak	309
30. Eva	323
31. Oak	339
32. Eva	351
33. Oak	361
34. Eva	371
35. Epilogue	383
Also by Bianca Cole	397
About the Author	399

Corrupt Educator Copyright © 2022 Bianca Cole

All Rights Reserved.
No part of this publication may be reproduced, stored, or transmitted in any form or by any means, electronic, mechanical, photocopying, recording, scanning, or otherwise without written permission from the publisher. It is illegal to copy this book, post it to a website, or distribute it by any other means without permission.

This novel is entirely a work of fiction. The names, characters and incidents portrayed in it are the work of the author's imagination. Any resemblance to actual persons, living or dead, events or localities is entirely coincidental.

Warning: the unauthorized reproduction or distribution of this copyrighted work is illegal. Criminal copyright infringement, including infringement without monetary gain, is investigated by the FBI and is punishable by up to 5 years in prison and a fine of $250,000.

Book cover design by Deliciously Dark Designs

Photography: Wander Aguiar Photography

1

OAK

The creek of metal bowing under extreme heat echoes through the night air, pushing me to run harder.

Fire.

The smoke billows in ominous clouds over the building, foreshadowing the darkness of the future, my future.

Ash.

As I round the corner and the building appears, all the air escapes from my lungs. The spark of blazing flames licks at the building's windows with a ferocity that looks untameable as the fire engulfs my entire life's work.

Ruin.

My legs ache from running the mile to the building as I struggle to draw clean air into my lungs. The smoke infects it like a disease, penetrating my lungs as rapidly as it destroys everything I've worked to build.

I'm too late.

It has spread to every part of the office block, including the top floor housing the server room, which is the hub and heart of my corporation. The sirens pierce through the air, nearing me and my headquarters, but I realize there's no hope. If the fire reaches the server room, my entire life's work is destroyed.

All I can do is watch as my empire burns to the ground. The Archer sign creaks violently as the inferno bends the steel, leaving it hanging onto the side of the building by a thread.

The corrupt assholes behind the fire have torn everything from me over one pitiful argument. I didn't want to provide my services to gangsters, as my business is legitimate, and that's how I wanted to keep it, but they wanted me to pay protection money to them. So, they've ripped it all from me for saying *no*.

Archer Data corporation's secure servers and entire net worth are in that building. We have nothing if the fire makes it into the server room. The Carmichael clan did this to me. They tore everything I built away from me at the flick of a switch.

My body shudders as I clench my fists by my side, longing to hit something or somebody. I grind my teeth together so forcefully it feels like I might shatter them as I stare at the destruction they've left in their wake. The crinkling of the paper between my fingers brings my attention to the letter they posted through my letterbox on Carmichael Enterprises' letter-headed paper.

Your empire will burn for this.

The second I heard my letterbox at this hour, I was sure it would be them after Jamie Carmichael's threat at our meeting two days ago.

Comply or suffer, Brett. It's your decision. We run this city, and no one gets by without paying their fair share. I will ruin you if you don't.

My refusal to work with criminals led to my destruction, but what man wouldn't fight against criminals?

People I despise. When I was old enough, I ran from the same type of people, leaving my home country behind and changing my name, establishing something on my own from scratch.

My name on the building, Archer, finally crumples under the heat as the last thread of steel holding it to the office snaps. I growl as it scrapes down the side of the building, screeching as it shatters the windows.

There's a darkness inside of me, which I've tried for a long time to bury, but it is tugging at my insides, longing to break free and wreak havoc on the Carmichael Clan. I may not be a criminal, but darkness reigns inside of me.

When I left the office, Jane told me she'd be working late tonight, but hopefully not this late. It's past two o'clock. Jane has worked at Archer Data Corp for seven years, and in all that time, I've ignored the cosmic pull between us, knowing that it's inappropriate for the

CEO to date his staff. My tastes in sex aren't conventional, and she wouldn't understand the darkness that resides in me. She couldn't have truly loved a man like me.

I shake my head, convincing myself she can't be inside. It's too late. She would have been long gone.

The police cars and fire department race into the parking lot, distracting me from my thoughts. They'll no doubt ask me to leave the scene, but I can't. My world is crumbling in front of my eyes.

One of the police officers exits the vehicle and approaches me. "Sir, are you the one that called us?"

I nod in reply. "Yes, this is my company's headquarters."

He nods. "Can I take your name, please?"

"Brett Oakley Archer."

The police officer scribbles my name on his notepad. "Thank you. How did you learn of the fire?"

My heart stutters in my chest as I fist the paper in my hand. The Carmichaels have the law enforcement in their pockets, so I won't tell him about the note. The only way to beat them is to play their game. I shake my head. "I went for a walk. I live a mile away, and I noticed the smoke coming from my building. That's when I rang."

He scribbles my account down before nodding. "Thank you. You're welcome to remain on this side of the barrier we're erecting. I assume no one is inside at night?"

"The cleaners work overnight. I don't know their schedules, though."

He glances at his watch. "Can you find out for me? We need to know if we may encounter civilians."

I pull my cell phone out of my pocket and call Jane's number. She should have those details with her. My stomach churns as it rings a few times before switching to voicemail.

"Jane, call me back. The office is on fire." I cancel the call, my hands shaking from a mix of shock and panic.

Numbness spreads through me like a disease, as I consider she may be inside. All those times that I refused her advances, all because I was too hell-bent on building my empire.

What if it's too late?

I ring Doris, my secretary, to check if she knows. She answers on the second dial tone, her voice sleepy. "Sir, what is it?"

"The building is on fire. Could anyone be in there?"

"How awful." She rummages around, and there's a click as she turns on a light. "The cleaners show up at about three o'clock."

"Jane mentioned she'd be working late, but I'd guess she'd be home by now, right?" I ask, swallowing hard.

Doris sucks in a worried breath. "Oh no, Jane regularly stayed in the early hours of the morning. I hope she isn't, but it's not impossible, Mr. Archer."

My hand tightens around my cell phone. "Thank you. Can you do me a favor?"

"Of course, anything, sir."

I clench my jaw. "Can you call the cleaning agency and call them off tonight for me?"

"Yes, I'll do it right now, sir."

"Thanks, Doris. Nobody will need to come in tomorrow.

"Leave it to me. I'll handle it, sir."

I cancel the call, feeling panic take hold of me again that Jane might be in the building. I'll never forgive those fucking Carmichaels if they took her from me.

The officer I spoke to earlier is lingering near the barrier they erected. "I have spoken to my secretary, and the cleaners come in at three o'clock. She's calling them off now."

He nods. "No one should be inside the building."

"The only person was my recruitment officer. She said she was working late, but I'd assume not this late." I swallow hard, glancing at the raging fire engulfing the building. "I haven't been able to get hold of her."

The officer nods. "Okay, I'll warn the fire department that there's a chance of one civilian."

I step back, staring at the shell of a building as the fire rages. It's at least half an hour until it appears like the firefighters are winning the fight.

The radio crackles on the officer's belt. "Body found, but no pulse. Ensure the paramedics are ready."

He takes it and replies. "Copy that."

My world spirals as I move toward him. "Who is it?"

He holds a hand up. "Stay there."

I glare at the man, scanning the office entrance, knowing deep down that it's her. Jane.

Three firefighters come out, and one of them carries a slim, lithe body slumped over his shoulder.

I rush forward. "Jane!" I shout, breaking through the tape to get through to her. The glimpse of burned bright blonde hair is the biggest giveaway that it is her.

"Mr. Archer," the police officer calls out to me, trying to stop me. There's nobody that could stop me as I sprint toward them, making the firefighter's eyes widen. "Stay back," One of them orders.

"I need to know who it is. Is she dead?" I say.

He gestures to the paramedics' ambulance. "Wait over there, please."

I swallow hard and do as he says, approaching the ambulance. They have a body bag ready, making the dark dread root even deeper into my soul.

"I don't think you should be here," the paramedic says.

I shake my head. "I own the company. Who is dead?"

The paramedic nods. "Okay, wait here."

The firefighter comes closer with the body and sets her down inside the open body bag. My stomach churns the moment I see her face. It feels like someone has punched me in the gut as I look at her serene, beautiful features burned and blackened by the fire.

"No," I cry, rushing forward.

The paramedic allows me to move toward her.

"Jane, I'm so sorry," I say, running my hand through her beautiful golden hair. A lump wedges in my throat so hard I can no longer speak. Tears flood down my cheeks as the impact of her loss hits me harder than the loss of my empire, which is proof I have been a fool staying away from her.

I never took her on a date, never kissed her beautiful lips, never had the warmth of her against me. I clench my fists by my side as grief twists into a fierce rage.

I bend down and whisper into her ear, even though she can't hear me, "I'll make them pay for this, Jane. I promise." A complex web of emotions flow through me as anger, guilt, and grief threaten to shred me apart at the seams.

The Carmichael clan is the most influential criminal organization in the state, which means I need to flee Georgia tonight if I stand a chance of getting revenge. The insurance will cover the fire damage, but Archer Data Corp will be in ruins once news spreads about the destruction of the servers.

"Sir, I apologize, but we require you to step away." A firm hand lands on my shoulder as I clutch onto Jane's freezing hand. As I stare at her, I realize I won't be able to attend her funeral. I have to leave now if I want to disappear.

I let go of her hand, tearing my eyes away from her beautiful face. Slowly, I step away, knowing this is the last time I'll see her. The last time I'll stand on Atlanta soil. I trust Eric, the company president, to handle the insurance company and fallout.

As of tonight, Brett Archer no longer exists. I will disappear off the face of this earth, untraceable. The Carmichaels won't find me until it's too late. I will tear their world down and hurt them ten times worse than they've hurt me.

Tonight, Brett Oakley Archer died. I have to become someone else for the second time in my twenty-eight years on this earth.

2

EVA

Five years later…

"I swear that isn't me," I say, standing in front of my father, who is holding a photo of someone who looks remarkably like me kissing the high school janitor. "Someone must have photoshopped it."

For a start, I don't think I've ever even spoken to the high school janitor in my life. As I stare at the photo, the sight of him churns my stomach. Not that I'm vain, but he's certainly not a man I'd be attracted to, weighing probably a hundred pounds more than he should and less hair on his head than I have on my legs.

Second, I've never kissed a boy in my life, let alone some random, balding, middle-aged man. It's hard to believe they think that's me.

"Eva Carmichael. You almost brought utter ruin on our family," my mother chides, shaking her head in the corner. "Don't think we're stupid enough to believe that isn't you." She steps forward and glares at me with her hard, stony expression. "How long has it been going on?"

I stare at my mother, dumbfounded, wondering if she believes I'd be in a relationship with the high school janitor. "I don't even know the guy." My parents are pathetic, as I don't have time for men.

I focus all my energy on my schoolwork, as I need to get into the best school I can to become a vet, much to their disgust. Even though they insist that will never happen, as my destiny is to inherit the family business, I plan to escape their grasp and follow my dreams.

My father slams a hand down on the desk. "Eva, don't lie to us," he roars. The look in his eyes is vicious. "You're eighteen years old. It's about time you took responsibility for your actions."

I swallow hard, trying to force the lump in my throat away. I hate that both my parents think I'm guilty of this.

"Did you sleep with him?" my mother asks, making heat spread over every inch of my skin.

"No," I cry, shaking my head. "I didn't even fucking kiss him."

"Language, Eva," my father quips. "I'm fed up with this." He glances at my mother. "I think you're right. We have no choice."

I glance between my mother and father, wondering what he means. "What are you talking about?"

My mom shakes her head. "It will be brutal, but I think she needs to learn a brutal lesson."

I swallow hard. "Would you stop talking about me as if I'm not even here?"

My father meets my gaze. "We're sending you to The Syndicate Academy in Maine," he deadpans.

It feels like my parents rip the ground from under my feet. "That's a thousand miles from here. From my friends," I protest, even though I don't have many friends here in Atlanta. "What the hell?"

My father stands, towering over me in all his height and grandeur. "You will go without another word. You're a Carmichael, and it's about time you learn what that means." He glances at my mother. "The only way for you to learn is to attend school with people like you."

I clench my fists by my side. "You mean the offspring of other criminals?" I shake my head. "I want nothing to do with your disgusting business."

My mother steps toward me and grabs my wrist forcefully. "Watch what you say, Eva. I can cut you off faster than you can walk out of this room."

I narrow my eyes at her. That's what I count on. My only crime is that I've been taking the blood money my parents give me monthly and saving all of it in a bank account they have no access to, which will be my college tuition. However, I'm not ready to draw that card yet.

I know their plan for me. My parents want me to marry a mob boss and allow another criminal to take over the family business, starting the cycle again. It's never-ending. There's no way I will continue it and force my future children into such a terrible existence.

Someone has to break the cycle, and I intend to be the one to end the tyranny finally.

MY HEART FLUTTERS in my chest as I stare up at the dark, intimidating building. Its cold stone and harsh lines only foreshadow what's waiting for me inside. The columns that flank the entryway all along the many meters of facade only add to its imposing effect.

I swallow hard, realizing I'm about to enroll in a school full of the spawn of murderous criminals who are probably exactly like my parents. "Please don't leave me here, mother," I say, pleading at her with my eyes.

Her expression hardens as she glares at me with no emotion whatsoever. "The Syndicate Academy is the perfect place for you to learn discipline, Eva." She tucks a stray strand of her hair behind her ear. "You need to learn what kind of behavior we expect of you as the *sole* heir to the Carmichael Clan." I hate when my mother calls me the sole heir, as all it does is remind me of my loss—our loss, and yet the way she says it, you'd think her child wasn't dead and buried.

Karl, my older brother, died two years ago. Unlike me, he took to the life of crime like a duck to water. Unfortunately, that was his undoing. At eighteen years old, he orchestrated a drug heist, trying to impress our poor excuse of a father, and the unruly bikers in Atlanta murdered him.

Despite our differences, I loved him more than anyone else. His death ripped a hole inside of me and left me as the sole heir to the Carmichael Clan, which means my parents will force me into an arranged marriage to some evil criminal mastermind who can carry on the family business since women *can't* possibly rule alone.

The criminal underworld still won't accept women as leaders in the twenty-first century. They plan to sell me off to someone who will benefit their business, but I have no intention of complying.

My mother clicks her tongue. "Come on. Principal Byrne is waiting for us."

Her high-heels clack against the stone of the steps as she rises toward the entrance of the gothic building. "Hurry now, Eva," she says, glancing over her shoulder.

I draw in a deep, steadying gulp of oxygen before stepping onto the first step. The towering arched entrance is ominous as I walk through it. Deep down, I'd hoped the cold, harsh exterior was only a front, but the walls of stone line the plain, bare corridors inside too. My mother's heels echo as follows the signs toward the principal's office.

"Keep up, Eva," she calls.

I hasten my steps after my mom, pulling my

cardigan more tightly around me. It's cold inside my new high school.

Who the fuck starts a new high school seven months from the end of their senior year?

It's insane. Although not as insane that my parents believe I've been sleeping with the janitor. My father even accused me of attempting to fall pregnant to ruin the family. It offends me they think I'd be stupid enough to get pregnant, even if I were sleeping with him. I have no intention of ruining my life before it's even started. Even so, it didn't stop my mother from dragging me straight to the doctor to have a birth control implant inserted in my arm. My plans don't involve a baby. They involve going to college and getting a veterinary degree.

My mother and father have controlled my life in every way since I can remember, forcing me to attend an all-girls school from primary age, so I don't get why they'd send me to a Co-Ed school now. They wanted to ensure I had no interaction with boys, but now they think I've stooped so low as to fall into the arms of my high school janitor.

The guy was also double my age. He's now been fired for something he didn't do, and my parents have flown me thousands of miles from my home. I don't know what's more offensive, they think I would prioritize a man over my studies, or they think my standards are that low.

Mother stops outside a door with Principal Oakley

Byrne's name carved into a brass plaque. She knocks confidently.

"Come in," a deep voice replies. A voice that sends shivers down my spine.

There is something unnerving about this school. I felt a sense of unease the moment I stepped over the threshold, but I can't put my finger on why. Perhaps it's the gothic style columns and dark stone that remind me of something out of a horror movie. It makes me feel like I'm entering somewhere dangerous.

My mother twists the doorhandle and swings open the door, stepping inside.

My heart hammers in my ears as I stare into the gloomy depths of the office in front of me. A sense of impending doom coils through me as I feel like I'm about to be thrown to the wolves.

"Come along, Eva," my mother calls.

I force one foot in front of the other and step into the dark office. It takes my eyes a moment to adjust. And then, it feels like my heart stops beating entirely. A pair of striking aquamarine eyes gaze at me. The man they belong to stands, drawing my attention to the bulging muscles straining against his simple white dress shirt. He has to be about six foot five tall as he towers over the desk. "Mrs. Carmichael, I presume?" he asks my mother, but his eyes don't move from me for a second.

"Yes, I'm ever so sorry that we're late, Principal Byrne." My mother shoots me an irritated glare as if it's my fault our flight was delayed. "Unfortunately, you're going to have your hands full with this one."

Unbelievable.

I'm being punished for something I didn't do. I've ensured I never stepped one toe out of line my entire life, and this is the thanks I get. They have uprooted me and turned my life upside down because of one stupid prank. As it is the only plausible explanation that I could come up with, Casey Hogan, my arch-nemesis in my previous high school, set me up with the photoshopped image.

The principal, who shouldn't be a principal at all, as he looks like a male model, continues to stare at me with an intensity that makes my stomach flutter. It's as if he is waiting for me to cower and break his gaze. "No student is too challenging for me." His voice is deep and as smooth as butter. This man is not your average principal, but the Syndicate Academy is not your average high school, from what I have read in the prospectus my mother gave me.

My mom laughs, and it's the fakest laugh I've ever heard. "No, I believe that's true. Your reputation precedes you."

"Indeed," he answers, still staring at me as if weighing me up.

I take in his sharp, beautiful features. My eyes move from his dark, curling hair to his solid, powerful jaw, which is peppered in a short, well-groomed beard. It looks like a master sculptor painstakingly carved every one of his features. He's that perfect.

"Eva," my mother scolds. "Answer the principal."

I meet my mother's gaze, realizing I don't know what he said. "Sorry, what?"

"Do you see what we put up with?" She shakes her head. "Principal Bryne asked you whether you like the look of the grounds?"

I swallow hard, shrugging. "They look alright." For the first time since I stepped foot into his office, I move my eyes away from his. The heat blazing through my body is impossible to ignore.

He clears his throat and moves his intense, brooding gaze to my mother. "How are Eva's academic abilities?"

Surely that's a question he could ask me. My mom opens her mouth to reply, but I cut in quicker. "I'm top of my class in all subjects." I keep my chin high and meet his intimidating gaze.

"She is, but that's not why she's here. We need her to learn discipline and stay out of trouble until she graduates." My mother clears her throat. "We can't have her ruin our reputation."

I give up with my parents. They don't trust me at all, despite never giving them a reason not to. Although, if they knew my ultimate plan to cut ties with them, they'd never trust me again. The moment some bitch at my school sets me up, they believe doctored evidence instantly.

"Of course not. Students in similar situations will provide Eva a good example to follow." His eyes flicker with an evil glint that sends shivers down my spine as he returns his attention to me. "There's a strict separation between the girls and boys in attendance during recreational times, as the boy's dorm is in a separate building entirely." He glances at me. "We also keep a strict watch on our staff."

Heat slams into me as I glance at my mother, realizing she told him what *supposedly* happened. "It's all bullshit that I kissed the janitor," I blurt out, making my mother gasp at my use of foul language. "Someone photoshopped the image, and my parents are too stupid to realize it." I'm not sure why I care what the principal thinks, anyway.

"Language, Eva. And don't speak of us with such disrespect." She raises her hand and slaps me hard across the face, something she likes to do to humiliate me, making a point in front of the principal.

I bring my hand up to my stinging face, grinding my teeth in annoyance.

When I glance back at the principal, there appears to be a glint of barely contained rage in his eyes as he glares at my mother.

Principal Bryne's expression turns severe as he tears his eyes off her and back to me. "I see what you mean. If Eva can't take responsibility for her actions, I'll teach her what happens to students who lie." My heart stills in my chest. There's a very serious threat in his tone, one which makes my gut churn with unease.

"I'm glad to hear it." My mother turns to me. "If I don't hear you're following every rule at this school, I will cut you off, regardless."

I don't respond to her, as I know it's an empty threat. My mother and father don't have any other heir, so their frequent promises to cut me off are bullshit, although I wish they weren't.

I want them to cut me off so I can follow my dream of becoming a vet. Even if they don't cut me off, I'm leaving and never looking back as soon as I've graduated from high school.

3

OAK

My nails bite into my palm as I clench my hands tightly, using the dull pain to control myself. There's a sinister part of me that craves to reach out, snatch Angela by her stupid ponytail, yank her over to me and wrap my hands around her throat until I crush the life out of her right in front of her daughter.

I close my eyes, drawing in a deep, calming breath. The mental picture of her life slipping from her eyes as I choke her while her daughter watches is satisfying, but it's not time.

There's a simmering inferno building under my skin, provoking the beast that lies in wait. Vengeance has never been this close. I can practically taste it on my tongue, but killing her here and now wouldn't come close to making her suffer enough.

Nothing short of deliberately and painfully

torturing her and her husband will suffice. When I've had my fun, I'll delight in obliterating the Carmichael family from the face of this earth.

"If that's all." She glances at her daughter. "Eva has a suitcase of belongings the chauffeur will bring in," Angela says.

I grit my teeth. "Yes, that's all." I gesture toward the door. "You may leave."

Angela's attention shifts to her daughter. "Behave." She turns around and strolls out of the office without a goodbye to Eva. Angela Carmichael is a selfish and heartless bitch, and I expect nothing else from a woman like her.

My gaze moves to Eva as her jaw clenches, and I notice a glimmer of anguish in her brilliant hazel eyes as she watches her mother walk away. I'd assumed that she may look like her mother, with those deep soulless brown eyes and jet black hair, but she is the opposite, with light hazel eyes and golden blonde hair that falls in waves around her shoulders.

The door slams behind Angela, reminding me I'm gawking at my pupil. It feels like talons rake down the inside of my body, trying to burst free as I allow Angela Carmichael to walk off campus alive. Five years I've waited to exact my revenge, and it hasn't been easy, even if I am a patient man.

I'm not surprised that Angela didn't recognize me. We met on one occasion, and I legally changed my name for the second time when I fled Atlanta five years ago. In the eyes of the law, I'm Oakley James Byrne rather than Brett Oakley Archer.

A name that has become second nature to me. Brett Archer died alone with Jane Williams and the Archer Data corp.

Angela is so self-centered that I never expected her to recognize me. A man she and her husband ruined without a second thought, hellbent on demonstrating the power they held.

My plan is dropping into place as she leaves the campus, leaving behind her sole heir in my hands. The key to everything. They're so worried about the reputation of their family that they've unwittingly delivered their daughter to the devil's doorstep.

I struck a chord with the superficial Carmichaels, causing them to forget their daughter is squeaky clean. The professionally doctored photo of her with the high-school janitor was all it took for them to move her to my academy in Maine.

Pathetic.

I needed leverage, and their daughter was the perfect target, even if I've yet to decide how to utilize her. My sole focus has been bringing her to this academy for the past year. Originally, my target had been her older brother, Karl, until he was murdered two years ago.

I plan to drag the Carmichael's name through the mud using their daughter before eliminating them.

Archer Daniels, the Syndicate Academy's gym

coach and one of my closest friends, has agreed to have a relationship with her to start it off, but as I look at the innocent little thing standing next to me, she doesn't strike me as a girl who would fall for his charm.

I glance out of my office window as Angela Carmichael walks down the steps toward the black town car she arrived in.

"I shouldn't be here," an angry voice murmurs next to me, drawing my attention back to the daughter of my enemy.

I'm surprised to find her bright hazel eyes fixed on me with a furious expression that few would dare give me. I intimidate most students, yet she appears undeterred by my presence. It's hard not to notice her natural beauty. Eva Carmichael is the polar opposite of her fake, self-centered mother in appearance. Nevertheless, she's a Carmichael, and all Carmichaels are the same.

"That's entirely untrue. You're the heir to the Carmichael clan." I stand taller and step closer to her in an attempt to intimidate her. "The syndicate academy is where you belong."

She holds her chin high, undeterred by my scare tactics. "I've got no interest in the family business." Mature wisdom in her unique hazel eyes makes her appear beyond her eighteen years.

"Words of a spoiled princess who doesn't understand the meaning of working for a living." I shake my head. "You'll learn some difficult lessons here, Eva."

Her jaw tightens, and she stands taller. She's not short but compared to my height, she is tiny. "I have every intention of working for a living once I graduate." Her brow furrows, and her fists clench by her side. "I will be a vet no matter what anyone says. I want nothing to do with my parents' deranged criminal organization."

Her outburst surprises me. Ironically, I teach students in the same situation I was in at eighteen before I ran away. No students in attendance are interested in living a straight and narrow life. They're usually as fucked up as their parents, if not worse.

"You shouldn't tell the other students that." I squint at her. "They'll prey on it as a weakness." I don't know why I warn her about the other students when my sole intention is to torture this girl, but we have some severely messed-up students in attendance. Girls and boys that would chew her up and spit her out.

She clenches her jaw. "Being better than your parents isn't weakness." Her eyes are blazing with anger now.

Her words pack a punch to my gut, as I was like her at one time. She's a hopeless romantic who believes there's an escape from darkness, but she is wrong and will learn.

"Your parents want you to take over the family business, and I'm here to mold you into a perfect leader for said business." I cross my arms over my chest. "You'll do as you're told while you're here. What happens afterward is up to you and your family."

I study her reactions closely, intrigued by the daughter of my enemy. She isn't what I expected at all. Instead of a smart retort, she holds her tongue and glares at me.

"Come. I'll show you to your dorm room." I gesture for her to walk out of my office.

She turns around and walks out, her hips swaying temptingly.

At that moment, I realize I'm staring unashamedly at her curvy figure and, particularly, her firm, round backside. Shaking my head, I walk after her and make sure I stay one step ahead. "Follow me."

Although far shorter than her mother's, Eva's heels clack on the stone floor, punctuating the air violently. The sound is all that falls between us as we make our way toward the girls' dormitory wing.

It's hard to believe I have the most precious thing to Angela and Jamie Carmichael after years of scheming. They ripped my world apart and dismantled the empire I established in minutes, as well as killed a woman I was too blind to recognize I loved.

The large insurance payout made it possible for me to purchase the Syndicate Academy from Artem Sidorov, ex-bratva commander who was pleased to retire at seventy-one. The school had a reputation for molding successful leaders, but I took it up a notch, extending attendance to every mafia, not only the Bratva.

I swipe Eva's keycard to enter the girls' dormitory wing and lead the way into the luxurious hallway. The dormitories are, of course, much like a hotel, as the families would expect nothing less for their beloved offspring.

There's an odd contrast stepping from the main school, which is cold and dark, into the west dormitory wing.

Eva's soft gasp is proof of that. A sound that draws my attention over to her as my pants tighten slightly. My brow furrows as I force my attention back to the corridor ahead, navigating my way through the labyrinth of rooms to hers.

Finally, I find room sixty-nine. "This is your room," I say, motioning to the door. I hold up the key card. "And this is your key." I swipe it over the panel, and it clicks open.

Her brow furrows. "Is this a boarding school or hotel?"

"All rooms have key card access for the students' protection." I shrug as she stares at me blankly. "It's impossible to pick an electronic lock," I add.

In the five years since I purchased this academy, we've had some incidents that would shock the most hardened criminals. In total, in five years, we've lost seven students to vicious attacks. Incidents shocked me to the core, but I guess it would never be easy bringing criminal families' heirs under one roof. I push open the door to her bedroom and step inside.

"You have your room, a small sitting room behind the first door and a bathroom behind the second, leading to a walk-in closet," I explain.

Eva follows me inside. "This isn't what I expected after seeing the rest of the school." She puts down her hold-all and walks into the room, where one suitcase is waiting. Considering she'll live here, she has few possessions.

"Is that all you brought with you?" I ask.

Eva glances up at me, a sadness in her eyes. "Yes." She shrugs slightly. "They only allowed me to pack one bag."

I clench my jaw, wondering what the stab in my gut is. Sympathy, perhaps? This girl has been subjected to parents like Angela and Jamie Carmichael. However, I refuse to accept she isn't like them deep down under her angelic exterior. A woman raised by evil doesn't grow up untouched by it.

I watch as she moves forward and gently runs her fingers over the cream silk linen on the four-poster bed. There's no denying that she is stunning, but it's a mask to what lies beneath–darkness and rotten evil.

"Listen to me, Eva," I say, my voice stern.

She spins around and meets my gaze, eyes wide. "Sorry, sir."

The word sir tugs at my insides as I feel myself thicken in my pants. No schoolgirls call me sir here, so perhaps the word appeals to the dominant side of me I buried long ago. My brow furrows as I stare at her, speculating why that word coming from this girl would affect me.

"Listen carefully. You will conform to the rules here, whether or not you like it." I close the gap between us, forcing her to step back against the wall. "I don't cower away from corporal punishment for those who don't obey."

Eva shudders, her eyes fluttering as a whoosh of air escapes her lungs.

The satisfaction coils through me at the first sign that she does indeed find me intimidating. I grit my teeth as another sensation other than satisfaction coils through me. A burning, forbidden lust that pools in the pit of my gut.

Her throat bobs as she swallows, and she shakes her head. "I don't have trouble with following rules and never have. My parents are gullible idiots who believe that I would ever have an affair with a middle-aged janitor."

I raise a brow. "It's pathetic to deny something when there's photographic evidence, Miss Carmichael."

Her eyes flash. "Not when Photoshop exists." She says it so matter of fact, glowering at me with admirable confidence.

"I can beat the denial out of you, Eva." I pause, staring at her for a few moments. "Don't think I won't."

She remains confident in her conviction. "It's not denial, sir. It's the truth," she says, turning from me.

"Are you disrespecting me?" I growl, snatching her wrist and yanking her back around.

Her eyes widen as they shift between my hand wrapped around her wrist and my face. "Please let go of my wrist, sir."

I search her eyes, ignoring her request. "Never turn your back on me again. Do you understand?"

When she doesn't answer me, the bit of control I had slips through my fingers. "I typically don't elect for corporal punishment on a pupil's first day." I move closer to her, urging her to take a step back, still holding her wrist. "However, you're testing my patience with your bratty attitude." I keep moving until the back of her legs hit the bed. "I asked you a question," I growl.

Eva's throat bobs, bringing my attention to her slender neck. "Yes, sir. I understand, but please, can you remove your hand from my wrist?"

There it is again. The tug between my thighs the second she says that fucking word. It's like throwing gas onto a bonfire.

"Since you asked politely." I lean toward her, inhaling her scent, which is a mix of lavender and jasmine that drives my urges wild. "Next time, you won't get off so easily." Our lips are mere inches away as she gawks at me with a mix of shock and fear and a hint of arousal. "Do you understand?"

Eva breathes a shuddering breath, nodding frantically. "Yes, sir."

I let go of her wrist and thrust my fingers through my hair. "Good." I stride toward the door to put some distance between us. "Get some rest. One of my colleagues will call on you in the morning and take you to breakfast at eight o'clock sharp." I glance at the clock on her wall to ensure it keeps time accurately. "Don't open this door to anyone until morning, no matter what."

The students have a tradition of hazing new pupils, especially pupils who begin halfway through the semester. My warning, I tell myself, is to ensure she stays out of harm's way, so any injury doesn't impede my plans.

Her brow furrows. "Why?"

"You and your questions are exasperating. Do as I say, okay?"

Eva nods in response. "Okay, sir." She flops down on the bed. "I'll get some rest."

At this rate, if she continues this sir lark, I'll end up fucking her like a beast as a welcome to the academy.

Eva rolls onto her front with her legs in the air, displaying her pink lace panties under her skirt. When she realizes I'm still lingering, still staring at her, she says, "Is there anything else you need, sir?" As she glances at me over her shoulder.

I clench my fists by my side, scowling at her. Either she realizes that she's flashing her underwear at me, and it's a deliberate attempt to turn me on, or she's too fucking innocent to know it. The jury is out on which it is.

"No, that's all." I clench my jaw, eyes still glued to her panties. "Don't open the door tonight." I step out of the room and grab the door handle, slamming it shut.

Eva Carmichael is different from what I expected as the daughter of my enemies. She affects me, which complicates things, as I can't be the one to scandalize her without possibly losing everything in return. My breathing, I notice then, is erratic as I rest my back against her door.

Archer is renowned for his wicked, errant ways. He isn't the school principal, and we brush his many affairs with pupils under the carpet. However, Archer having his way with a pupil is entirely different from me crossing that line. It could ruin me for the second time, and I'll be damned if I allow another Carmichael to ruin me.

4

EVA

A knock at my door forces me to sit up straight. "Who is it?" I wonder if principal Byrne has returned, remembering his warning not to open the door.

He's the scariest man I've ever met, and I've met some nasty characters through my parents' work, but he's also the most beautiful man.

"It's your next-door neighbor," a voice calls back.

I stand and approach the door, considering opening it after the principal's warning. "Oh, what do you want?" I ask.

"I wanted to introduce myself. I'm on your left. There is a moment of silence.

My brow furrows as I speculate why Principal Bryne would advise me not to open the door. If I wish to fit in, I have to be friendly, and refusing to open the door isn't a good way to make acquaintances.

I open the door to a small, pretty girl with red hair. "Hey."

She smirks. "Hi, you're Eva Carmichael, right?"

I clench my jaw and nod. "Yes, who are you?"

"Jeanie Doyle," she says, holding out a hand for me to shake.

I regard it anxiously. "As in Doyle from Chicago?" I ask, realizing she's related to the Callaghans of Chicago. I know every child in here is the product of high-profile criminals. The exact reason I'll never fit in, but at least it's only for seven months.

She tilts her head. "Yeah, are you going to leave me hanging here?" She glances at her hand.

I shake it, and she clutches so fiercely it's like she's trying to break my bones. "It's nice to meet you," I say, reclaiming my hand.

She smirks, but it's a malicious smile that sends shivers through my body. "You shouldn't have opened the door," she says as two girls appear on either side of her.

Dread hammers into me as I slam the door shut in their faces, but the two girls stop me, pushing it open. "What do you want?" I swallow my fear.

One of the new girls cracks her knuckles. "To welcome you to the Syndicate Academy."

My father's voice rings in my head as I stare at the three girls who wish me harm.

You need to learn how to fight your own battles, Eva.

When I was six, my parents enrolled me in boxing

classes, even though I had no interest in it. They forced me to continue until I was sixteen, and my teacher guaranteed them I could hold my own in a fistfight. Perhaps I'll finally be able to use the skills I learned. Although, three on one will be tough.

I take a step away from them, preparing myself for an attack. "I don't want any trouble." I hold my hands up.

One of the other girls smirks. "Too bad it found you."

I ball my fists and hold them in front of my face. "Bring it."

They all laugh at me, which only angers me.

Jeanie is the one to strike first, rushing at me and jabbing me in the stomach. I step away and then punch her in the face, taking her by surprise.

One of the other girls comes for me and punches me in the chest. I grab her wrist and twist it hard, bringing my knee into her stomach.

She groans as I let her go, pushing her back into the other girl.

Jeanie moves forward again, eyes flashing with rage. "Not bad for a rookie."

I narrow my eyes at her. "I'm not a rookie."

She laughs. "I heard you're a fucking snowflake who has never even killed anyone." She tilts her head to the side. "What heiress of a clan hasn't killed by the time she's eighteen?"

My stomach churns. "You're sick if you think it's something to brag about, taking someone else's life."

Jeanie glances at one of the other girls. "Can you believe this?"

She shakes her head. "Bitch doesn't deserve to attend the Syndicate Academy, if you ask me."

I glare at them both. "No one asked you."

They exchange glances. "She needs teaching a fucking lesson," the other girl says, cracking her knuckles.

I hold my fists in front of me as they taught me. It's not in my nature to be aggressive, but I'll defend myself.

She comes at me and jabs at my left side, which I block easily. The girl gets impatient, throwing a jab at my right too fast. I slam my fist into her stomach hard, making her grunt as she doubles over.

"Fuck this," Jeanie says, rushing for me fast.

She tackles me to the ground, landing punch after punch. I struggle to push her off, but her strength overwhelms me as she gets about three solid blows in before I can fling her off me.

Blood trickles from my busted lip. "What is wrong with you?" I ask, struggling to believe these girls delight in hurting others. It makes no sense, but my brother was the same, determined to prove himself deserving of the depraved empire my parents built.

"Nothing," Jeanie replies. "What did you expect from an academy full of mafia heirs?"

I didn't expect this kind of shit on my first night here. The fact is, I will stand out like a sore thumb because I have no plan to take over my parents' business.

The tallest of the girls steps forward. "If you think this is bad, you'll be surprised." There's a cruel edge to her tone as she reaches into her pocket, pulling an object out. She's so fast all I catch is a flash of metal as she lunges forward, stabbing the knife into my right leg.

I scream in agony as she pulls it out, making blood fly into the air. My stomach churns at the sight of my blood spurting from the deep wound as I take a step backward, which only serves to make it bleed more.

The pain is terrible as I put weight on my leg, so I balance on one leg, knowing they might attack again and I won't be able to fend them off. "What the hell?" I say, glaring at them as a foreign rage infects my blood. "As if it wasn't unfair, three against one, you bring a knife, too?"

The same girl who stabbed me smirks and steps closer, twirling the knife in her hand. "Because you fought, you get special treatment."

I hop backward on my one good leg, knowing that I'm only delaying another painful attack. My eyes flit to the doorway, which now has an audience gathered outside of it, but no one comes to my aid.

The tall girl comes for me again, and I dodge her but only just, falling over in the process and landing flat on my ass. The jolt sends a shot of excruciating pain through my leg, and I growl, irritated that I can fight these sickos off.

Would they kill me?

I wouldn't put anything past the students of this nuthouse. This place should be illegal, but cops are as corrupt as the criminals like all authorities in this world. Money is the root of all evil, and if you have enough, it doesn't matter what heinous crimes you commit. It will all disappear if you have money.

The girl grins down at me, moving the knife toward my other leg. She holds my gaze, enjoying the fear that radiates from me.

She moves to stab the knife into my other leg, but I disarm her, pulling the knife from her hand when she least expects it. I point the knife at her, waving it. "Get the fuck back."

The girl smirks. "Or what? Are you going to stab us?"

I glare at her, a dark hatred simmering beneath my skin. "Yes, stay the fuck away from me."

The same girl pulls something out of her pocket and flicks her wrist, opening a switchblade. As I try to formulate a plan, my heart pounds in my ears. I may be more of a liability if I stand as the blood pours from the stab wound, but I try to get to my feet. I topple back over onto my ass, to the amusement of my attackers.

"What a pathetic wuss," Jeanie says, glancing at the other girls. "What shall we do with her?"

My head swims from the blood loss, making me dizzy. I'm not sure whether these girls would even think twice about murdering me. I tighten my grasp on the knife in my hand, remaining focused.

"Out of the way," the principal booms. "All of you, back to your rooms."

The girl drops the knife onto the floor next to me, her face paling as she jumps away as if someone slapped her. She's worried about being caught by the principal. It wouldn't have surprised me if this were part of the curriculum, as they nurture brutality and darkness.

The principal's piercing aquamarine eyes find mine, and the anger in them is blazing. I can't work out if it's directed at them or me.

"You three will report to Professor Nitkin." He glares at them. "He'll be in charge of your punishment."

The three girls pale, and Jeanie scowls at me with a burning hatred. They turn and leave, so I'm left alone with Principal Byrne. Once they're gone, he turns his attention to me.

"What did I tell you, Eva?" he asks.

I draw in a shaky breath, wincing as my ribs hurt from the beating I took. "Not to open the door." I remain on the floor, feeling tiny as he towers over me.

His eyes are wild with rage as he moves toward me, closing the gap. "And what did you do?"

"I opened the door." Shame coils through me as I keep my gaze down on the floor. "I'm sorry, sir."

A soft growl escapes Principal Byrne's lips as he crouches next to me. It's a sound that scares me, but it also has a strange effect on me I can't quite understand. His earthy, musky scent infiltrates my senses as he gets as close as he did before.

He chucks his jacket onto my bed and pulls his tie off before unbuttoning his shirt, making heat filter through my body.

"What are you doing?" I ask.

His eyes narrow, concentrating on the wound on my leg. "I need to create a tourniquet fast on this stab wound. You're losing too much blood, and I fear they hit an artery."

He pulls his shirt off, and it's impossible not to admire his muscled body and dark tattoos that spread down his arms and to the left of his chest, even while I'm bleeding out, or perhaps it's because I am bleeding out since it's making me a little light-headed and dizzy.

He tears the arm off his shirt and retrieves a pen from his jacket pocket, making quick work to use the fabric and the pen to tourniquet the stab wound. It's evident he's done it before, as the tourniquet stops the blood flow instantly. Once done, he slips his shirt back on despite missing an arm and buttons it up before sliding the jacket on.

He meets my gaze, crouching in front of me. "Put your arms around my neck."

My eyes widen. "S-Sir?"

He shuts his eyes and breathes a long, shuddering breath, scaring me. "I said, put your arms around my neck." There's a deadly edge to his voice.

I swallow hard, hesitating to touch this brute of a man at all. He's so handsome it is intimidating, especially this close.

His jaw clenches, and eyes flicker open, finding mine. The intensity in those aquamarine depths sends a foreign sensation to my gut. "Don't make me say it again."

Slowly, I slide my arms around his neck as the warmth of his skin burns through me, making me realize how cold I am. I shiver, my body craving his warmth as my head swims. He's right. I've lost a lot of blood as I shut my eyes, my body wanting to shut down.

Principal Byrne slides one hand under my knees and the other around my back, lifting me as if I weigh nothing. "Stay with me, Eva. Whatever you do, don't shut your eyes."

My stomach flutters. The hard press of principal Byrne's muscles against my body as he holds me close is intoxicating. His warmth is safe and comforting, even though this man scares the living daylights out of me. He's intense, brooding, and intimidating, but I sense that's how he likes it, for the students to fear him.

"Where are you taking me?" I ask, breaking the silence between us.

His jaw clenches as his attention remains ahead of us. "I won't tolerate dumb questions."

I bite my bottom lip, focusing on anything but my new principal's gorgeous face. Up this close and personal, it's kind of impossible to ignore. He's beautiful, and the way he's carrying me is intimate and makes me heat from the inside out. Not to mention, he smells divine of musk and pine and something I can't quite put my finger on. My thighs squeeze together as my desire for him elevates.

"I think I can walk on it, sir," I suggest as I feel my entire body heating at the prolonged proximity to him, the heat between my thighs building as a sense of awareness prickles over my skin.

Principal Byrne shakes his head. "I've seen my fair share of stab wounds, and if you try to walk on it, you will do more damage than good and lose more blood."

I swallow hard, wondering how often people get stabbed here at this academy. "I guess students often get stabbed here, then?" I ask, wishing my voice didn't sound so pathetically terrified.

His jaw clenches, and he nods. "Yes." That's all he says as he carries me straight out the front entrance of the cold, stately school and opens the passenger's side of a large SUV with one hand before gently placing me into the seat. "Belt on." He slams the door, making my heart thud against my rib cage.

I do as he says, sliding the belt on and clicking it into place.

Principal Byrne walks stiffly around the car and slides into the driver's side without looking at me, turning on the engine. The purr of the engine is all that falls between us as he drives through the wrought-iron gates.

5

OAK

*I*t's not uncommon that I'm ringing the parents of new pupils on the first morning to report an incident, but I can't understand why I have to for Eva.

I warned her not to open the door, yet she ignored my warning. Running a hand through my hair, I pick up the phone on my desk and dial Jamie Carmichael's number. I grip the plastic so hard I'm surprised it doesn't snap in two.

The dial tone rings, and within a few moments, Jamie Carmichael answers. "Hello." I'd recognize his voice anywhere.

"Mr. Carmichael." I clear my throat. "It's Principal Byrne from the Syndicate Academy."

He sighs. "Oh, for God's sake. What's she done now?"

I clench my free fist, suppressing a growl that attempts to break free. Eva is nothing like the other students—she's innocent, considering she's the daughter of two of the most dreadful people I've ever met.

"A few girls attacked Eva in her dorm. She's in the hospital at the moment as she sustained a knife wound to her left leg, a cracked rib, and some superficial bruises." I pause for a moment. "I have to inform you of all incidents that occur on campus."

Jamie Carmichael clicks his tongue. "Excellent. Hopefully, it will force her to stand up for herself in the future."

Stand up for herself?

I clench my jaw as I know the words I want to say would anger him.

For a girl who insists she wants nothing to do with the world she was born into, she fared well against three of the most violent girls in school. Eva fought back, but they outnumbered her three on one. Not to mention, the girls brought a knife to the fight, tipping the scales in their favor.

I'm not surprised that her father's reaction is so insensitive. The two of them deserve to rot in hell.

"Indeed. It was purely a courtesy call," I grit out, struggling to contain the rage rising to the surface.

He tuts. "Don't tell me the next time Eva's injured." There are a few moments of silence. "I only expect to hear from you if she's dead, and then I will kill you myself." He slams the phone done, inflaming the fire exploding inside of me.

When I planned my revenge, it went differently to this. Instead of a desire to torture and harm their daughter, I can't help but pity her. I slam the phone down on the receiver and massage my temples.

I grab a paperweight from my desk and hurl it across the room. It hits the wall and shatters into fragments. None of this is going as I planned it. Eva Carmichael is supposed to be like her selfish parents, and yet I'm struggling to see her as anything other than a victim of their willful neglect.

I grab the bottle of scotch off my desk and pour myself a glass, savoring the way it scars my throat. It's unorthodox for a teacher to drink on the job, especially since I have classes to attend in an hour, but I don't give a shit.

Eva has been haunting me since I set eyes on her for all the wrong reasons. She's strong and knows what she wants. Her determination to become a vet is endearingly innocent and admirably brave, even if she's naïve to believe she'll ever break away from her parents. They will hunt her down if she tries to run.

My office phone rings, and I see it's the hospital calling on the caller ID. "Hello, Oakley Byrne speaking."

"Mr. Byrne, it's Doctor Kenward." There's a brief silence. "I'm calling regarding Eva Carmichael."

"Yes." I swallow hard as I recall her wide hazel eyes following me as I left her alone at the hospital. A part of me felt guilty, which is absurd. I couldn't have spent my night at the hospital with her.

He sighs. "The knife wound missed any major arteries, but we can't be sure whether there's any nerve damage."

I grind my teeth together as those three girls went to town on Eva more than most girls, and I believe that's because she fought back.

"How long should she be in?"

"She needs rest, but we'd prefer to keep her in for a few days to be sure," he suggests.

"Can't the nurse tend to her here?" I ask, not wishing her to stay away from the academy any longer than she already has.

There are a few moments of silence. "Whatever you prefer, as long as your nurse is confident enough to deal with the knife wound." Elaine Jasper is our resident nurse, and she has dealt with so many outrageous injuries. Stab wounds are her specialty at this school.

Eva's wounds were bad, but nothing she couldn't handle. Since it was Elaine's day off yesterday, I had no choice but to take her to the local hospital. "I'll confirm with her and let you know later." I don't want to make him suspicious about what goes on in this school.

He clears his throat. "Am I right in thinking this was an accident?"

There's suspicion in his tone, which is why we don't use hospitals. "Yes, Eva fell in the kitchen with a knife and stabbed herself," I deadpan, assuring there's no uncertainty in my tone. "We will be more careful with who can enter the kitchen in the future."

"Indeed." There are a few moments of silence between us. "Well, I will await your nurse's decision." He cancels the call.

I sigh heavily and close my eyes, rubbing my temples. It would have been far easier if Eva's brother, Karl, had remained my target.

With her brother, the Apple didn't fall far from the tree. He was exactly like his parents, but I'd struggled to get him to the academy. His father wanted him deeply involved in the family business from a young age, and all my efforts were in vain. It wasn't long after my last attempt to get him to join; I heard the news of his passing and knew I had to turn my efforts toward their daughter.

Eva Carmichael.

An innocent flower in a field full of dark, poisonous ivy. It makes no sense how she remained seemingly untouched by the darkness, but it makes using her more difficult.

Under her innocent facade, there has to be that same relentless selfishness that her parents embody, and I'll unearth it. I don't believe she is as perfect as she appears on the surface, and I intend to tear her apart and reveal the truth before bringing her worthless family down along with her.

My heart pounds hard against my rib cage as I head toward Eva's hospital room. The prospect of seeing her has an unwanted effect on me. As I reach the room and glance into the window, I feel my stomach tighten.

Eva sits upright in bed, reading a book on veterinary science. Most girls would sit there scrolling through their phones on mind-numbing social media all day. I'll give her one thing; she's devoted to her dreams.

I hate that my admiration for her grows, especially as that admiration works against me. She will be collateral damage in my quest for revenge, but it would be easier if she were easy to dislike.

I draw in a deep breath and walk through the open door into her suite. She doesn't notice me at first. "You're coming back with me, Eva," I announce, crossing my arms over my chest.

Her beautiful hazel eyes widen as she looks up at me. "Oh, I thought I was supposed to remain here for a few days, sir."

I clench my jaw, feeling that desire tighten its hold on me at the use of that fucking word. "Why do you call me sir, Eva?"

Her brow furrows. "It's what I've always called my

teachers." She shrugs. "I guess it's natural in the south."

She's unapologetic about it and doesn't ask whether she should stop. Deep down, I don't want her to. "I see." I keep my arms crossed over my chest. "Nurse Jasper is back today at the academy, and she'll take care of you in the infirmary."

Fear flashes into her eyes, and her throat bobs as she swallows. Understandably, she fears returning to the school after what happened. "Don't worry. Those girls won't go anywhere near you again," I assure her, walking closer to her bed. "I guarantee it."

I notice both a mix of curiosity and relief in her expression. "How can you be sure?"

I sit in the chair next to the bed, clenching my fists in balls to stop myself from reaching for her. "Professor Nitkin punished them. They wouldn't dare touch you again."

Her delicate throat bobs as she swallows again. "I see."

A tense silence surges between us as we both stare at each other, electricity snapping through the air.

Her brow furrows. "Did you tell my parents?" Her voice is hesitant.

I can't understand why I feel guilty about the answer. "I spoke with your father. He told me not to tell him of any more injuries you may sustain."

A flash of sadness enters her stunning eyes, but it's gone in an instant as she clenches her jaw. "Of course he did." She glances at her hands on the bed, clenching her fingers together.

It's hard not to pity her, which is a complication I don't need. The heir to the Carmichael clan is the polar opposite of the people who wronged me five years ago, but it may be a front. I'm not ready to believe that she's untouched by the darkness she grew up around.

"Are you ready to leave?" I ask.

Her lips purse and she squints at me. "Once I'm dressed... Although, I'll need the nurse to help me get my pants on."

I swallow hard at the mention of her needing to dress, which means she's practically naked under the thin hospital gown. "I'll search for one."

"Thanks," she says, returning her attention to the book.

I leave the room and search for a nurse but don't see one. A young woman sits behind the reception desk, so I approach. "Excuse me, is there a nurse available to help my student dress?"

Her brow furrows as she glances at me. "They're all busy. There's been a terrible road accident, and all the staff is helping down at ER."

I clench my jaw. "Can you help?" I ask.

She shakes her head. "I'm not permitted to leave the desk unattended. We have a lot of confidential files here."

I sigh heavily, pinching the bridge of my nose. "Fine." I walk away, back toward her room.

Eva's lying on the bed with her eyes shut and wrist against her forehead. I grind my teeth together at the thought of having to help her dress. I don't have a choice.

I clear my throat as I walk inside, making her jump.

Her brow furrows. "No nurse?"

Fuck.

"There's been a nasty accident, and there's no staff currently available."

Genuine concern enters her expression. "I hope no one is too badly hurt." She moves to the side of the bed unaided and swings her legs out, grimacing. "I'll handle this myself, sir." She watches me expectantly. When I don't move, she clears her throat. "Would you mind staying outside?"

I shake my head. "You can't get dressed alone." My jaw clenches. "I'll help."

Her eyes widen, and her cheeks turn bright red. "T-that won't be necessary, sir."

"You can't dress in your state." I grab her bag. "Do you have something that won't put pressure on the wound?" I feel my heart pounding in my ears at the thought of helping her get dressed.

Eva still looks shocked as she shakes her head. "I'm not sure. Maybe a skirt, but it's freezing, isn't it?"

A skirt shouldn't be too difficult. I nod in response. "Yes, but the car has heating, and we'll get you straight into the infirmary." I open the bag, find the skirt, and grab a blouse and a sweater. "Do these work?" I ask.

She looks redder as she nods. "Yes, but I need underwear too, sir."

Fuck. Eva is telling me she is buck naked under her hospital gown.

"Oh, of course." I search through the bag and find a black lace bra and matching black thong that make my cock harden in my pants. I clench the fabric so hard in my hands, imagining her in just this, staring up at me innocently as I kiss every inch of her soft skin.

What the fuck is wrong with me?

This situation couldn't be more inappropriate.

I clear my throat, place the clothes on the bed, and stand by her side. "Can you stand?"

Eva shrugs. "I haven't tried without help."

My heart is beating so hard it feels like it's trying to break through my rib cage. "It's probably best if you remain seated," I say.

She nods in response. "Yes, sir." Her cheeks are flushed a deep crimson as she watches me, her lips slightly parting as our gazes remain locked.

I swallow hard and grab the black thong, kneeling before her.

The position makes it impossible not to imagine forcing my mouth to her center while I make her scream my name. I push the thoughts from my mind and lightly lift her wounded leg first.

Eva winces, proving she couldn't have dressed alone. Bending over would have been trouble enough, especially with her bruised ribs.

I slide the fabric over her left ankle and then her right before gently pulling them up her thick thighs. My cock is hard and throbbing with need as my fingers skim over her soft porcelain skin. When I get them to the top of her thighs, Eva grabs my hands in hers, eyes wide. Her tongue wets her bottom lip. "I think I can handle it from here, sir," she murmurs.

I clench my jaw, wishing she hadn't stopped me. All I want is to slide my finger through her center and feel how wet she is. The way she shudders at my touch is proof enough that she's aroused. Add to that her erratic breathing as her chest rises and falls violently and the red flush of her cheeks. I sense she's probably dripping wet for me.

I clear my throat, trying to focus. "Of course." I remove my hands from her panties and clench my fists by my side, turning my attention to the skirt.

Eva winces, squirming to get her thong on. They differ from the pink lace panties she wore the day she arrived.

"Ready?" I ask, holding the skirt.

She nods, sucking in a deep breath. "Yes, sir."

I wish she wouldn't be so fucking polite right now. Ignoring the swell of my cock as I crouch in front of her again, I lift her left foot, sliding the skirt through it, before lifting her right and doing the same.

Eva winces again, but I can't focus on that. All I can focus on is not tearing the thong and skirt off and burying my head between her thick thighs. My impulses are so primal that it feels like they're trying to burn me alive from the inside out. I'm on the edge of losing control.

I allow my fingers to skate over her skin more this time as I drag her skirt up slowly, needing to feel her for as long as I can.

She gasps quietly as my fingers coast over her inner thighs deliberately. Her wide, innocent eyes shoot to mine, which snaps me out of it as I let go of the skirt. She wiggles it the rest of the way, zipping it on the side.

"Can you handle it from here?" I say, glancing at the bra and blouse.

She swallows hard. "I don't think I will put the bra on. My ribs are sore."

I nod in reply and grab the bra, stuffing it back into her bag. I can see the outline of her nipples in the hospital gown that she's wearing. At least the sweater will hide them from my view.

"Do you need help with the blouse and sweater?"

A part of me wants her to say yes. The idea of seeing her beautiful, puckered nipples makes me mindless with need.

She shakes her head. "No, sir. I can manage. If you wait outside, I'll give you a shout when I'm ready."

I stand there battling my primal urges to take this girl here and now. "Of course." I turn and walk out of the room, shutting the door behind me. I rest my back against it, pinching the bridge of my nose.

What the fuck have I gotten myself into now?

Eva Carmichael is the epitome of innocent temptation, and I'm not sure I can resist taking a bite out of the forbidden fruit, fruit which I intend to destroy along with her family. My desire for her is a complication I don't need.

6

EVA

An awkward silence fills the car, underlined by the engine's roar as Principal Byrne drives toward the academy. He shouldn't have been the one to help me dress in the hospital, as it's inappropriate.

My body tingles from the way his fingers delicately skated across my skin. It was as if he was working to turn me into a molten pool of desire, even if that probably wasn't his intention.

I can still sense that sexually charged tension now, but I can't work out if it is from my side or whether it's just wishful thinking; I mean, Principal Byrne is the most attractive man I've ever met, but I'm also high on pain meds.

There's no way a man like him would be attracted to me, especially since I'm his student, a student whose parents sent here because I allegedly slept with the janitor at my last school. He might assume I'm a hussy who will sleep with anyone, and perhaps he's testing the waters. It wouldn't shock me, as this school isn't conventional.

Principal Byrne keeps his eyes on the road with such intensity. His large fingers are wrapped tightly around the wheel, turning his knuckles white.

I don't understand why he is so angry. "Have I done something wrong, sir?"

He tightens his grip, eyes narrowing but remaining fixed on the road. "No, why do you say that?"

I swallow hard, twirling a curl of my hair around my finger. "You always seem so angry." I shrug as his piercing aqua eyes shift to me briefly. "I thought maybe it's because you have an issue with me."

There's a soft rumble from his chest as he shakes his head. "I'm not angry, Eva."

I laugh. "You could have fooled me."

His grip tightens further, the leather squeaking under pressure. The tension in his shoulders and the tight set of his jaw as he grinds his teeth indicate he's lying to me.

The silence stretches between us as he doesn't intend to continue the conversation, focusing on the road with fierce intent.

I gaze out the window, observing the town disappear as we head into the tree-lined forest, where the Syndicate Academy is hidden from prying eyes.

"Maine is beautiful," I say, peeking at the principal.

It's so different from Atlanta's concrete jungle that I've grown up with. "Have you seen a black bear, sir?"

He shakes his head. "I don't have time to venture into the woods."

I feel disappointed he doesn't hold a conversation with me, but I sense that Oakley Byrne is a man who prefers not to participate in small talk.

"What do you do for fun, then?" I ask, wondering if he does anything other than teach and run the academy.

"Fun?" He scoffs, a smirk playing at the edge of his lips, despite his attempt to contain it. "I'm too busy for fun."

I wrap my hair around my fingers, focusing on the beautiful man sitting next to me. "That's a shame. Life is too short to be dull." I swallow hard, thinking about my late brother. His life had barely begun when those bikers took him too early. It's cruel, and although we were so different, we'd been close since childhood.

"I have little free time, considering my duties at the academy." His voice is softer, and when I glance at him, the tension has eased.

"Life will flash by faster than you know," I say, shaking my head. "You should always carve time for yourself."

His eyes meet mine, blazing with an emotion I can't identify. "That's true." He smiles a real smile for the first time, and the sight beats the oxygen from my lungs. It is breathtaking. "Perhaps I'll do that. What do you do for fun? And you can't say study, as that doesn't count."

I sigh, glancing out of the window. "I love to read."

He smiles. "What's your favorite novel of all time?"

I scrunch my brow, struggling to pick. "That's a tough question. I love Jane Eyre by Charlotte Bronte."

I see him roll his eyes at that.

"But I enjoy all genres, not just romance." I shrug. "What is it you enjoy?" I ask, interested in learning about the enigma of a man.

The tension returns as he clears his throat. "I like to paint."

Paint.

I wasn't expecting him to say that, as he's so serious.

"Really? What do you paint?" I ask as he pulls through the enormous wrought-iron gates onto the long, winding driveway of the academy.

He runs his large hand across the back of his neck. "I've not painted for years, but I used to love painting people."

"Wow, you must be talented. Did you paint portraits?"

His eyes move from the drive to me. "Nudes mostly."

"Oh, I see," I mutter, heat flaring through my veins and lighting me on fire. "I was about to suggest you paint me, but that wouldn't be appropriate." I don't know where that came from, but I regret it instantly.

He gives me a heated glare. "Definitely not," He

grits out before pulling into a parking space in front of the gothic building. He exits the car and walks around, opening my door.

He slides an arm around my back and the other under my knees, lifting me as if I weigh nothing.

I hook my arm around his neck to support myself, enjoying the warmth of his body against mine.

I sense him turn rigid against me as he carries me in through the front entrance to the school, but instead of turning right, he turns left.

"Shouldn't I try to walk?" I ask.

A muscle in his jaw ticks. "No, your chart said you need to stay off your feet until the stitches heal, other than briefly washing and using the bathroom."

He carries me up a few flights of stairs until he comes to a grand double oak door with the word 'infirmary' carved into a wooden sign.

Principal Byrne turns around and backs through the doors, which swing inwards before turning back around.

The infirmary looks like a plush private clinic with rooms lining either side of a grand waiting room at the front filled with overly expensive furnishing.

He carries me to the third room on the right. "This is you," he says, setting me down gently on the bed. "Nurse Jasper will be by in a minute to help you settle in."

"Oh, okay." I smile at him, feeling uncomfortable as he lingers next to me, his aquamarine eyes fixed on me intensely. When he says nothing else, I break the silence. "Thank you for everything, sir."

He clenches his fists by his side and nods before walking away.

I sigh heavily, as no matter what he says, he always seems angry around me.

The clack of heels approaching warns me that this Nurse is on her way. A small, mousy brown-haired woman appears in the doorway, smiling softly. "Hello, dear. I'm Nurse Jasper, and I'll be looking after you." She hurries over to me. "Shall I help you change?" She asks.

I nod, wishing that Principal Byrne had to help me undress, too. The intensity of that moment and the soft brush of his calloused fingers against my inner thigh still resonates with me.

I've never had a proper crush on anyone before, except for Jamie Orly in sixth grade, but he hated me. Perhaps it's a pattern with boys and men I have a crush on, as I'm not sure the principal likes me either.

Principal Oakley Byrne, however, is the most beautiful man I've ever met. I think getting over my crush on him will be impossible, especially after seeing him shirtless and feeling his body against mine and his hands so close to such an intimate part of my body.

I dreamed of him last night, and something tells me he'll probably appear in many more dreams to come, especially after today.

I SPENT the next four days entertaining myself with reading for my final SAT exam. If one positive came out of my injury, it's the free time to study what I want.

The syndicate academy doesn't bother with SAT exams, but I've registered to sit the exams at a nearby high school next year and have my admission ticket.

In the eyes of the law, I'm currently homeschooled rather than attending some fucked up academy for heirs of criminals.

Someone clears their throat at my door, startling me. I didn't even hear it open.

I look up, and I'm met with those piercing aquamarine eyes that have haunted my fantasies since I met him.

Oakley Byrne.

"Hello, sir," I say, heat spreading through my body as a tingle ignites over every inch of my exposed skin.

"Hello, Eva," he says. My name sounds filthy from his lips, but it's probably my imagination. His gaze is intense as if he wants to burn a hole through me with it. "How are you?"

I swallow, breaking the eye contact between us as need surges through my body, heating me from the inside out. "I'm doing a lot better, thank you." I've never been as intensely attracted to anyone as I am to Principal Byrne.

He moves closer, shoving his hands in his pants

pockets, which draw my eyes to the bulge at his crotch. My stomach flips as I imagine how incredible it would be to see this God of a man *buck* naked.

"Nurse Jasper informs me she hopes you'll be well enough to start classes in three days." He pauses a foot from me.

I smile and glance up at him, nodding. "Yes, sir. I'm looking forward to leaving this room."

"I'll bet," he says, glancing around the small yet comfortable room. "Normally, you select your subjects on the first day of the semester, but since you're starting mid-way through, I need to confirm which classes you wish to attend."

My stomach twists as I know this school doesn't cover the normal subjects you'd expect. It's about teaching the students to be criminal masterminds, which I have no interest in.

"I see." I clasp my fingers together in front of me on the bed. "Do you want me to pick now?"

He nods, stepping forward and placing a form and pen affixed to a clipboard in front of me on the bed. "Yes, I need to ensure there's room in the classes you pick." There's tension in his shoulders as he steps away. "I'll just sit here in case you have questions." He stiffly sits in the chair at the end of the bed, watching me with an intensity that makes me shiver.

I shuffle under his gaze before picking up the piece of paper. My stomach churns as I read through the lessons, none of which you'd find at Columbus Highschool, where I used to attend.

"Interrogation? Torture?" I ask, eyes widening. "Is that for real?" My eyes find the principal's, and he's staring at me with an odd glint in his aquamarine depths.

"Of course. What did you expect?" A small smirk twists onto his lips, making my stomach flutter. "Geography?"

I shake my head. "No, it's just…" I realize what I'm going to say sounds ridiculous, so I cut myself off.

"Just what, Eva?" He asks, standing and walking to the side of the bed.

"This isn't what I want," I murmur, staring at the paper. When I glance up at principal Byrne, there's a softness in his eyes that takes me aback. I swallow hard.

His hand rests on mine, sending sparks through my veins. "You have to make the best of your situation."

I clear my throat. "Very true, sir."

The muscle in his jaw tenses again as he pulls his hand from mine and sits back in his seat. "Do you have questions about the subjects?"

I shake my head, unclipping the pen from the clipboard. "Six subjects in total?" I question, meeting the principal's intense gaze.

"Of your choice, yes." He runs a hand across the back of his neck. "All students must take Physical Education, English and Math and your six chosen subjects."

I'm surprised to hear they teach Math and English here. The list has fifteen different subjects, all of which don't interest me in the slightest. I pick those that don't sound too terrible, avoiding interrogation and torture like the plague.

Combat Training.
Leadership Strategy.
Money Laundering.
Strategical Planning.
Anatomy.
Law.

Once done, I glance up and find Principal Byrne watching me like a hawk. It's rather unnerving, as this man knows how to intimidate, but perhaps because he's so beautiful, it makes his stare more terrifying.

"Finished," I say, passing him the sheet of paper.

He takes it and quickly scans my choices, raising a brow. "Combat training?"

I cross my arms over my chest. "After what happened to me, I'd say I need it, wouldn't you?"

The edge of his lip lifts, but he quickly turns stern. "I'd say you held your own against three very vicious girls."

My heart thuds harder at the compliment. "It never hurts to improve," I say, looking anywhere but at him. "Is there space in these classes?"

He clears his throat. "Yes, there's space." His brow furrows. "You'll have to watch out for Archer, though, the combat training tutor." He regards me with an odd look. "He has a thing for blondes."

My brow furrows. "Are you suggesting my teacher might hit on me?" I ask, finding it a rather odd thing for him to say.

He nods. "He is renowned for it, and since you're legal…" He trails off, shaking his head. "Just keep your wits about you, is all I'm saying."

Despite my bewilderment, I nod. "I will do. Is there anything else you need, sir?" I ask.

His nostrils flare at the question, and his eyes almost seem to burn into me. "No, Eva. Rest and get better. I'll see you in class." He strides out of the room, back straighter than an ironing board.

I let out a heavy breath once the door shuts, finding it hard to compose myself around such a devastatingly handsome man.

Get a grip, Eva.

The man is my professor.

Nothing will ever happen between us, no matter how much I want it to.

7

OAK

I stand in the doorway into my classroom, watching Eva through the small window.

It has been nine days since she arrived at the academy, but this is the first lesson she has attended. Among other subjects, I teach leadership strategy, which she won't be too interested in, but none of the subjects that we cover here will interest her.

Nurse Jasper has given her two crutches to aid walking as her stab wound heals. She believes Eva may have sustained some nerve damage, but only time will tell.

Eva sits at the front of the classroom next to Dimitri Jakov, staring at her like a hungry wolf ready to pounce. My stomach tightens as I clench my fists by my side.

Thankfully, Eva appears unaware of his attention as she doodles on a small notepad in front of her.

I uncurl my fists and reach for the door handle, turning it and entering the classroom. I fix my gaze on Eva, who doesn't look up as I walk in.

The giggles erupt from the back of the classroom as they chatter together. All the girl's eyes land on me with schoolgirl lust, except for one.

Irritation coils through my gut at how little attention she pays me.

I place my briefcase next to my desk, unbuttoning my jacket and slinging it over my chair.

When I glance up again, she still hasn't looked at me.

The other girls in the class regard me as I unbutton my cuffs and roll my sleeves up to my arms, hating the chatter that explodes from the back of the room.

Eva's eyes remain on her notepad as if she's in a trance.

I clear my throat. "Get your books out and turn to page fifty-six," I order.

Eva remains still, doodling away in her notebook. She's in her own little world, as she doesn't react.

I walk toward the desk, clenching my fists by my side. Even once I'm a foot from it, she still doesn't notice me. "Eva, did you hear me?"

The moment I say her name, she breaks out of her daze, eyes shooting up to meet mine. "No, I'm sorry, sir." I can see she's been drawing a detailed image of a bird, labeling its anatomy as she goes.

My jaw clenches at the use of that word that seems to have the power to unravel me.

Jeanie Doyle and Anita Henderson, two girls who attacked Eva on her first evening, snicker behind her. Jeanie moves toward Anita, whispering something which makes Anita laugh. It only serves to elevate the simmering rage pulsing through my veins.

I glare at the pair. "Do you have something to say, Jeanie?" I ask, fixing my attention on her. "Or do I need to send you back to Professor Nitkin?"

Jeanine pales, shuffling in her seat under my gaze. "No, I'm sorry, Principal Byrne."

"Good," I say. And then I move my gaze back to Eva, who glances at me with an odd expression, her book now out on the desk. "Page fifty-six, and don't make me repeat myself again."

Eva's throat bobs as she swallows as she quickly navigates to the correct page. "Yes, sir. I apologize."

Desire rages through me like a wildfire burning through the forest unrelentingly, making it hard to turn away from her.

I grit my teeth together and walk back to my desk, subtly adjusting myself in my pants. In the five years since I bought this exclusive school, I've never desired one of my students. The last student I expected to desire was the daughter of my enemy. The student whose family I intend to ruin.

I grab my marker pen and write the names of three historical leaders on the board.

Attila the hun
Ghengis Khan
Queen Mary I

"We immortalize these three leaders in history because they all have one similarity." I turn to face the students. "Can anyone tell me what that is?"

Natalya is the one who answers. "They were ruthless about what they wanted." Natalya Gurin is one of the brightest students at this school. She'll make a great leader, but I fear it'll be in vain.

The Bratva is a highly misogynistic organization based on archaic traditions that I don't believe will allow a woman to run it, even if she is Mikhail Gurin's only heir.

I nod. "Exactly right. History was not kind to these leaders, but for us, they are perfect role models."

Dimitry nudges Eva, which draws my attention to them as he whispers in her ear.

Eva's cheeks flush red, revealing he said something inappropriate. Dimitry is renowned for being a serial flirt with the girls.

"Dimitry," I bark.

He jumps, straightening in his chair.

I cross my arms over my chest. "If you have something to say, tell the entire class."

A whisper of a smirk graces his lips. "I don't think you'd like to hear what I said, professor."

My blood heats at the look on his face, making it boil beneath my skin. I'm ready to explode, anger clawing at me. I pace toward them, setting my hands on his desk.

Dimitry shrinks in his chair as I loom over him.

"Repeat what you said now."

Despite his cocky attitude a moment ago, he pales. He's all talk and no bite. "I said I'd love to welcome Eva to the academy after class in my dorm room." Green envy slices through me that he'd even consider trying to make a move on her.

The class laughs at his comment. "Out," I bark.

Dimitry's brow furrows. "Professor?"

"It's disrespectful to speak to a woman that way." I nod toward the door. "Professor Nitkin has a free period. You'll tell him I sent you."

Dimity pales as he looks at me in disbelief. "Isn't that a bit harsh—"

I slam my hands down on the desk. "Now, or I'll send you to him every day until you learn your lesson."

Dimitry stands and collects his books, walking out of the room. When I return my attention to the class, every face looks shocked. Gavril Nitkin is our most feared professor, as he's sadistic with corporal punishment. Even our most ruthless students fear being punished by him.

I clap my hand. "Does anyone else have anything degrading to say to their classmates?" I ask, remaining stood in front of Eva.

The silence is deafening as she stares at me in surprise. I let my gaze move to her for a few moments, observing the way her cheeks are more flushed and her chest rises and falls violently.

"Good," I say when no one speaks. "I want you to read page fifty-six to page sixty-five." I turn away from Eva and return to my desk, sitting down behind it.

My harsh punishment for Dimitry is unusual, and I know that if he'd said it to any other girl in this room, my reaction would have been different. Pure jealousy reared its ugly head, drawing more questions to light about my questionable urges toward Eva. I've never been so viscerally attracted to a woman before I set eyes on her. She's under my skin, which is a terrible complication I don't need.

I notice Jeanie leans over and mutters something to Anita again.

"In silence, unless you want to join Dimitry." I glare at them, forcing them to shut up.

I find my attention pulled straight to Eva. Her cheeks are still flushed, and her hair is a little messy since she pulled her fingers through it nervously. Everything about her is alluring in the worse sense of the word.

I intend to embroil Eva's family in scandal, but not myself along with them. If I were to engage in a sexual relationship with a student, the academy's reputation would falter.

My initial intention was to use Archer Daniels. However, that would be problematic when my jealously rears its ugly head. It leaves me up the creek without a paddle, as I'm unsure how I'll use this alluring creature to get my revenge.

The entire class read the book, including Eva, who looks lost in the pages, her eyes tracking the words with wide-eyed and innocent surprise.

The book is controversial, hence why we use it here. It details the greatness shown by ruthless tyrants from history. Men and women that most people regard as inhuman monsters, but we can learn a lot from their past leadership concerning running a criminal organization in the modern world.

Natalya has finished reading.

"Once finished, I want you to write a short two-page essay in favor of one of the leader's you've just read about that inspires you the most."

Eva's brow furrows as she tears her eyes from the book and turns a page in her notepad. My heart skips a beat as I track every graceful movement she makes, lifting her pen and innocently tapping it against her bottom lip. The image is unbearable as all I can think about is my hard cock parting them as I slide it inside.

Eva glances up, our eyes locking in a heated gaze as she realizes I'm watching her. Even as her eyes widen slightly, I can't bring myself to look away until she finally does, forcing her attention to the notepad on her desk as she writes her essay.

Her cheeks are practically crimson now as she stares with such intensity at the desk, but I still can't bring myself to tear my eyes away from her.

After a few minutes, she glances up again and practically shudders when she sees that I'm still fixated on her like an addict. Her slender throat bobs as she swallows hard, licking her perfect, plump lips.

She raises her hand, drawing my attention to her firm breasts in her tight blouse, which is a size too small as gaps appear between the buttons. A vision of me ripping it apart and throwing her onto her back on my desk floods my mind.

"What is it, Eva?" I ask.

"Can I use the restroom?"

My cock is semi-hard beneath the desk, and I know she only wants to use the bathroom to get away from my intense gaze. I tilt my head to the side slightly. "Of course. Do you need help with your crutches?"

Her nostrils flare as she shakes her head. "No, sir."

I nod toward the door. "Be quick. You must finish this essay before you leave."

"Of course." her lip trembles before she pulls it between her teeth. She grabs her crutches and makes her way as fast as she can out of the room, leaving me reeling over my urges.

I adjust myself in my pants and focus on the book before me, knowing that Eva won't finish this essay before the end of class. It means she'll have to stay late with me alone during her lunch break. My cock throbs at the prospect.

I tap my fingers on the desk as I read through an essay from my previous class on leadership enforcement methods, trying to ignore the dark storm raging to life in the pit of my stomach.

It's ten minutes before I hear the clicking of Eva's crutches on the floor outside, growing closer. Fifteen minutes remain of class, and she hasn't even started her essay yet. She finally makes it to the classroom and enters, sitting behind her desk. Eva's eyes remain fixed on anything but me as she picks up her pen and writes.

Natalya clears her throat, drawing my attention to her. "I've finished, Professor."

I smile despite the unease settling deep in my bones. "On my desk, please." I glance at my watch. "You may go to lunch early. Anyone who hasn't finished their essay by the time the bell rings will stay during their lunch." My attention flicks over to Eva, whose cheeks are flushed pink as she scribbles faster.

A few minutes pass, and quite a few of the students finish before the bell, sliding their paperwork onto my desk and leaving. There are four students left when the bell rings. Eva, Jeanie, Anita, and Alexi.

Jeanie and Anita finish within a few minutes, walking up to the front and passing me their essays. Alexi and Eva scribble fast, but I can tell Eva is behind him, as she's written only three-quarters of a page to his one and a half pages.

Alexi clicks his pen and stands, shouldering his rucksack.

Eva watches him as he hands me his essay before

slipping out of the classroom and shutting the door behind him.

Alone.

I draw a deep breath and slowly slide my hand to my crotch, pawing myself through the fabric as I leak into my boxer briefs.

Eva does something to me that no other woman has done before. I feel like a neanderthal, ready to throw her over my shoulder and rut into her over my desk.

Her cheeks are flushed as she scribbles faster, keeping her eyes fixated on the paper.

"Don't rush, Eva. I don't want to grade a shit essay because you couldn't wait to get to lunch." My desire for her consumes me as I slowly and silently unzip my pants under the desk and pull the length of my cock out, stroking it up and down in forceful jerks as I watch her.

Her eyes shoot up to meet mine, but I continue stroking myself under the desk. I'm thankful it's solid at the front, so she's unaware of what I'm doing.

"Of course, sir."

I groan softly, hearing her call me sir. My eyes don't leave her angelic face as I stroke my cock harder, faster, fantasizing about all the dirty things I want to do to her.

Eva focuses hard on the sheet of paper, scribbling at a more acceptable pace. Her tongue slips between her lips slightly as she concentrates, making it impossible to get the mental picture of her tongue worshipping the length of my cock out of my mind.

I curse under my breath as I feel my release rushing closer.

Eva glances up, brows pulling together slightly as she stares at me for a few beats, before returning her attention to the essay she's writing.

Every stroke of my hand down my throbbing shaft sends me closer as I pick up the pace, running through a mental movie of her writhing and naked on my desk, begging me for my cock. "Fuck," I mutter, losing a sense of where I am and who else is in the room.

My cock grows in my palm as my release rushes for me. I grunt, grabbing the edge of the desk with my free hand and unleashing every drop of my seed onto the underside of my desk, panting for air. I was so wrapped up in my pleasure that I hadn't even sensed Eva's approach.

"Are you alright, sir?" She asks, brow furrowed as she stands over the desk, holding her essay in her hand.

I shove my still semi-hard cock into my pants and nod. "Yes, Eva. Fine," I grit out, wondering what the fuck came over me. "Leave the essay on the desk."

She places it on my desk and leaves, her hips swaying in the most cock-stirring way as she walks right out the door.

I sigh heavily and grab some tissues off my desk to clear up the mess I made underneath it. My breathing is labored and frantic.

I've never been so out of control—so fucking insane. My heart is pounding so hard it feels like it's trying to break out of my chest. Eva Carmichael has some sick and twisted power over me—power I need to overcome if I'm ever going to get my revenge on her family.

8

EVA

"Hey, I'm Natalya," a girl says, sitting next to me in the cafeteria. "Thought you could use some company."

I smile at her but can't help the paranoia that sweeps over me. The last time someone introduced themself to me, I ended up stabbed and in a hospital bed for a week.

"Don't worry. I'm not a psycho like Jeanie, Kerry, or Anita." She grabs her fork and digs into her vegetable lasagne, clearly sensing my unease.

Natalya was in my class with Principal Byrne before lunch. I noticed she was one of the few people to answer his questions, and she was the first to leave after finishing her essay. She's a motivated student who wants to do well, like me. The only difference is she wants a life of crime.

"I saw you in my leadership class," I say.

She nods. "Yeah, ignore assholes like Dimitry. He'll regret it after being sent to Nitkin."

"Who is professor Nitkin?" I ask.

It's not the first time I've heard his name since Principal Byrne sent my attackers to him.

"He's a fucking sadistic hardass." She gazes at me and shrugs. "If you do well and keep your head down, hopefully, you'll never see that side of him." She sighs. "It's only idiots like Dimitry who get sent to him for punishment."

I nod in response, observing my new acquaintance. She is very attractive with dark brown hair and equally dark eyes, and her skin is tanned and flawless.

"How long have you attended the academy?"

"Since I was little." She smiles. "My brother sent me here when I was eight years old."

My eyes widen. "Wow, that's young. Didn't you miss home?" I ask, wondering how it would feel to be shipped off to boarding school from such a young age. When I was little, my childhood was charmed even if my parents were strict until I learned about all the nasty secrets my family hid from me.

She laughs, shaking her head. "No, it was a relief to be away from it, especially after my mother left for Russia. I love my brother, but he didn't have time to spend with me while he was trying to run our late father's organization."

"Oh, I'm sorry about your father," I say, realizing

that despite my parents' lack of care for me, at least they've always been there.

She shakes her head. "Don't be. I like life as it is." There's a wistful smile on her face as she sighs. "Enough about me." She tilts her head. "Who starts a new high school halfway through the first semester of senior year?"

I raise my hand. "Me, it would seem."

She laughs, putting me at ease. "You don't say. Why?"

"It's a long story."

She glances at her watch. "Well, we've still got twenty-five minutes of lunch break to kill."

I laugh. "True." I swallow hard, trying to work out how to explain the crazy story that landed me here. "It's pretty ridiculous, to be honest."

"Spill," she says, smiling encouragingly.

I hesitate for a moment before nodding. It feels like the floodgates open as I tell her about the doctored photo of the janitor and me and how my parents went crazy. I tell her I'd never even spoken to him, let alone slept with him and that it had to be Casey Hogan behind it, as she's always hated me.

Natalya listens until I'm finished. Her brow furrows as she glances at her watch. "Not such a long story, after all." She smiles. "That sucks, though, that your parents wouldn't listen to you." She shrugs. "I've only just met you, and I can tell you're telling the truth."

"You can?" I ask, surprised to hear she believes me.

Natalya nods. "Yeah." She glances around briefly to check no one is listening. "If I were you, I'd be on alert. Someone wanted you here at this academy. That's my bet."

My brow furrows. "I assumed it was a prank by Casey at my old high school."

Natalya shakes her head. "Sweet, Naïve, Eva." She sighs heavily. "The world we operate in, coincidences like that don't happen. Someone wanted you to attend this school." She places a hand over mine and squeezes. "Be careful, is all I'm saying." Her brow pulls together. "I get the sense you aren't like other girls here."

We are going to get along well. "Okay, I will." I smile at her. "Thank you for sitting with me."

She laughs. "It's nice to have someone new to speak to. The people here are so boring and predictable, except my two best friends, Adrianna and Camilla." She smiles. "I'll introduce you to them tonight at dinner if you'd like." She pulls her class schedule out of her bag, groaning. "I've got combat class next with Archer. How about you?"

I pull mine out too and glance at the next period. "Snap." I smile.

Natalya shakes her head. "It's not something to be happy about. Archer is a harsh trainer. Even if he jokes most of the time, he pushes everyone to their limits." Her brows pull together as she glances at my crutches. "Although, I'm pretty sure you'll have to sit this class out."

"I guess I'll have to watch then?" I ask.

She rolls her eyes. "Yeah, lucky bitch."

I laugh at that. "Most people wouldn't call me lucky for being stabbed."

"Touche." She chuckles. "But you're lucky to get out of combat training." She stands and shoulders her bag. "We should get a move on, as we don't want to be late."

I nod and grab my bag, hoisting it over my shoulder. And then reach of my crutches, which are in Principal Byrne's hands.

My heart stops beating in my chest as he stares down at me intimidatingly. I don't know what it is about this man, but he has a way of stealing all the oxygen from the room he's in.

"Sir, can I have my crutches, please?" I ask.

Natalya's eyes are wide as she glances between him and me.

"You're in no condition to participate in combat training yet." His grip stiffens on my crutches as he makes no move to return them. "Your mother reiterated the importance of you learning discipline." He fixes his pale aquamarine eyes on me with an intensity that makes me shudder. "It's a lesson we teach in the earlier years, but I'll give you one-on-one tuition on it while you're not fit for combat training."

My cheeks flame at the thought of having one-on-one time with this god of a man.

Natalya's mouth drops open as she stares at him. I

guess it's not standard for pupils to be given one-on-one training. Her gaze moves to mine. "Looks like I'm on my own for this one." She smiles. "See you later?"

I nod in response, feeling too embarrassed to articulate a response.

Natalya walks out of the cafeteria, leaving me alone with the principal, who looms over me. He's still holding my crutches in a vise-grip.

"Can I have my crutches, please, sir?" I ask again.

A muscle in his jaw flexes every time I call him sir, but I can't figure out why. Perhaps he's not used to southern students at this school, as I haven't picked up many southern accents.

"Of course." He passes one crutch into my right hand and the other into my left, his skin brushing mine momentarily as he does. Heat coils through me as I try to ignore the electrical spark that zaps through my body.

It's crazy how his touch affects me.

"Thank you." I struggle to my feet clumsily, peering at him once I'm steady. "Shall I follow you?"

His nostrils flare as he nods. "Yes, we'll go to my office." He turns his back on me, ready to walk out.

"Not a classroom, sir?" I ask. The idea of being in that small, dark office alone with him makes me anxious.

His back turns rigid as his steps away falter. "All the classrooms are full this period." There are a few moments of silence. "Follow me."

I swallow hard, following him in silence out of the cafeteria and down a dark corridor toward his office. The click-clack of my crutches on the cobblestones is the only sound that echoes through the silence. My palms are already sweaty, and my heart is practically drumming against my rib cage with each step I take.

This man is too intimidating and too beautiful to be alone with. He both scares and thrills me. The way he watched me earlier today in leadership class was bordering on predatory.

He comes to a halt outside of his office, slipping a hand into his jacket and pulling out a key.

I watch as he slides it into the lock, turning it slowly. The click echoes through the cold, stone corridor. The thought of being trapped in his tiny office with him for an entire hour makes butterflies take flight in my gut.

"After you," he says, his voice as smooth as butter. I hate that his voice sends a prickle of goosebumps rising over every inch of exposed skin.

What the hell is wrong with me?

I walk past him, closer than I should as my arm brushes against his jacket. The click of the lock turning behind me sets me on edge. That toe-curling, masculine scent of him infuses the air, making desire shoot right between my thighs.

Why would he lock the door?

I lean on my crutches awkwardly in the center of his office, waiting for him to tell me where to sit.

"Have a seat here," he says, pointing to the sofa.

I swallow hard and stumble over, gently propping the crutches against the sofa before sinking into it.

He sits down next to me, closer than I expect.

"I don't think I have any books for this lesson, sir," I say, keeping my gaze on anything in the room but him.

I notice a photograph in a frame of a beautiful, blonde woman smiling. An ache ignites in my chest, one I can't understand. I wonder if that's his wife and don't know why I care whether he's married. It's none of my business.

"No, Eva." His voice cuts through my thoughts, warning me of his proximity. "This is a practical lesson."

I whip my head around, meeting his gaze. My brow pulls together. "What is that supposed to mean, sir?"

His jaw clenches again, and he shakes his head. "I'd prefer you call me Oak, Eva."

My heart flutters in my chest at his request to call him by his first name. "That seems a little inappropriate." I meet his intense gaze.

He chuckles, and the sound turns me into a molten puddle of desire as I clench my thighs together tightly. His attention moves to my legs as if sensing how aroused I am right now. "No, what is inappropriate is you calling me sir all the time."

My brow pulls together. "It's polite, not inappropriate."

He growls, his face turning dark. "Discipline doesn't come easy to you, does it, Eva?"

I realize at that moment that his asking me to call him by his name was my first test, and I failed. "No," I reply, my head hanging. "I guess it doesn't."

He clears his throat. "I'm the authority figure in this room, and if I tell you to call me Oak, what should you do?"

I lick my dry lips. "Call you Oak," I reply.

"Good girl," he says, and his praise heats my blood. He tilts his head. "Do you maintain this silly pretense that you didn't make out with your high school janitor?"

The question catches me off guard as I sit up straighter, rage flooding through my veins. "Pretense?" I question, digging my fingernails into the palm of my hand. "It wasn't a pretense. Someone set me up."

"Don't lie to me, Eva," he says, his voice lethal. There's a threat in each syllable that he utters.

"I'm not lying." I hold my chin high. "It's the truth, and nothing you can say will change that."

"As I expected," he murmurs, walking toward his desk.

My heart slams against my ribs in apprehension of his next lesson. "I'm serious. Get an expert to analyze the photograph." I grind my nails vigorously into my palm. "They'll confirm it's not genuine."

His aquamarine gaze meets mine. "That may or may not be true, but I've seen the photograph, and it looked convincing to me." He pulls a ruler from the drawer, making my heart skip a beat. "I teach discipline through one method." He slides the plastic across the palm of his hand.

What does he intend to do with that?

"What method?" I ask, my heart racing at one-hundred miles an hour.

A dark smile twists his beautiful lips, and the flash of evil I'd seen the day I arrived at the academy ignites in his eyes. "Pain."

I swallow hard as he moves closer. "You're asking me to lie about that photograph." I've never been a good liar. I hate lying.

He tilts his head. "Discipline is about following rules, Eva. If I ask you to stop lying about the photo, then that's what you should do."

I shut my eyes, inhaling a deep, shuddering breath. I won't allow this ass to make me lie about that photograph, no matter what he does. "But I'm not lying," I grit out.

He tuts. When I open my eyes, he's standing a few feet away.

"W-what are you going to do?" I ask, loathing how my body shakes with fear.

There's a smirk on his lips, which fills me with dread. "I told you we don't shy away from corporal punishment here, Eva." He places his palm out flat and smacks the ruler against it. "Hand out for me, please."

I swallow hard and lay the flat of my palm out.

He brings the ruler up and then smacks it against my palm so hard it takes the air from my lungs. The strike stings as I stare in shock at the principal. "Are you going to stop lying to me, Eva?"

I grit my teeth and harden my gaze, glaring at him. "I'm not fucking lying."

"That'll be two more for that language," he growls, grabbing my other palm and pulling it flat next to the other. He brings the ruler down in quick succession over both palms, making me cry out. "Now, tell the truth."

I glare at him with a newfound hatred, feeling such conflicting sensations when I look into his aquamarine eyes. "I am telling the truth," I grind out.

Six more strikes follow, harder than before. I feel tears pooling in my eyes.

He clicks his tongue; the sound making rage simmer in my gut. "I think I need to be harsher." His aquamarine eyes blaze with evil intent as he stares at me, making my stomach churn with nausea.

He won't rest until I admit to something that isn't true, which goes against every instinct and moral in me. I will not admit to doing something I didn't do.

This is going to be a very long hour.

9

OAK

It takes every ounce of restraint within me not to bend this beauty over the desk and spank her ass with the ruler until she's so sore she won't be able to sit for days.

I'm a sadistic son of a bitch because I know she's not lying, but I can't help myself. The darkness inside of me demands I make her hurt, punish her for being the offspring of the two people who tore my world apart. And yet, there's a small part of me that wants her close, begging me with those beautiful, bright hazel eyes to stop.

"Are you ready to tell me the truth?" I ask, halting my assault on her red palms.

Her eyes narrow, and she holds my gaze without a word.

"Do I need to take this punishment a step further?" I ask, searching those eyes for fear.

If she fears me, she doesn't show it. "What the hell is that supposed to mean?"

I narrow my eyes. Eva seems so unaltered by the pain I've inflicted. There's a part of me that is desperate to push her more, see how long she will hold out, and I'm so close to following that instinct. Everyone has a breaking point, and I want to see how long she will take the moral high ground.

"I'll give you one more chance, Eva."

Her eyes narrow. "Or what?"

It's as if everything she says is designed to bring my darkness to the surface. "I'll hike up your skirt and paint your ass red until you tell me the truth."

Her jaw unhinges, eyes going wide—finally reacting to me, even if it took longer than it should have. "Are you insane?"

I cross my arms over my chest, glaring at her to make her realize how serious I am. "Bend over."

Eva's throat bobs softly, and her nostrils flare as she shakes her head. "I'm sorry, but that will not happen."

Despite the fear flaring in her hazel eyes, her voice is as calm as ever. "Don't make me ask twice, Eva. You will not like what happens if you do."

She moves suddenly, jumping to her feet and hobbling toward the locked door of my office without her crutches.

"Eva, don't be foolish," I growl, grabbing the crutches and following her. "You're going to be more damage to yourself."

Her entire body stiffens when she tries the handle, only now remembering that she saw me lock it earlier.

"What do you think you are you doing?" I ask, moving toward her, as her shoulders sag and she supports herself against the door.

My cock is harder than a rock, tightly confined in my boxer briefs. It's highly inappropriate that I locked us in here together, let alone asked her to bend over for me. "If you don't bend over my desk in the next five seconds. I'll strip you bare and tie you to it," I growl.

Eva's eyes are wide and full of pain as she turns around to face me, looking shell-shocked by my threat. "Are you being serious right now?"

The question feeds my rage as I stalk toward her. "Did it sound like a joke?" I growl, grabbing hold of her wrists and yanking her against me, placing the crutches in her hands.

A gasp escapes her plump lips as she shakes her head. "I'm telling you the fucking truth. You're being an asshole for not believing me, just like my parents."

"What did you call me?" I glare at her.

Her throat works as she swallows hard at my tone, and she doesn't repeat what she said.

"Bend. Over. Now." I clutch her wrist tighter between my fingers. "Final warning. I won't ask again."

Her cheeks pale as she nods slowly, as if only now realizing how *serious* I am. Each hobbling step she takes toward my desk is slow and hesitant as I watch her walk away before glancing over her shoulder.

I don't waiver as I hold her gaze.

Eva places the crutches against the desk and bends over my desk carefully, not putting pressure on her wound and trying to hold the hem of her skirt down over her ass. She fails, badly.

My cock strains against the zipper of my confining suit pants at the sight of bare skin and a narrow strip of black cotton. I grind my teeth to avoid groaning as I step toward Eva, who is trembling.

Once I'm a foot away from her, she finally speaks, "Sir, this isn't necessary."

I smirk, as she has a lot to learn when it comes to discipline. "It's necessary. What did I tell you to call me, Eva?" I ask, lifting the hem of her skirt all the way to rest on her back with the edge of the ruler.

I can't stifle the soft groan that escapes my lips at the sight of her thong and her practically bare, perfect, firm ass.

"Oak," she murmurs. "Please, don't do—"

I bring the ruler down on her left ass cheek hard and fast, silencing whatever plea was about to escape her plump lips. And then I do the same on her right ass cheek. Both times, she squeals in pain. "Oak, please stop," she mutters.

I draw in a deep breath. "Why? Are you going to admit the truth?"

"Never," she spits. That feisty fire I've grown to enjoy resurfacing as fast as it disappeared.

I spank her ass with the ruler harder, twice on each cheek in quick succession.

She whimpers, her thighs trembling.

I narrow my eyes as I notice a wet patch forming right between her thighs, telling me this is turning her on, although it's supposed to be a punishment.

I move the tip of the ruler between her thighs and stroke it down her wet seam in the cotton, making her gasp. "Eva, this isn't supposed to be pleasurable," I say coldly.

A strangled half-scream comes from her lips as I gently bring the rule down flat against her wet, fabric-clad arousal.

"Such a dirty girl." I slide the tip of the ruler over her red skin. "It's proof that you were so desperate you fucked your school's janitor." I spank her ass cheeks again, watching the way her skin reddens.

The welts are beyond erotic, and all I want is to rub my hands over her skin, caressing the pain away before giving her more. "And now you're getting wet for your principal, aren't you?"

"No," she snarls, her body tensing. "You're a fucking psychopath."

I chuckle at her outburst and spank her repeatedly until she is panting from the mix of pain and pleasure.

"Stop," she cries, her voice a mix of anguish and pure lust. "Please, Oak, stop this."

I place the ruler down on the desk she's bent over

and move closer. "Have you learned your lesson yet? Are you going to tell me what I want to hear?"

The bell rings at that moment. "I have to get to my next class," she breathes.

"I want you to tell the truth. Tell me what you did with your janitor, you dirty girl," I growl, as the reins on my control snap.

"I've already told you. Nothing," Eva grinds out.

"Stand," I order.

She does as I say, grabbing her crutches and straightening up to pull the hem of her skirt down.

I grab her shoulder and force her to turn to face me harder than I should, considering her injury. Our bodies are so close we're touching as her chest rises and falls with sharp intakes of breath. "I want you in this class every day, including weekends. I'll send you a schedule via email. Some days you will have to cut lunch short."

"I don't think this is what my mother had in mind when she asked you to discipline me."

I raise a brow. "Your mother told me to use any means necessary, and I will, Eva. Don't think that I won't."

She shakes her head. "In seven months, I will walk out of this godforsaken school and leave behind my parents' name." Her eyes blaze with purpose. "I will enroll myself in veterinary school before they know what has happened and never return to Atlanta."

My hands remain tight around her shoulders as I yank her closer, pressing her body against mine. I search her eyes, wondering if she believes that. Her parents will hunt her down and drag her right back home. It's hard not to admire her courage, though. "They'll never allow it," I say, regretting it as a flash of sadness enters her eyes.

"I don't care. I want nothing to do with their disgusting business." Her lip curls up. "I'll flee this country if I have to."

I raise a brow, doubting even fleeing the country would evade the reaches of the Carmichaels. They're powerful and have many allies across the globe. "How does this have anything to do with you telling me the truth, though, Eva?" I ask, realizing we've both gotten sidetracked.

Her nostrils flare. "How many times do I have to tell you someone photoshopped that dumb photo?" She clenches her free fist by her side.

"Deny it all you like. I've seen the photo and don't believe you." It's a low blow since I had the photo doctored myself, but I have to break her resolve if I'm going to use her against her parents. "I will spank the answer I want to hear out of you if it fucking kills me."

"You'll never hear that answer from me." Her eyes flicker with defiance as she leans back. "So, you'll have to kill me instead," she says, her voice level and calm.

My eyes dip to her plump, cherry lips, making her bite them temptingly. Tension flares between us as I move my eyes back to hers, seeing the flaming desire raging in those beautiful hazel depths. My cock throbs, desperate for release. I want to fuck this girl right here.

How the fuck can I spend five years planning the Carmichael's ruin only to be spun into a three-sixty the minute I set eyes on their daughter? I clench my jaw, trying to remind myself that this seductive little vixen is, in fact, the offspring of my enemy.

"Oak?" She breathes my name. Her eyes fixed to my lips, which have inched precariously close to her own.

Her breath tickles my face and inhale her intoxicating floral scent.

"Is there perhaps another reason you spanked me?" Eva asks, licking her lips. "Do you feel it too?" Her wide, innocent eyes observe me.

"Feel what?" I snap, wondering what she's going on about.

She shakes her head, flicking her blonde hair over her shoulder. "I'm probably imagining it."

I move my hand to her hips and dig my fingertips into them, wishing my cock wasn't so hard that it's drained all the blood from my fucking brain. "Imagining what, Eva," I bark, my patience slipping.

Her cheeks turn a deep crimson that matches her welted ass as she murmurs, "The chemistry between us."

Fuck.

My only goal when buying this academy was to destroy her family, but now lines are blurring. This girl is flirting with me, stumbling right into my hands. The only problem is that to ruin her, I'd have to ruin myself.

"Be careful, Miss Carmichael." I let go of her hips and take a step away, drawing in a deep breath not infected with her sweet, floral scent. "You don't know who you're messing with."

Her chin rises as she glares at me confidently. "Perhaps you are the one who should be careful, Oak." She walks past me with her crutches as elegantly as her injury will allow toward the door, which is still locked. And then I hear a jangle of keys as she leans on one crutch and slips the office door key into the lock.

The little viper stole them while I spanked her.

She turns around and glares at me. "Catch." Eva throws them at me, forcing me to catch them. And then she hops with such purpose right out of my office, looking magnificent despite the crutches and leaving me aching for her like I've never ached for anyone, slamming the door behind her in her wake.

"Fuck's sake," I mutter to myself, turning around and digging my fingers through my hair.

What the hell am I going to do with Eva Carmichael?

It's the fucking damn question of the century. Everything has seemed certain and my path clear until Eva stormed into my life, like a tornado sweeping into my world and turning everything upside down.

I need to learn how to rein in my desire for her. Otherwise, a Carmichael may destroy me for the second time.

10

EVA

Natalya sits down next to me in our law class, smiling. "You look like someone pissed in your cheerios."

I shake my head. "Shit lesson with Byrne," I mutter, my hands and ass still stinging from his assault. It's hard to believe that they get away with such brutal punishment at this school. The harder thing to believe is the way he touched me afterward. The things he said bordered on sexual.

And now you're getting wet for your principal, aren't you?

My heart is still hammering a little uncontrollably as I think about how it felt to be at his mercy.

Her brow furrows. "Can't have been as bad as combat training." She sighs heavily. "Archer was grumpy today."

Oak was a complete and utter asshole, but I don't want to go into detail. "Who takes this class?" I ask.

"Byrne."

My stomach dips, hearing his name.

"He teaches law, discipline, and leadership."

Fuck.

"Great," I murmur, swallowing hard as my fear and arousal blend at the prospect of seeing him again. Three times in one day is too fucking much.

Her brow furrows as she notices the fading welts on my palms. "

"Did he hit you?" Natalya asks.

I nod in response. "Yes, apparently, that's standard practice here."

Natalya nods. "Oh, it is, but Byrne isn't typically the one who carries out corporal punishment. That's Nitkin."

I sigh. "Great, so I get the special treatment then."

Her brow furrows. "It's a little odd. Why did he hit you?"

"Because he's an asshole," I mutter.

At that moment, Principal Byrne walks into the classroom.

Natalya chuckles softly. "Tell me about it later." She opens her book to page eighty-five, which must be where they're at in this class. The chapter is titled *forensic science.*

A shudder races down my spine as I realize this class teaches these students how to evade the law, remaining on the wrong side of it without getting caught.

Principal Byrne keeps his eyes off of me. Even so, I

feel my cheeks heat in his presence, thinking about how I spoke to him. I'm not sure what got into me, but it happens whenever I'm with him. The desire to push against his authority and annoy him.

The way he touched me was nothing short of erotic, even if it was with a ruler. No teacher should treat a student that way, but this isn't like a normal school.

He spins and writes murder on the board. "Can anyone tell me how you avoid being charged with murder?"

Natalya's hand shoots up.

"Natalya," he says.

She draws in a deep breath. "The most important thing is to ensure you leave no traces of DNA at the scene."

"Exactly." He claps his hands as his eyes land on me. "Eva, how do we ensure that?"

My brow furrows. "I'm sorry, sir, I'm new to this, so I'm not exactly sure."

"You should have caught up while you were hospitalized." His nostrils flare. "And what did I tell you to call me?"

I swallow hard. "I assumed that was during discipline class."

"You assumed wrong." He folds his huge, muscled arms over his chest. "Everything you learn in that class, I expect you to bring to all of our classes together."

I nod in response. "Okay."

His eyes narrow. "Okay, what?"

Natalya shifts next to me as if she's uncomfortable on my behalf.

"Okay, Oak," I grit out, digging my nails into my stinging palms.

Many whispers break out when I address our teacher by his first name, but the asshole smirks. "Good, now Natalya, tell me the answer."

Natalya gives me an apologetic glance before saying, "Always wear gloves, shoe covers, and ideally something over your hair to avoid any coming lose at the scene."

Oak nods. "Correct." His piercing eyes meet mine for a moment.

I glare at him as hatred stirs inside of me. This man is a complete and utter asshole. He may be beautiful, but he's rotten to the core. There was no world in which his beating was necessary, yet he did it anyway.

Sick son of a bitch.

I squeeze my thighs together as he looks away.

The sickest part of it all is that his punishment made me so damn wet. For a brief, delusional time, I wanted him to pull my thong down, shove his cock inside me, and take my virginity. It's all I could think of, and even now, two hours later, I'm still desperate for release.

I've still got one more class, and then I'm going to disappear into my room for a very long, hot *shower*.

"What class do you have next?" I ask as we meander down the hallway, Natalya slowing down her pace so I can keep up with the crutches, as I finally escape Byrne for the day.

Natalya smirks. "Anatomy, with Nitkin." She shakes her head. "Can't fucking wait."

I glance at my timetable, noticing I have the same. "Me too." I raise a brow. "What's so bad about anatomy class?"

"You will see," she says, smirking at me. "Come on."

She places a hand on my shoulder and steers me down the corridor, where a boy marches right toward us, piercing blue eyes fixed on Natalya.

"Fuck," she murmurs.

"What's wrong?" I ask.

Before she replies, the boy speaks, "Well, well, look who we have here." He smirks, and it's a cruel smile that sends shivers down my spine. "Gurin always has to latch onto the newbies because she has no fucking friends."

His two friends chuckle in response.

"Go away, Elias," she mutters, trying to urge me past him.

Elias holds his muscled, tattooed arm out in front of her, stopping her dead. "That's rude, Natalya. Introduce me to your friend." He has dark, messy hair that curls over his forehead. The dress shirt he's wearing is only buttoned up three quarters so you can see the dark tattoos scrolling over his skin, and he has the arms rolled up his forearms revealing more ink. He's wearing a pair of black pants and ridiculously expensive Italian leather shoes.

Her eyes are blazing with hatred as she glares up at him. "Take your hands off me before I land you in the infirmary."

He laughs. "I'd like to see you try." His attention moves to me. "Elias Morales. Who are you?"

I swallow hard, my attention moving between him and Natalya. "I'm Eva Carmichael."

He shoves Natalya back and steps closer to me. "Beautiful for an Irish girl," he murmurs before glancing back at his friends. "Let me introduce you to Rosa Cabello and Nikolai Kushev."

The girl has onyx hair, which is dead straight and falls to her waist. She has dark brown eyes and tanned skin, complemented by the beautiful red halter neck top she wears and a pair of emerald green pants. Nikolai stands close to Rosa with his arm around her back and hand resting on her hip.

His hair is bright blond and medium length, curling just over the lapel of his smart dress shirt, partly covering a dark tattoo that disappears beneath it. His skin is pale, and his blue eyes are icy as he regards me warily, his free hand shoved into the pocket of his black pants.

Elias clears his throat, drawing my attention back to him. "You should be careful about who you make friends with." He glares at Natalya hatefully, but there's something else in his eyes too. Desire, perhaps?

"Yes, I will be." And then I use my crutches to move away from him before saying, "I certainly won't be friends with you, that's for sure. I'd rather be friends with a fucking corpse." I hold my chin high, despite being certain this guy is dangerous.

Natalya gasps softly beside me.

He tilts his head, eyeing me dangerously. "Is that right, Carmichael?" His gaze moves to Natalya. "I'm sure I can arrange that."

I move forward and hit him in the shin with one of my crutches, forcing him out of my way. "Now, move the fuck out of our way." Natalya follows as I move around him. "We don't have time for assholes," I call back.

"Shit, you may regret that, Eva," she murmurs once we're out of earshot.

My brow furrows. "Why?"

She shakes her head. "Elias Morales hates people who stand up to him, and that was your first encounter." Her lips draw into a tight line. "He was trying to hit on you, and you made him look a fool."

"Is that why he hates you?" I ask.

"No, he had it out for me before I even spoke to him."

I glance back down the corridor to find the three bullies are no longer there. "He doesn't scare me. If he has a problem, fuck him."

Natalya smiles. "You are incredible. We're going to be good friends. I have to introduce you to my friends Camilla and Adriana at dinner." She laughs. "They were already going to love you, but when I tell them you stood up to Elias, they'll probably worship you."

My stomach flips a little, and I wonder if I've made a mistake talking back to that boy. The thing I hate the most in this world is bullies. We make it to the classroom, both a little breathless.

Natalya leads me over to a seat at the front and slumps down in it. "Are you alright?"

I nod. "Yeah, this place takes some getting used to."

She chuckles. "It's all I've ever known."

I shake my head. "Is Elias like the resident bully?"

Natalya nods, her face turning serious. "He's had it out for me ever since he arrived here in fourth grade."

"Why?" I ask.

Natalya shrugs. "Beats me. I did nothing to him. He just hated me at first fucking sight." She sighs heavily. "I think it's because he hates how smart I am."

It might have something to do with Elias's crush on the beautiful Russian. I'd know the look he gave her anywhere.

A sharp knock on wood echoes through the classroom, drawing everyone's attention to the front, where a tall, dark-haired man stands, glaring out at us all with unique hazel eyes.

"Page Seventy-five," he orders, his voice stern and accented.

Natalya quickly grabs her book and thumbs to the page. There's an unusual atmosphere in this class. The unease in the air is palpable amongst all the students.

Nitkin.

He sure as hell does command fear, as I can practically smell it seeping off of every student in the room.

I grab my book and turn to the requested page before glancing back up at the notorious Professor Nitkin. He is undeniably attractive—as hot as any male model. "What is it with all the teachers here being so hot?" I murmur in question to Natalya.

Her eyes widen. "Don't talk in this lesson unless you want to be punished." She glances up at Nitkin as he writes on the board. "I don't know, but you're right. Pretty much all the staff are hot, even the women."

I chuckle at that.

Suddenly, Natalya grunts as something hits the back of her head. "Ouch," she says, placing a hand where it hit and turning around to glare at Elias, who is staring at her with his piercing blue eyes.

"What you looking at, Gurin? I'm hot, but there's no need to stare."

Natalya's normally calm features turn furious as she glares at the heavily tattooed boy, shaking her head. "Perhaps you should go fuck yourself, then."

The shock on his face is amazing, as it seems my standing up to him in the corridor got her confidence up. I give her a soft nudge and a knowing smile, and she shrugs. "What's the worst that can happen, hey?"

A bang on our desk makes both of us jump as the Professor glares down at us. "Do you two already know all you need to know about the liver?"

My stomach churns at the tone of his voice. And I shake my head. "Sorry, sir. I'm afraid not."

His eyes narrow. "You are new. What's your name?"

"Eva, sir."

He nods. "Welcome, Eva. Now pay attention, or I'll make you carve up the liver, no matter how little you know about it."

My brow furrows, and I wonder what he's talking about until he whips off a lid from a silver platter at the front. "This is a human liver."

I stifle a gasp, wanting to ask where the fuck he got a human liver from, but I know I won't like the answer. Also, I don't get the sense that this is a class where you ask questions. A shiver travels down my spine as I stare at the bloody organ. I hold a hand over my mouth as nausea rolls through my stomach.

"Where can we find the liver on a human body?" Nitkin asks.

Not even Natalya puts up her hand in this class.

"No one?" He asks.

I hesitantly put my hand up, as biology was one of my top classes at my last school. After all, I want to be a vet.

"Yes, Eva."

"The right side of the abdominal cavity, just below the diaphragm, sir," I say.

He claps his hands; the sound makes me jump. "Right." His gaze roams over the entire class. "And who can tell me the best way to damage the liver?"

My heart skips a beat as I realize what this anatomy class is all about.

How could I be so stupid?

I'd hoped it would be like biology, but it appears it's all about working out the best way to murder people, essentially a class in killing. It couldn't be more contrary to my desire to learn how to save animals' lives. I hate this fucking place. Natalya might seem like a nice girl, but this is what she's interested in, becoming a criminal, just like my parents.

Can I be friends with someone like her?

A part of me wants to be, as she's been so friendly to me, but the other part knows what these students will become once they graduate—killers, drug dealers, and, worse.

"Natalya. You must know the answer to this?" Nitkin presses.

She nods in response. "Yes, the best way is to stab through the front of the chest where there's no protection from the ribs, but this can be challenging in a fight." She shrugs. "If you are going to do that, you may as well aim for the heart."

My stomach twists at her cold and calculated answer.

Elias is right. I need to be careful who I'm friends

with here, as it's easy to forget that criminals surround me.

"Over here," Natalya says, leading me through the busy cafeteria toward a table near the back, as my crutches clack on the cafeteria floor, making me long for the moment Nurse Jasper tells me I can walk without them. "I can't wait for them to meet you."

My stomach churns, as I've never been very sociable. The idea of meeting new people, especially the people that attend this fucked up school, scares me.

She heads straight toward a table where two girls sit, chatting. One has dark chestnut brown hair, and the other has golden-brown hair, each beautiful in their own right.

"Girls, I'd like you to meet my new friend, Eva," Natalya announces.

They both turn and smile at me. "Hey. Is this the famous girl who stood up to Elias in the corridor?" The golden-haired girl says.

Natalya smiles widely. "It is. Eva, meet Camilla," she gestures toward the girl with golden-brown hair.

"Nice to meet you," I say.

She then signals to the darker-haired girl. "And Adrianna."

I give her a nod.

Camilla pulls a seat out next to her. "Come and sit with us."

I smile and place my crutches against the table and take the seat, trying to ignore my anxiety.

"So, what exactly did you say to Elias?" She asks.

I shrug. "He told me to pick my friends carefully."

"And she told him she won't be friends with him, as she'd rather be friends with a fucking corpse," Natalya cuts in.

Camilla's eyes widen. "Shit. I hope he didn't take it personally."

"Not to mention, she called him an asshole after hitting him in the shin with her crutches," Natalya adds.

My brow furrows. "Why? What would he do?"

Adriana snorts. "What wouldn't he do? The guy is a psycho." She glances at Natalya. "Haven't you told her what he's done to you in the past?"

Natalya shakes her head. "Let's not talk about that right now." She bites her bottom lip. "I may have told him to fuck himself in anatomy class."

Adrianna whistles. "You must be a glutton for punishment, Nat. He won't let that slide from *you*."

She shakes her head. "It's about time I stood up to him. In seven months, I will have graduated and never have to see him again."

Camilla sighs. "True." Her eyes scan the cafeteria as if she's searching for imminent danger. "I'm starving. Let's get some food."

After anatomy class, I wonder whether I should

hang out with anyone here. I grab my crutches and follow the three girls up to get our food, feeling a little on edge. They are all criminals or future criminals if they've yet to commit any crimes. Natalya helps me out, grabbing two trays so she can carry my food for me.

We return to our table and sit and eat the food, which is ridiculously good for cafeteria food, chatting together for longer than I expect. All the while, I struggle to relax, knowing what these girls are capable of.

It doesn't make me feel any less alone in this crazy school, despite finding friends. I don't belong here, but thankfully I only have to endure it for another seven months.

11

OAK

Tension coils through me as I walk toward the girl's dormitories, searching for Eva.

She's attended every discipline class I put on her schedule for a little over two weeks until today. Eva was supposed to be at my office twenty minutes ago, and she didn't show up. Her injury is a lot better now, as she's been off the crutches just under a week, after Elaine Jasper confirmed she has no nerve damage and his healing nicely.

I searched for her in the library, cafeteria, and courtyard, to no avail. Her room is the only place I haven't checked.

Today's lesson is the first period, so I assume she either forgot or overslept. Either way, I intend to drag her out of bed and spank her perfect little ass.

Normally, I wouldn't go seeking my students. I'd punish them for not turning up by sending them to

Professor Nitkin. Eva is mine to punish, mine to inflict pain on. I know I'll never send her into his hands.

As I open the door to the girls' dormitory, I'm met by two girls who blush the moment they see me.

"Morning, Principal Byrne," they say in chorus.

"Morning," I grunt, holding the door open so they can slip out into the corridor.

The dormitory wing is quiet, as most girls should be in class. I walk to room sixty-nine and knock on the door. Silence is the response, so I knock again, harder this time.

A groan echoes from the other side, followed by soft footsteps nearing the door. The door swings open, and Eva's eyes go wide when she sees me.

I feel my cock throb in my tight boxer briefs at the sight of her in an almost sheer pale gold nightgown. Her hard nipples are visible through the fabric. It takes all my self-control to drag my eyes to her face, rather than lower, to find out if she's wearing a thong.

Eva folds her arms over her chest. "Sir, I mean, Oak… What are you…" She stops and glances back at her clock. "Oh shit, I'm sorry." She shakes her head. "My alarm must not have gone off."

I stand there, unable to speak, as my body battles with my mind. All I want to do is shove Eva into her room and fuck her over and over until she screams my name so loud the entire school hears us.

I clench my jaw. "It's not acceptable, Eva." I force

myself to keep my gaze on her beautiful eyes. "The more discipline classes you take, the worse you get."

She sighs heavily. "Sir, I—"

"Oak," I growl.

"Shit, Oak, sorry."

My eyes narrow. "You have a very dirty mouth, too." I take a step closer to her, pushing her to take one back into her room.

"I'll get dressed and be in your office in five minutes."

I shake my head. "We don't have time for that." I narrow my eyes at her. "I'll teach you in here."

Her face pales, and she shakes her head. "That's very inappropriate."

"I don't care." I take two more steps before turning and slamming her door shut. The moment it is shut, her sweet floral scent invades my senses, making it difficult to concentrate. My eyes scan her room, landing on the vibrator flashing on the nightstand.

Dirty little girl.

Eva clears her throat, looking mortified that I noticed the vibrator. Quickly, she scrambles over and grabs it, shoving it into the nightstand. "I wasn't expecting company," she mutters, looking adorable when she turns that deep pink color.

"Tell me what you've learned these past two weeks in our classes."

Her tongue darts out over her bottom lip before she

sighs. "I've learned that you enjoy inflicting pain." She shrugs. "That's about the sum of it."

I narrow my eyes. "That is all?"

She nods in response, keeping her chin held high. "Pretty much."

"You're supposed to be learning that lying has consequences."

"I know lying had consequences, but I've told you I'm not lying."

I run a hand through my hair. "Perhaps I need to take a different approach."

Eva's throat bobs softly. "What kind of approach?"

I glare at her. "I'm not certain yet." I turn around, knowing that being in her room with her is extremely dangerous. "Follow me."

"But, I'm not dressed."

I don't turn around. "Grab a robe and follow me." When she doesn't move, irritation claws at my insides.

After a few beats of silence, she rushes over to her bathroom door and grabs a robe, slipping it on.

"Where are we going?" She asks.

"No questions," I say as I lead her out of her bedroom and down the corridor.

I walk toward the adjoining chapel of the school, knowing two boys got into a bloody fight last night. Eva isn't responding to physical pain, but perhaps forcing her to scrub blood off the floor might have a better result.

The moment we enter, Eva gasps at the blood splattering the floor. "What happened here?" Her eyes are wide as I glance at her over my shoulder.

"Two boys fought last night." I grab a bucket and scrubbing brush out of the closet. "Fill this up from the tap." I nod at a small sink toward the back. "And get to work."

Eva's eyes move between the bucket and my face multiple times before she sighs and grabs it off me. She's on the mend from her injury, so being on her hands and knees for half an hour shouldn't do any damage.

I sit on the pew directly in front of the bloodstains, watching as she fills her bucket. If she's surprised by me sitting so close, she doesn't show it. Instead, she pulls her white gown off and places it next to me, giving me a pointed look. "I don't want blood on it," she says before sinking to her knees with a slight grimace and scrubbing the bloodstained floor.

My body blazes with heat at the sight of her in that slip.

Eva is bent over with her back to me, which gives me a tantalizing view of her pretty little ass and pussy nestled between her thighs, even if the sheer fabric somewhat obscures it.

I rub a hand over my cock, cussing under my breath. It strains against the bounds of my pants, yearning to be freed and buried in my pupil's tight virgin pussy. The obscenity of having such disgusting thoughts in the school chapel only turns me on more.

I'm going to hell.

When I'm certain she can't see, I rub myself through my pants harder. The desire to pull my cock out and masturbate until I reach my peak and then shoot my cum over her full ass is so strong, but I don't allow my desire to rule me.

Instead, I clench my jaw tight and remain satisfied with the gentle rub of my hand over my aching length.

Eva moves around innocently, peering over her shoulder now and then. Her butt wiggles from side to side as she scrubs, making me so hard it feels like I might die if I don't find my release.

I clear my throat and speak, hoping it will distract me. "Tell me, Eva. Did you have similar punishments at your last school?"

Her brow furrows as she glances at me over her shoulder. "Of course not. It was a normal school."

"Surely, teachers punished pupils for bad behavior."

"Never me. I've never been punished until I came to this hellhole."

Her sincerity is refreshing, but it irritates me that every time she speaks her mind, it only makes me want her more. "Is that right? I find it hard to believe."

She turns her attention back to the spot she's cleaning. "I don't care if you believe it or not. It's the truth. Something you have no regard for."

I've never allowed a pupil to speak to me the way

she does, and yet, no part of me wants to punish her for it. I want my sick and twisted way with her.

"You missed a spot," I say, pointing to a small splatter of blood in an area she'd moved away from.

Her eyes narrow, and then she crawls over to it, facing me, huffing under her breath. I stifle a groan at the sight of her hard nipples, pointing through the almost sheer fabric.

"What was that?" I snap.

She shakes her head, smiling innocently. "Nothing, sir–I mean, Oak."

I grip hold of the pew beneath me so hard it's a wonder the wood doesn't bow and snap as she turns her full attention back to the job at hand. The next fifteen minutes are sheer torture as I save every image of her on all fours in my mental picture gallery, holding them in my memories so I can work out my frustration straight after we're finished.

With five minutes to spare, Eva stands and announces, "Finished."

I tilt my head to the side. "Have you learned your lesson yet?" I ask.

Eva glares at me. "Not sure what lesson it is I'm supposed to be learning. I've told you the truth, and it's you that isn't accepting it."

I flex my fingers, wondering why she doesn't tell a little white lie and be done with it.

Is she that incapable of bending the truth?

"Come here," I order, glancing briefly at the clock

on the wall. If I'm too long, Eva will be very late for her next class, as she needs to get dressed. "Over my knee, Eva."

Her body turns rigid. "Sorry?"

I flex my fingers to stop myself from grabbing her and forcing her over it. "I said, over my knee."

"I heard you, but that—"

I grab her wrist hard and yank her across my lap, groaning as I feel her wriggle against the press of my erection. The scent of her so close makes it impossible to control myself as I lightly lift the hem of her nightgown.

She fights against me. "Oak, I don't have any panties on."

"Good," I growl, lifting the hem right to her hips.

She glances at me from over her shoulder, brow furrowed. "Where is the ruler?" She asks, her voice so quiet.

The dark, monstrous part of me delights in the sound. "I forgot it, so my hand will have to do."

Her eyes widen. "Isn't that a little—"

My hand lands on her right cheek before she can finish the question.

Eva recoils, squealing softly. The sensation of my hand striking her is no doubt different from the wooden ruler I've used on her for the past two weeks. It's impossible to deny the need to caress her ass cheeks in my hands, stroking the skin after each spank.

Eva's thighs tremble as her arousal glistens

between her thick thighs. It takes all my willpower not to touch her there, not to bury my face in her pretty little cunt.

Eva has control over me that's she not even aware of. Each time I punish her, I feel a little more of my control slip. I know I should put a stop to her daily lessons, but it's as if I'm powerless.

"Oak," she practically moans my name, making my cock throb against her abdomen. She wriggles again, trying to fucking kill me.

"What?" I rasp, struggling to maintain my position as an authoritative figure rather than a lover. I want to tell her to moan my name while I fuck the innocence right out of her on the chapel floor.

Her thighs clench together. "I've already told you the truth," she breathes.

"Wrong answer," I say before bringing my hand down on her ass again, allowing my fingers to move closer to her center. "Stand. Up." I grit out. If I don't stop now, I will impale myself in the sweet, innocent little virgin before she can say the word *no*.

Eva trembles as she returns to her feet, straightening up. She reaches to pull the hem of her nightgown down, but I grab her wrist to stop her.

"No," I order.

I can feel the tenuous grip on my control slipping as I take in the beautiful sight of her so bare for me. A few moments tick by as memorize it like a masterpiece of art. When I move my eyes back to her face, I realize where her eyes are fixated; on the thick outline of my erection.

I clear my throat, snapping her out of it. "You are dismissed."

Eva's eyes flash with disappointment as she licks her lips before nodding. She pulls the hem of her slip down, grabs the robe, and wraps it around herself. Without another word, she rushes away from the chapel and me—away from the monster who wants to devour her whole and spit out her fucking bones.

If Eva knew the truth, she'd run for her life and never look back.

12

EVA

I rush down the hallway toward my next class, knowing I'm already late for English with Professor Jameson. By far, out of all the teachers, she is the nicest of them.

Not to mention, she teaches both math and English, the two normal subjects at this God-forsaken school.

After Oak spanked me over his knee, I had to rush back to my dorm, dress as fast as I could, and run back out.

He is insane. He may be hot as hell, and at first, the idea of being bent over daily and spanked by such a dominant, sexy man fed a dark fantasy of mine, but as our lessons carried on, I wondered what he was getting out of it. Now, it seems he's changed tactic, which I'm reminded of as I glance down at my still red fingers. My skin crawls at the memory of how much blood there was on that floor. I've tried to scrub the blood off them, but I didn't have enough time.

When I first met Oak, I couldn't stop thinking about how good it would be to cross the line between teacher and student, but the saying, be careful what you wish for, is fitting for this situation. He never crosses that line, but he flirts with it, and I can see the longing in his eyes afterward.

Today was just as bad. Oak watched me bend over in my slip as I scrubbed the floor, and I could see that dark lust in his eyes. Then he hauled me over his knee and spanked me with his hand…

I don't have the words to explain how erotic it was and how wrong it was for my principal to do that to me. I can still feel the phantom press of his hard erection against my abdomen. If there's one thing that I'm certain of, Oak gets off on inflicting pain.

I shake my head as I hasten my footsteps, rounding the corner only to bump straight into Elias. A dark smirk spreads onto his lips. "Look who it is. Eva Carmichael." His eyes narrow. "Do you realize who you are fucking with?"

I tilt my head to the side. "Not really, and I don't care. I'm late for math." I try to sidestep around him, but he steps into my path.

"No one talks to me the way you did and gets away with it." He cracks his neck. "Now you've made Gurin think she can talk shit to me too, which I will ensure never happens again."

I cross my arms over my chest. "Get out of my way."

His fists clench by his side before he wraps his fingers around my neck, practically lifting me off the floor.

I struggle to draw in any breath, staring into his soulless blue eyes. My heart hammers so hard as I thrash my legs toward him, trying to break free by any means possible.

"Listen to me, you little bitch," he growls. "Natalya is mine to torment and always has been. Mine, do you understand? If you step in one more time, I'll fucking kill you." His eyes narrow. "Do you under—"

"Morales," Oak's roaring voice cuts through the corridor. "Drop her now," he growls.

He obeys, literally dropping me on my ass.

I groan at the impact and struggle to get to my feet, but before I can, Oak hauls me up himself.

"What the fuck are doing assaulting a girl in an empty corridor?" Oak asks.

Elias smirks at him. "Sorry, sir, but that's what this school is all about." He tilts his head, glancing at me. "How is she going to take over an organization if she can't hold her own against others?"

"Nitkin, now," Oak roars, rage stirring in his eyes.

Elias' eyes darken. "No."

I'm shocked to hear Elias stand up to Oak; however, Oak isn't, or if he is, he doesn't show it. "Your games are tiresome, Elias. Report to Professor Nitkin before I haul you there myself."

Elias glares at me before returning his attention to Oak. "Why? What school rules did I break?"

He has a point. This school doesn't have any rules, not in the traditional sense.

Oak glares at him, standing taller as he squares up to the brutal young man. "Since I'm the principal of this school, I can decide what I punish you for, Elias." I doubt it's rare for pupils to challenge his authority. After all, he's teaching psychopaths how to run their criminal empires.

Elias' eyes move to me and then back to Oak, and he smirks. "I've had Natalya Gurin in similar holds while you walked by without a word, and yet, this beautiful Irish girl comes along, and you are defending her." He strokes his chin as if thinking. "Interesting, Byrne." His eyes move to me. "It would appear you have a secret admirer," Elias says.

I feel my cheeks heat but say nothing in return.

Oak merely glares at him with his arms crossed over his chest and legs wide apart, waiting for him to do as he's told.

Elias remains irritatingly cocky, glaring at him. "Do you want the school to know that you have a crush on a student, Byrne?" He asks.

Oak's jaw works. "Your accusations are unfounded. Get to class before I throw you out of this fucking school," he says, his voice oddly calm.

Elias smirks in response and then heads down the hallway, escaping punishment from Nitkin.

I stare up at Oak, brow furrowed. "Why didn't you force him to go to Nitkin?"

His bright aquamarine eyes meet mine, and there's a mix of guilt and confusion in them. "Don't question me, Eva." I watch as his fists clench by his side. "Get to class. You're going to be late." His tone is cold.

I lick my bottom lip. "Is it because what Elias said is true?"

He growls, hands moving to my hips as he pushes me up against a nearby locker. "What exactly do you believe he said that is true?"

My stomach flutters anxiously as I stare into his beautiful eyes, wondering what demons haunt him. Oakley Byrne is deeply tormented. The rage that often works itself to the surface is proof of that.

"That you have a crush on me," I say, my voice sounding more confident than I expected.

His lips curl into a wicked smirk, one that makes dread sink like a lead weight in my stomach. "Is that what you hope, Eva?" His nostrils flaring. "That I want to fuck you?"

I shake my head. "You were hard when you—"

His fingers wrap around my throat and squeeze, cutting the words off mid-sentence. "Don't," he growls.

I try to claw at his fingers, but he doesn't let go.

"You are my pupil. That is all. Now get to class

before I send you to Nitkin." He winces at the threat before releasing a hold on my throat.

I draw in a deep gasp of oxygen before scurrying away from him. For the first time since we met, I'm scared of him.

There's always been this darkness surrounding him, but this was the first time I've seen it in action. I don't speak again, rushing toward Professor Jameson's classroom as rapid as I can without a glance backward.

I reach for my throat, the ghost of Oak's fingers lingering. His touch differed from Elias', but it didn't make it any less terrifying.

Someone has already shut the door to the classroom as I round the corner.

Great.

I walk up to the door and turn the handle, which draws everyone's attention to me. "I'm sorry I'm late, professor."

Professor Jameson scowls slightly. "Don't let it happen again, Eva." She nods to my seat at the front next to Camilla, and I take it.

Camilla frowns at me. "What happened to your neck?" She whispers.

I reach for it and wince slightly, finding it sore. "Elias," I say.

"Shit," she mutters. "You're lucky you aren't in the infirmary. What happened?"

Heat coils through my veins as I meet her questioning gaze. "Byrne came along and stopped him."

Professor Jameson claps her hands. "Girls, you are supposed to be reading The Tiger in the Smoke, not chatting."

"Sorry, professor," I mutter, grabbing the book out of my rucksack and placing it on the table.

I quickly flip to the page I was up to in the book and focus my attention on it. My heart is still frantically beating in my chest, not because of my run-in with Elias Morales. I run my fingers over the place where Oak wrapped his palm around my throat, remembering the heat that surged inside of me.

What the fuck is wrong with me?

All I should have felt when Oak touched me so aggressively was fear, and yet my gut tightened and desire flooded my veins. When Elias did the same thing, I was scared, yet I was scared when Oak did it but turned on too. It's so confusing. It made me hot and bothered and unbelievably needy for him.

I try to focus on the words on the page, but they all blend into one. My mind is scrambled by what happened in that corridor. Not to mention what happened in the chapel.

Camilla nudges me slightly. "What happened to your hands?" She whispers.

I glance down and see that she's noticed the bloodstains. "Discipline class with Byrne involved me scrubbing blood off the chapel floor," I respond quietly, making sure Professor Jameson doesn't glance back up while I speak.

"Ew, gross," Camilla says, shaking her head. "I guess he didn't let you leave with enough time to scrub the blood off you." She leans closer to me. "Did he say who was involved?"

I shake my head. "No, just that two boys fought."

She nods and flips her page in the book before glancing back at me. "I heard it was two kids in seventh grade."

I raise a brow. "Where did you hear that?"

A slam of a hand against wood makes us both jump as we glance up at Professor Jameson. "What did I tell you, girls?" Her eyes narrow. "Do I have to seat you two separately?"

We both shake our heads in unison. "No, sorry, Professor," Camilla says before focusing her attention on the book.

"It won't happen again," I assure her.

She looks unconvinced, but waves her hand dismissively.

I glance down at the book's page, but again, all I can think about is Oak. The way he acted in the corridor was both horrifying and exciting. Two things that shouldn't go hand in hand, yet I'm quickly learning that with Oak, everything he does seems to get me hot and bothered.

I can't work out if it's because he's forbidden or because, for some strange reason, I'm drawn to him, connected to him in a way I've never been with anyone.

13

OAK

I flex my chest muscles, stretching out my back, as I watch the clock's hand strike one o'clock in the afternoon.

Time for my lesson with Eva.

My fingers drum impatiently on the desk as I wait for her to arrive. Eva has been late for every one of our discipline sessions since we started just over two weeks ago, and it doesn't matter how much I try to instill that fear in her. She will not bend to my will.

She's stronger than expected. Every time I punish her, I come that much closer to snapping the line I have on my control. It's as if she's trying to taunt the beast to come out to play. After our first session, I assumed she may have worn more discreet underwear, but she wears the same skimpy little thongs each time.

After yesterday's in the chapel and then in the corridor, I fear she may not turn up. The fear in her eyes was as real as I've ever seen it, and it made me sick to my stomach. I'm a sick son of a bitch, and I know it.

I've made her attend discipline class every day, even on weekend, because I have a twisted need to touch her daily and inflict pain on her as I watch her panties get wet. I affect her as much as she affects me, but the question is, what the fuck am I going to do about it?

The big hand moves to two minutes past, and I clench my jaw. Yesterday, Eva forced me to find her in her dorm room, but I know she's up and somewhere in this school now. She had two classes this morning. If she keeps pushing the boundaries, I'll snap.

Sweet, innocent Eva doesn't want the beast that lurks behind the man. After her mother and father were through with destroying me, the darkness I'd tried to contain ruled me for the first few years—darkness I now have tenuous control over.

I reach for the ruler in the drawer of my desk, but instead of pulling it out, my fingers skate over the leather riding crop I brought in here the day after I spanked Eva for the first time. A more sensual implement, but one I think I need to use on Eva. Her lack of progress means I need to be harsher with her, as she knows what I want to hear, but she won't break.

Forcing her to clean the floors was perhaps even less effective. The determination in her eyes was even fiercer afterward.

The large hand hits ten past, and I stand, pacing the floor.

Who the fuck does she think she is playing with?

If she isn't here in one minute, I'm going to search the school for her, and when I find her, I will drag her by her neck right to this room and make her wish that she'd never disobeyed me.

I open the door, barreling out of it, only to smash straight into Eva. The impact knocks her to the floor as she winces.

Shit.

"Eva, are you okay?" I ask, kneeling next to her. The building rage inside me twists to a slight simmer in the background.

She looks a little stunned for a moment before nodding. "Yes, sorry, were you going somewhere?"

I stand and hold out a hand for her to take, not answering her question.

She looks hesitant, and that fear I saw yesterday remains as she takes it and allows me to pull her to her feet.

"Inside, now," I order.

Her eyes flash at the sudden authoritative tone of my voice, but she doesn't throw back a retort, passing me and heading into my office.

Once the door is shut, she says, "Well, you've already bruised my ass today, so it looks like I'm off the hook."

I narrow my eyes at her. "Not even close." I glance

at the clock. "You were over ten minutes late. This insubordination is becoming tiring, Eva."

She tilts her head, brow furrowing. "Were you coming to find me, Oak?" she asks, a flirtatious tone to her voice, as if she isn't scared about the way I treated her yesterday.

Over the past two weeks, she slipped easily into using my first name. I enjoyed it at first as using it made her squirm, but now it sounds natural and not as entertaining. Surely she isn't stupid enough to push the subject again, not after I lost it with her.

"Bend over, Eva," I order.

Her nostrils flare, and a flicker of amusement enters her brilliant hazel eyes as she walks toward the desk and slowly bends at the waist, hiking her skirt up.

A deep growl rumbles through my chest when I see her perfect little pussy bear for me. I squeeze my erection, feeling so uncomfortable as my cock lengthens. "No thong today, Eva?" I ask.

Eva glances over her shoulder. "You've already seen me buck naked." She shrugs her shoulder. "What's the point? It's more comfortable, anyway."

I can't contain my desire as I step toward her. "Perhaps this is your way of admitting the truth. Tell me what I want to hear, and this all ends now."

Eva shakes her head. "I'm a virgin who hasn't kissed a boy, let alone a man."

I groan, finding it almost impossible to believe that

Eva is *that* innocent, that untouched. "Don't lie to me," I say, but my voice sounds strangled.

"Never," she murmurs.

I feel the reins on my self-control slip as I move closer before spanking her bare ass cheek with my hand and then massaging the skin. "Such a dirty girl," I say.

Eva moans softly, arching her back in invitation.

"Tell me what I want to hear."

If Eva were like her parents, she would have lied to me long ago. No matter what I do to her, she stays firm in her conviction, which only makes me want her more. "Never," she rasps, but that fierce tone is laced with lust.

It takes every ounce of control not to slide my fingers through her bare pussy. Instead, I reach for the riding crop and lash her ass with it hard.

Eva yelps, her hips rising from the desk. "What the fuck was—"

I strike her again and again until she's panting and whimpering. It's the only way I know how to stop myself from touching her, making her mine. None of this was part of the plan to destroy her family.

I should throw her to Archer and be done with it, but the mere thought makes the darkness rise to my surface, threatening to tear apart all that I've worked for.

"Tell me, Eva." I set the riding crop down and gently massage her welted ass with the palm of my hand, shutting my eyes at the soft feel of her skin against my rough hands.

Eva whimpers softly before shaking her head. "When will you accept I've been telling the truth from the start?" She glances over her shoulder at me, a mix of anguish and longing in her eyes. "The only man that has ever seen me this naked is *you*."

I growl softly, parting her ass cheeks to get a better view of her virgin cunt. "Is that right, baby girl?" I ask, the nickname escaping me before I can stop it.

A strangled moan escapes her lips. "Yes," she breathes, her thighs trembling. "Only you." Wetness dampens her inner thighs, as I know she's been anticipating this moment as much as I have.

"Have you been fantasizing about this?" I ask, feeling my mind waging war on my body, which has no intention of listening. The words unleash a tornado raging beneath my skin as the climax of the storm brews dangerously.

"Oak," she breathes my name, still watching me over her shoulder. "I—

I spank her ass again, making her whimper. "If you lie, I'll know," I murmur.

She keeps watching me over her shoulder, eyes full of desire. "I want you," she breathes.

Those three words tear me apart as all my common sense eludes me. Eva is tempting the beast to come out and play. "Have you been using that vibrator on this pretty little pussy and thinking about me, Eva?" I ask, gently running a finger through her soaking wet arousal.

"Yes." Her throat bobs as she continues to hold my gaze. "I've played with myself every night since we met, imagining you inside of me."

I growl and pull her to her feet, yanking her against me.

"You are walking a dangerous line, Miss Carmichael."

She licks her bottom lip, drawing my eyes to them. "Perhaps that's what I want. Danger," she murmurs.

My self-control obliterates as I crash my lips into hers, kissing her with pent-up and dark frustration. I let my hands slip lower to her ass, gripping each cheek hard as I pull her against me, wanting her to feel how hard she makes me.

Eva moans as her lips part for me, allowing my tongue entrance as I search her mouth. It's as if I'm starving for her, and I need to suck the very essence of her into my body, infect my blood with her.

My common sense is no longer working as I slide my fingers between her thighs, feeling how wet she is. "Fuck," I breathe against her lips before trailing them lower to her neck.

Eva is wetter than any woman I've ever had in my arms—so fucking wet. I let my finger delve into her warm heat, making her gasp. "Oak," she moans my name softly, making me even harder.

After the way I snapped at her in the corridor

yesterday morning, it's a surprise she is here. It's a surprise she hasn't stayed far away from me.

"This is one time I want you to call me sir, Eva," I growl against her skin.

Her eyes flash with such longing as she nods. "Yes, sir."

I groan and capture her lips again, drowning in the utter deliciousness that is my student.

The student who is the offspring of my enemies. Reality snaps through me like a firm belt against my ass. I push away from Eva, startling her.

"Sir?" She stares at me with confusion and disappointment, her throat bobbing softly as she swallows.

I shake my head. "I'm sorry, I shouldn't have—"

Eva doesn't allow me time to finish as she pushes forward and pulls my lips back to hers. "You should have," she murmurs before slipping her tongue into my mouth tentatively.

The kiss is different, innocent, and uncertain as I allow her to lead it, allow her to kiss me at her pace. I softly place my hand on her hips, drawing her closer to me. This moment is perfect, wrapped in her arms, but I can't stave off the darkness and the need to dominate as I tighten my fingers on her hips and force her to turn around, making her gasp as I hike up her skirt and slide a finger through her soaking wet cunt.

Eva gasps, glancing at me over her shoulder. "Sir?"

A loud knock comes at my office door, breaking

through the cloud of insanity that had taken over my mind.

I step back away from her, dropping the hem of her skirt. My finger is still wet from delving inside of her tight virgin pussy.

What the fuck am I doing?

14

EVA

I bolt upright, my heart hammering so hard it feels like I'm about to go into cardiac arrest.

Oak straightens, returning to his side of the desk and sitting in his chair. "Who is it?" He calls, then mouths to me, "Sit in the chair, Eva."

I swallow hard and sink into the chair opposite him, feeling my cheeks heat.

"It's Professor Jameson."

My stomach dips as I wonder if she heard me moaning the principal's name.

"Come on in," Oak calls, barely appearing affected by the fact we almost got caught in a rather uncompromising position.

I shift uncomfortably in my seat, remaining rigid as I face forward, pretending to focus on a textbook on Oak's desk. Ever since we started this fucking lesson, he's hardly touched this book. All he has done is spank me since the first day and now...

I can hardly think about what we just did and what it means.

"Hi, Oak." She stops when she sees me. "Oh, I apologize. I thought you were alone."

Oak shakes his head. "No, I teach Eva discipline in her free periods, since she is new to the school."

Professor Jameson smiles at me, but there's an edge to it. "Hi, Eva."

"Hi, Professor."

"Shall I come back later, Oak?" She twirls a strand of her strawberry blonde hair through her fingers flirtatiously. "I wanted to discuss arrangements regarding the winter formal." She flutters her eyelids, and I suddenly have the urge to stand up and punch her in the face.

My stomach churns at the mere thought of violence. My desire for Oak is becoming a bit of an obsession. Professor Jameson seems like the perfect woman for him, smart and beautiful and most importantly, about his *age*.

"Sure." He pulls out his timetable. "We can discuss it after school in the staff room with Archer and Gav."

I notice the disappointment on her face, but she quickly masks it with a fake smile that doesn't reach her eyes. "Of course." She nods at him. "See you later, then."

He grunts as she turns away and walks out of his office, shutting the door behind her. It's as if the moment she leaves, Oak's demeanor changes entirely. His shoulders sag slightly, and he gets to his feet, pacing the length of his office.

"Are you okay, Oak?" I ask.

He stops pacing and stares at me with a look of pure anguish. "No, Eva." He shakes his head. "I'm not okay."

I watch as he walks back to his desk and sits down, staring at me.

"I'm sorry." He shoves his hands through his dark, thick hair. "What happened was inappropriate."

I open my mouth to tell him I'm not sorry, but he holds his hand up to stop me.

"Listen." His gaze turns stern. "You will speak of this to no one, and from now on, we will not have discipline lessons together."

His declaration makes my stomach dip and my chest ache. "But—"

"I said listen," he growls.

I fall silent, twiddling my thumbs in my lap like a naughty little child. That's how he's making me feel right now.

"You will forget this ever happened, and we will stay out of each other's way." His eyes are cold and unfeeling as he stares at me. "It was a stupid mistake."

The words punch me hard in the gut as I feel tears gather in my eyes, but I don't allow them to fall. Instead, I hold my chin high and meet his stony gaze, allowing him to see all the emotions I currently feel.

"I never wanted to come here, Oak." I shake my head. "This isn't where I belong, and even though I have friends, there's always one thing that stops me from ever fitting in." I sigh heavily. "I'm nothing like them. I never want to be a criminal. I never want to be the head of my family." I swallow hard as Karl's face flashes into my mind. "Do you know the one thing that made this school bearable?"

Oak doesn't reply.

I feel the pain clawing at my throat like claws scraping down the inside. "You," I murmur, holding onto the tears that so desperately want to fall. "You were the only good thing." I laugh at that. "Sounds ridiculous, considering that you've inflicted pain on me every day for just over two weeks." There's a slight shift in Oak's eyes, but it's not clear what he's thinking. "I guess that's how fucking pathetic I am that I clung to you, even when you hurt me." I stand and throw the discipline textbook onto the desk. "Goodbye."

I walk out, and only once I'm in the corridor do I allow the tears to fall down my cheeks. A small, pathetic part of me had hoped Oak might have stopped me, might have told me he feels the same.

Who am I kidding?

Principal Oakley Byrne is out of my league and always has been. I don't know why he kissed me and why he touched me the way he did, but it's clear it has nothing to do with the way he feels about me.

He probably hates me just as much as my parents.

It's my life story. Everyone I care for tosses me aside. The only person who didn't was Karl, and he's gone.

I rush through the corridor to my dorm, knowing I can't face any more classes this afternoon.

Fuck it.

If they punish me for it, so be it. I don't care anymore. I want out of this place and out of my parents' lives. All I want is to start afresh somewhere no one knows me—a second chance, but I know that despite my plan to escape them, it's probably wishful thinking.

There's no escaping my parents' reach simply by running away, which means I need a new plan—a fail-proof one.

I HAVE NO MORE lessons for the rest of the day, so I head to the library to meet with Natalya.

"Hey, over here?" She whispers.

I smile when I see her surrounded by books. "Hey." I take a seat next to her. "What are you studying?" I ask quietly.

"Interrogation," she replies.

I raise a brow at the response.

She shrug. "It's a useful skill in the Bratva."

I nod in reply, twiddling my fingers anxiously as I need to ask her a question. "Can you keep a secret?"

Her eyes shoot up to meet mine, and she smiles wickedly. "What kind of secret?"

I shake my head. "A very important one. Can you keep one?"

She nods. "Of course. You have my word."

I swallow hard. "I don't want to be a part of my parents' business or lives."

Her brow furrows. "Really? What do you want to do then?"

"I want to become a vet, but I'm not naïve enough to believe running from them would be easy."

She contemplates. "No, it wouldn't be easy." Natalya puts down her book, looking at me seriously. "Your parents are renowned for having global connections, not just national."

"Yeah, that's the problem." I meet her gaze. "How could I get away with it?"

Natalya drums her fingers on the table. "I know you want to keep it a secret, but Camilla might be the only one who can help." She shakes her head. "She has the means for someone to disappear. After all, her family specializes in trafficking.'"

My stomach churns at the way Natalya talks of it so easily. "Trafficking?" I confirm.

Natalya nods. "Yeah, the Morrone crime family has been in charge of the biggest women trafficking ring in North America for years."

"Don't you find it hard to accept that women like

you and me are being taken from their homes and sold?"

Natalya tilts her head slightly, considering the question. "Yes, in all honesty, but thankfully my family doesn't trade in people."

"What do they trade?"

She purses her lips together before saying, "Everything else."

I shake my head. "I can't stand it, Natalya. The injustice of the world that my parents are forcing me to be a part of. If my brother were still alive…"

"Then what?" Natalya pushes.

"I'd hope my parents might have allowed me to live how I wanted."

Natalya looks skeptical. "Doubtful, you still would have been useful to marry off and strengthen the family's relations with some kind of criminal organization."

"True." I sigh heavily, knowing that she's right. My parents are too heartless and self-centered to consider letting me live my life the way I wanted.

"Seriously, though. Camilla is the woman to ask." She shrugs. "You may hate what her family does, but she's the only person I know who has the means to make sure you disappear so that your family can't trace you." Her brow furrows. "You're going to wait until the end of the school year, though, right?"

I nod in response, knowing that the money I've saved is more than enough to pay my college tuition to become a vet, but I hadn't factored the heavy cost of having someone else help me flee my parents. By the time I've finished school here, I should have enough for both.

Although my parents have never cared for me much, they have always given me money, and a lot. "How much do you reckon something like that would cost?" I ask Natalya.

She raises a brow. "I'm sure for a friend that Camilla will do it as a favor, as long as she can convince her father." She shrugs. "If not, she won't charge much."

I let out a breath I was holding, wondering if my new plan would be enough to escape their clutches. "Do you reckon I'll need to leave the country?"

Natalya grabs my hand and squeezes. "Don't worry about it right now. I'd say probably, because your parents have a lot of influence, and I don't know how easy it is to disappear from them in America, but we'll deal with it when we come to it." She smiles. "And, of course, me, Adrianna, and Camilla will visit no matter where you end up."

I laugh at that. "I thought I was supposed to be untraceable?"

Natalya rolls her eyes. "Not to your friends."

It defeats the object in my eyes, as if people from school know where I am, then that means my parents can try to extract that information. Although Camilla, Adrianna, and Natalya are all from equally powerful crime families, I doubt they could interrogate them.

"Are you sure about this, though, Eva?" Natalya asks.

I nod in response. "I've been sure about it since I can remember." I sigh heavily, running a hand through the ends of my hair. "I'm not cut out for the life my parents want for me."

She shakes her head. "Few are."

I raise a brow. "What about you?"

"I feel a duty to my family and my brother." She shrugs. "Whether I can live up to the expectations remains to be seen. I'm a brilliant student, but I have put nothing into practice." Her brow furrows. "I don't think I have to worry about taking over for a long while, though. After all, my brother is only Thirty-one years old."

"That's young to be in charge."

"He was twenty-one when our father died."

"And he's been in charge ever since?" I ask.

Natalya nods, a sad look in her eyes. "It forced him to grow up fast. Few twenty-one years olds have that much responsibility thrust onto them." She sighs. "I've always felt bad for Mikhail. His life isn't his own."

"Won't he have an heir, anyway?" I ask. "Someone who can take over?"

"I always said that to him, but he's adamant marriage and children aren't what he wants." She smiles, but it doesn't reach her eyes. "Although I hope he finds a girl to make him happy. He deserves some happiness in his life."

It's hard for me to think that men like her brother or my parents deserve anything but suffering. They hurt, kill and maim daily, so how can someone like that deserve anything? They're criminals.

Instead of voicing my disgust, I nod in response. Natalya may be a good friend, but I know we'll never see the world the same way. I'm thankful that she can understand why I want to leave, and she's willing to help me. It's more than I've ever had before.

15

OAK

What the hell have I done?

Five years of planning could all go to shit. I kissed Eva Carmichael. A terrible act that I can't stop replaying over and over. It has consumed every waking thought for the past three days.

Thankfully, it happened on a Friday, so I had the weekend to sulk in my cottage over it, but now it's Monday.

Somehow, I've avoided running into her since I don't have classes with her on a Monday, but tomorrow I will have to face her in leadership strategy class and law.

The despair was written all over her face when I threw her out of my office and canceled the rest of our one-on-one lessons. Her little speech shocked me to the core and for a horrible reason.

It made me realize why I'm so drawn to her. She

reminds me of myself at her age, desperate to escape by any means necessary—desperate to be better than the people who raised her. The innocent daughter of my enemies reminds me of myself.

How can I destroy someone so innocent, so utterly against all that her parents stand for?

I've been running through all the ways I could destroy the Carmichaels, hellbent on destruction as the primary aim, but I never considered a different angle. Help Eva be free of her parents and rub it in their faces before murdering them, of course. The question is, would Eva stand by me if she knew what I wanted to do to her family?

She may declare to hate what they've done to her, but how deep does that hate run?

I push a hand through my messy hair, shaking my head. It takes a certain person to stand by the murder of the people who brought you into this world, and I'm uncertain Eva is that kind of person. She's good and pure.

Archer gives me a nod as he enters the staff room. "Alright, Oak?" He calls.

I'm so distracted that I mumble my response, which catches his attention.

"What's up?" Archer asks, slipping into the chair opposite me.

I meet his gaze and shrug. "Nothing." I rub a hand across the back of my neck. "Just trouble with a pupil."

He nods slowly, watching me intently. "Is it the Carmichael girl?"

I clench my fist at the mention of her. Archer is one of only two people who knows why I bought this school and my plan to get revenge on Eva's family. Gavril is the other. "Yes."

"Are you still intending to send her to me to…" He trails off rather than saying it.

"No," I practically growl.

He raises a brow, a small smirk on his face. "Why not?"

I glare at my friend, gritting my teeth. "Because I'm not, okay?" I snap.

His eyes widen, and he holds his hands up. "Alright, calm down." He runs a hand through his hair. "If I didn't know any better, I'd say you have the hots for the girl?" Arch says.

"Shut it," I say, rubbing my temples. "I don't want to talk about it."

Archer chuckles in response. "You look like a man who needs a fucking night out and a lot of alcohol."

I meet my friend's gaze. "Is that an invitation?" I've heard of worse ideas.

"Why the fuck not? We haven't been out in ages." He pulls his cell phone out. "I'll see if Gav wants to join." He types a text to him and fires it off.

"You're right. I think it's exactly what I need." A night of drinking with my friends might help get my mind off of Eva Carmichael and the crazy line I crossed with her three days ago.

Arch smirks and nods toward the door. "Perfect. I'm going to get cleaned up and have something to eat." He moves for the door out of the staff room. "Meet back here at eight o'clock?"

I nod in response. "Sure. See you then."

Arch walks out of the staff room, leaving me alone with my chaotic thoughts.

I never foresaw such a ridiculous complication. There's something deep that connects me to the girl I wanted to ruin, the girl I wanted to destroy in the name of revenge.

THE BAR ARCHER picked is heaving with kids, as it's popular with the local college. Typical Archer always makes sure there are a lot of hot young college girls around for him to pick from.

Gav looks as uncomfortable as I feel as we step inside. "Is this the best place for us to grab a drink?"

I nod in agreement, glancing around. "It's a little loud."

Archer shakes his head. "Sorry, grandpa, but this is the hottest place in town."

I glare at him. "In case you forgot, we're teachers at a nearby school, not frat boys."

He laughs. "Both of you need to lighten up." He

shakes his head and leads the way toward the bar. "It's not like we'll run into any of our students."

Hopefully, he's right. None of us are stupid enough to believe that students don't sneak off campus. The students aren't permitted to leave the grounds unless they have permission, but that wouldn't stop them.

We've caught kids doing exactly that, but it doesn't mean we'll run into any here. There are another ten clubs in the town which makes the chances slim, even if this is the hottest place in town, as Arch put it.

"Usual?" Archer asks, glancing at me.

"Yeah, whiskey, neat."

He laughs, shaking his head. "Never can change it up. Can you?"

"Why should I? I like whiskey."

Archer orders my whiskey, a vodka for Gavril, and a manhattan for himself. He likes to think of himself as sophisticated, even though most of the time he's an idiot, a loveable idiot, but an idiot all the same.

"Let's find a booth, somewhere we don't have to shout to hear each other," Gav says, glancing around the room.

I spot a booth in the corner and point to it. "Over there."

Gav nods and leads the way to the booth, shoving through the college kids crowding the place. Once we get to it, he growls. "This is the last time I let Archer pick where we go."

I laugh. "Agreed."

"What did you agree to?" Archer asks, slumping down on the far side of the booth with his drink.

"That this is the last time you choose where we go for a night out," I say.

He shakes his head. "Both of you need to chill."

I sip my whiskey, trying to forget about Eva Carmichael and the broken expression on her face after I kicked her out of my office. It's impossible to erase the image, especially after how good it felt to kiss her, touch her. I ruined it all by telling her it could never happen again, which is what a man in my position should do, even if it's not what I want.

"Oi, you're here to unwind and not think," Archer says, clapping me on the shoulder. "Stop thinking about the Carmichael girl!"

Gav's brow shoots up at that. "Eva?"

I glare at Archer and then sigh. "Yeah, it seems the girl I intend to ruin to get to her parents is irresistible."

Gav laughs. "She's cute, for sure, but I wouldn't have expected her to be your type."

That irritates me as I sit straighter, staring at him sternly. "And what exactly do you think my type would be?"

He rubs a hand across the back of his neck, leveling his gaze at me. "Older than twenty-one." He glances at Archer. "My two closest friends are perverts."

Archer holds a hand to his chest. "How dare you?"

Gav laughs. "It's true."

I raise a brow. "Are you telling me you've never found a student attractive?"

There's a flash of something in Gavril's eyes, but it quickly disappears. "No, they're too young, too immature."

It's what I would have said over a month ago. However, now I've met Eva, she's all I can think about. "I thought that too," I mutter.

"Has anything happened between you two?" Archer asks, suggestively quirking his brow.

I swallow hard. "I kissed her in my office."

Gav spits his vodka out, but Archer looks unsurprised.

"You did what?" Gav asks, shaking his head. "I thought you wanted to ruin her family. How does that work if you ruin yourself as well?"

I narrow my eyes at Gavril. "Hence why I canceled all our one-on-one discipline classes and chucked her out of my office."

"Sounds like you did one thing right," Gav says.

I dig my nails into the palm of my hand, trying to quieten the darkness swirling beneath the surface.

"I'm not so sure. It's clear that you like Eva, so why don't you be the one to ruin her reputation?" Archer's head tilts to the side slightly. "Or is it because you care for her?"

I grind my teeth, wishing that he wasn't so perceptive, even if he acts like a clown most of the time. "Perhaps." I shrug. "I'm not sure. All I know is she's not what I expected." I meet Gavril's questioning glare. "She's not a spoiled mafia princess." I draw in a deep breath. "She nothing like them."

"Are you forgetting what her parents took from you?" Gavril asks, almost sounding angry.

I know my two friends are invested in my plan, and they want to see me get my revenge on the two pieces of shit that burned my world to the ground. However, everything has become blurred and unclear ever since I met Eva. What once was as simple as anything is so fucking complicated, I can't make heads or tails of anything anymore.

I knock back the rest of my whiskey and slam the glass down on the table. "Enough of this. I agreed to come out because I want to forget about it, not talk about it." I wave a server over, and she takes my order for another round. "Let's get drunk and forget about the Carmichaels."

Gavril brings his glass up to his lips and sips, watching me cautiously.

Archer nods and knocks back the rest of his drink. "Here, here." He smirks at me. "Let's get drunk."

Gav nods in agreement. "Sounds good to me." He knocks back the rest of his vodka as another round arrives.

I signal the server before she leaves. "Keep them coming every twenty minutes and put them on my tab," I say, handing her a fifty-dollar bill.

She smiles, batting her eyelashes. "Of course."

Before I met Eva, I may have flirted back, perhaps seduced her after her shift, and taken her back to my cottage. The mere thought of taking anyone other than Eva there makes me sick to my stomach. It's a very odd feeling. One I can't understand.

There is no way I can ever take Eva back to my cottage, no matter how badly I want to. She's a pupil, and I'm the head of a nationally renowned school. The mafia families are rather forgiving of scandal in the halls of SA, but a scandal involving a principal maybe something people can't overlook.

If I let my obsession with Eva rule my actions, I may end up destroying everything I've built this time. There would be no one to blame except for me.

16

EVA

"Get dressed. We're going out," Natalya announces, waltzing into my room with Camilla and Adrianna following close behind, all of them in dresses.

My brow furrows. "Going out where?" The idea of going out right now makes my stomach churn.

All I want to do is curl up into a ball and sleep. It's what I did all weekend since the kiss with Oak, and I can't face the idea of going anywhere. I saw him in the corridor today, but he didn't see me. My heart ached at the sight of him, and tomorrow I have to sit in his class, twice.

"Elias has hired a minibus, and he's invited us to join him in town," Natalya says, shrugging. "As well as ten other people."

I glance at Camilla, wondering what's going on.

"And you think it's wise to accept an invitation from that nutcase?" I never told Natalya about what happened in the corridor when he accosted me and only let me go because Oak interrupted us.

There's a flash of something in Natalya's eyes as she shrugs. "We're eighteen years old and stuck in this school twenty-four seven. I want out."

Camilla and Adrianna exchange concerned glances, but they doesn't say anything.

"Fine, give me time to dress, though."

Natalya shakes her head. "Why do you think we're here? To help you pick out your outfit and get ready."

I swallow hard and nod. "Okay, I don't have many dresses with me." Even at my last school, I was never the girl who picked out dresses with my friends. My group of friends were too interested in studying or staying in watching movies. We were not the girls that went out, which my parents were thankful for.

Camilla walks to my closet and pulls open the door. "I'm sure we'll find something." She moves clothes aside, sifting through each piece. "Perfect," she says when she comes to my cream mini-dress with sleeves and a plunging neckline that is very revealing. My cheeks heat at the mere thought of putting it on, as I got given it as a gift by one of my father's friends who was a total pig.

"I'm not sure that will suit me," I say, shifting my weight from one foot to the other.

"Nonsense," Camilla says, walking over with it. "You'll look gorgeous."

Natalya nods. "I have to agree with Camilla. You will look hot in that."

"Agreed," Adrianna adds.

I sigh heavily, glancing between the girls in my room and the dress before finally giving in. "Fine, let me try it on."

I wriggle out of my joggers and pull off my shirt, throwing it on the bed. Then I slide the dress on and turn to Camilla. "Can you zip me up?"

Camilla smiles and nods as I turn around to allow her to do it up.

"There. Spin around and let us see," she says.

I turn around, feeling almost naked as I do.

Adrianna whistles. "You look hot."

Natalya nods in agreement, and Camilla stares at me with a half-open mouth. "Drop dead gorgeous," Natalya says.

I heat at their stares and shake my head. "I'm not sure about it." I flatten my palm over the fabric. "It's a little too revealing."

Camilla loops her arm with mine. "Nonsense. It's perfect, and we've got to go, or we'll be late."

I grab my winter coat off the back of the door as they usher me out of my room, rushing down the corridor. "How are we getting out of here without being seen?"

Natalya grins wickedly. "You're going to learn some SA secrets tonight." Instead of taking a left and heading out of the dormitory, we turn right deeper into the girls' wing.

My stomach dips when I see Jeanie, Anita, and Kerry up ahead. The three girls who attacked me on my first night in this godforsaken place.

"What the fuck are they doing here?" I murmur to no one in particular.

Camilla answers. "Unfortunately, they're friends with Elias."

"I don't like this," I say.

Adrianna squeezes my arm. "Don't worry. You've got us now."

They're standing in front of a large portrait of a woman. When they see us, their eyes narrow. "Look who it is," Kerry says, sneering at us.

Jeanie steps forward, eyes moving between us. "When Elias told me he'd invited you, I thought it was some sick joke."

Natalya squares her shoulders and lifts her chin. "I'm not sure why the fuck he invited you."

Jeanie shakes her head. "Come on then. Who's going first?"

"After you," Camilla says.

Jeanie narrows her eyes before pulling at the portrait on the wall. To my surprise, it swings open to reveal a laundry shoot. She glares at the four of us before climbing in and disappearing. Her two friends, Kerry and Anita, disappear after her.

"What the hell is going on?" I ask as Camilla moves to climb in after them.

She glances at me. "The laundry shoot takes us to the back exit of SA, where the minibus is waiting." With that, she launches herself after the three girls.

"If I'd known those three were coming, I'd never have agreed," I say to Natalya.

She rolls her eyes. "They're all talk, no bite."

I glare at her. "Tell that to my leg." I nod toward the leg they stabbed.

"Sorry, they did a number on you."

Adrianna is the next to climb in and disappear.

"But that's because they fear you." She nods toward the shoot. "You next."

I give her an incredulous look, as I thought I might weasel my way out by going. "I'll go last."

Natalya shakes her head. "No, you won't."

I grind my teeth and haul myself into the shoot, glancing down it nervously. "Are you sure this is—"

Natalya shoves me, pushing me down the shoot.

I scream as I fall down the slide into a bundle of dirty laundry at the bottom. "Gross," I say, as I quickly jump out of it.

"Did you scream?" Camilla asks.

I shrug. "Natalya pushed me."

Adrianna laughs. "Classic, Natalya." She gives me a

pitiful look. "She did the same to me the first time we used this escape route."

Camilla looks sheepish. "That might be my fault. I did it to her on her first time."

We both laugh as Natalya appears from the shoot, quickly jumping out of the laundry.

"I hate the landing every time," she says, glancing at the dirty laundry. "It fucking stinks."

We all laugh at that, only to be cut off by Anita whistling at us. "Hurry. Everyone is already on the bus."

The door at the back of the laundry room leads to an enclosed courtyard where the minibus is parked. Elias is leaning against it with his arms crossed over his chest. His nostrils flare the moment he sees Natalya. "Kept me waiting, Gurin," he says, pushing off the bus and walking toward her. He wraps an arm around her and claws her against his side. "Never do it again," he says, his tone menacing.

My brow furrows, and I'm about to say something when Camilla yanks me onto the bus. "What's going on with those two?"

Camilla shakes her head. "I don't know, but when I questioned her, she got all defensive."

Adrianna leans forward. "If I've learned anything about Natalya, let her reveal things in her own time. If you push her, she'll snap."

I sit down next to Camilla and ask, "You once asked

Natalya if she'd told me about what Elias did to her. What did he do?"

Camilla meets my gaze and then glances at Adrianna.

Adrianna shrugs. "It's not exactly a secret."

Camilla sighs. "Elias tormented Natalya for years. He would call her names, physically hurt her, belittle her in front of everyone, humiliate her." She glances to the front of the van, where Elias has pulled Natalya onto his lap. "The bastard even stabbed her pretty badly a couple of times."

I gasp at that. "What the fuck for?"

Adrianna cut in. "He said she needs teaching a lesson for being a teacher's pet."

Camilla nods. "He's been a complete jerk to her from fourth grade until maybe a year ago when things became tamer." Her brow furrows. "He even kind of left her alone at the end of last year."

I watch as he messes with Natalya's hair as she sits in his lap. "But we can't work out why." She shrugs. "But after you stood up to him, something changed, and he's started messing with her again. Natalya gets all closed off about it any time we bring it up and won't discuss it, but we have a feeling he has something over her."

"Like what?" I ask.

Adrianna shakes her head. "We have no idea. We wish we did."

"I think he has the hots for her," I say, sort of to myself.

Camilla laughs, thinking I'm joking. When I give her a serious look, she shakes her head. "There's no way Elias likes Nat like that. He's been too fucking cruel over the years."

"Just what I see as an outsider." I shrug. "It was my first thought when he came up to us in the hallway that day."

Adrianna contemplates me. "Fuck, maybe Eva's right." She shakes her head. "It sounds fucking crazy, but we've been too close to it all these years."

I nod. "Not to mention when Elias attacked me in the corridor—"

"What? When did that happen?" Adrianna asks.

"Last week, I told Camilla." I bite my lip as I remember how Oak came to my rescue, only to wrap his fingers around my throat. "But something he said was odd."

"What was it?" Camilla asks.

I glanced around to ensure no one was listening. "He said, 'Natalya is mine to torment and always has been. Mine, do you understand?' He said it like a jealous boyfriend."

"What the fuck?" Adrianna says, shaking her head. "If that boy likes Natalya, then he is fucked in the head for the ways he treated her all these years."

I nod in agreement. "He clearly has issues."

Dimitry Jakov, who I hadn't even noticed, sits down

in the seat in front of me, leaning toward me. "Who has issues?"

Adrianna and Camilla glare at him. "It's called a private conversation, Dimitry," Camilla says.

Dimitry smiles lazily, glancing at me. "Is that right?" He runs a hand through his dark, short hair. "It's called a public bus, though."

Adrianna shakes her head. "Ask her out and stop messing about," she quips.

My brow furrows as I wonder who exactly she means.

Dimitry reddens and shrugs. "Okay, will you save me a dance, beautiful?" He asks, looking right at me.

My stomach churns at the thought, but I'm supposed to be going out to forget about Oak. Perhaps a harmless dance and a bit of flirting with a nice, attractive boy my age won't harm. "Sure," I say, smiling.

He smiles back, looking relieved. "Great, see you on the dance floor." He then returns to sit with a few guys sitting right at the back.

"Ugh," Camilla says, shuddering. "Why would you agree to dance with him?"

"Why not? He doesn't seem terrible."

Adrianna laughs. "That's because you didn't know him when he was younger." She gives Camilla a pointed look. "In all fairness, Jakov has grown up pretty handsome, don't you think?"

Camilla wrinkles her nose. "I'd say that's a stretch too far for me."

I laugh. "Fair enough, but it's only a dance. It's not like I've agreed to date him."

And I know I never would, not when all I can think about is one very forbidden man. A man I should have never thought of in that way, but now life feels utterly hopeless if I never get to kiss him again.

17

OAK

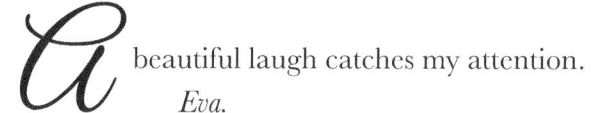

A beautiful laugh catches my attention.
Eva.

I search the bar for her, desperately trying to find the source of that laughter. Perhaps it's someone who sounds eerily like her, but deep down, I know that's not true. No one sounds like her. My eyes land on a large table near the back, where quite a few of SA's students are gathered, but I don't see her.

I nudge Gav. "Looks like we have some rule breakers."

The smirk that twists his lips is devilish. "Oh, I do love punishing rule breakers." He rubs his hands together, making me shake my head.

"Perhaps we can have some fun with them?" I suggest.

Gav's brow furrows. "What do you have in mind?"

"Sit with them a while and make them sweat." I shrug. I know my suggestion is motivated by spending time with Eva. Since entering my classroom, she's been stuck to Natalya Gurin's side, and I can see Natalya from where I'm sitting.

Gav runs his hand through his hair before smiling. "I like your thinking. The moment I sit down with them, they'll shit themselves."

I laugh, nodding. "Let's do it then." I glance over at Archer, who is currently wrapped up in a young blonde girl at another table. "I'll tell Archer."

Gav raises a brow. "Not sure there's much need. He's a fucking idiot."

I get up anyway and approach him. "Arch."

He turns away from the woman he'd been kissing and raises a brow. "What?"

"We have students at the bar who Gav and I are going to join and torment." I glance at the girl he was making out with. "Wondered if you wanted to tag along?"

His eyes widen slightly at the mention of students at the bar. "Where?"

"Over in the back. About fourteen of them." I tilt my head. "Do you want to join us or not?"

Archer glances at the blonde and then back at me. "Sure. Sorry, sweetheart." He peels himself out of her grasp. "Maybe another time." He winks and then follows me back to our table.

Gav's already on his feet, fists clenched as he glares over at the table of delinquents. "Ready?"

I nod. "Follow my lead." I step toward the table, moving through the crowd toward the table of students. My steps almost falter the moment I set eyes on Eva Carmichael. She's wearing the sexiest dress I've ever seen, in cream fabric and cut low to stress her perfect breasts. The sleeves are long, which adds an elegant touch to the outfit.

A soft roar claws up my throat as I notice Dimitry sitting next to her with a hand resting casually on her thigh.

Motherfucker.

I march toward the table and take the seat directly opposite Eva. The moment she notices me, her face pales. "Shit," she mutters.

Her exclamation draws Dimitry's attention as he lets go of her thigh, inching a little further from her.

I clear my throat. "I didn't realize all of you had clearance to leave the grounds," I say, my voice calm despite the chaos blazing inside of me.

Anyone who hadn't noticed me does then, as Arch kicks a guy off one stool and sits down, crossing his arms over his chest. I notice he keeps his attention solely on Adrianna Vasquez.

Gav remains standing, but most of the students watch him warily. It's insane how much fear the Russian professor can inspire.

It's Elias Morales who speaks. "I did." He lifts his chin and levels his gaze at me. "After all, we're eighteen years old. We can do what the fuck we want."

I raise a brow. "That may be so, but you are all too young to be here legally."

Elias laughs. "Who the fuck gives a shit about legal? The academy is about teaching everything that isn't legal." He gets a few snickers from his classmates, but most of them are too fearful of Gav to laugh.

"Touche," Arch says. "How about we join you?" His eyes still don't move from Adrianna, who's looking anywhere but at him.

"If you think you can handle it, old man," Rizzo, a new kid who started this semester, says.

He's as cocky and stupid as Elias. Archer, however, is always one to see the humor in anything. "You know I could kick your ass even after sinking two bottles of scotch, Rizzo."

Rizzo laughs and passes him a bottle of vodka. "Help yourself." He sits back in his chair, a cocky smirk still plastered on his face. Either he's fearless or plain stupid, as Gavril is staring at him like he's ready to tie him to a torture rack.

Archer pours himself a large glass of vodka and leans back, sipping it.

I remain still, eyes focused solely on Eva. If I don't control my anger, I might launch myself over the table, pummel Dimitry into a pulp and claim Eva over the fucking table in front of her classmates.

My cock throbs at the mere thought, which shows how fucking far gone I am. The forbidden aspect only adds to my desire. Eva should run for her fucking life.

The server I'd tipped earlier finds me and sets her hand on my shoulder at that moment. "I had to track you down," she whispers before placing the glass of whiskey in my hand.

A few of the boys at the table wolf-whistle, but I straighten and nod in thanks. I'm painfully aware that Eva's eyes are on me now, even though she had another man's hand on her thigh moments ago. I grit my teeth and glance at her again to find she's glaring at the server with similar angry jealousy.

I smirk at that and lean toward her again, realizing that my actions will annoy Eva. "Why don't you get everyone a round on me," I whisper into her ear and give her another fifty-dollar bill. It's childish, as if I'm fucking eighteen again, but I can't help it.

She nods and winks before heading off to get more drinks.

It's an irresponsible move. As their school principal, I shouldn't be buying these underage students drinks. However, Eva's presence here only hazes my judgment and makes it hard to think of anything else.

"So, how the fuck did you lot sneak off campus?" I ask, glancing between every pupil at the table.

A few of them pale, most grin in drunken pride.

"I'm afraid if we told you that, professor, we'd have

to kill you," Elias says, grinning at me with that cocky smirk I'd love to punch off his face.

To my surprise, he has his arm lazily draped over Natalya Gurin's shoulder. The same girl he has spent years tormenting. Natalya looks a little uncomfortable, suggesting that perhaps she's not here by choice, or at least not in Elias' arms by choice.

Elias has a lot to prove. He may be part of the Estrada Cartel family, but he's only a cousin and doesn't share the Estrada name. It means that while he's a big fish at this school, out there in the real world, he's not such a big deal. He's ninth in line to lead the Estrada Cartel, behind his six cousins and two older siblings.

"I'd like to see you try, Elias," I say evenly, holding his gaze. "A few have tried, none have succeeded."

He snorts at that. "Yeah, right, old man."

I clench my fists at my side, moving my gaze back to Eva, who Dimitry is fawning over. He leans forward and whispers in her ear. "Dimitry," I bark his name.

He straightens, eyes wide. "What?"

"Did you forget what happened the last time you whispered something inappropriate to Miss Carmichael?"

His face pales, and his eyes dart to Gav, who is observing on his feet, arms crossed over his chest. I notice the way his gaze fixes more than once on Camilla Morrone. Perhaps my friend isn't so immune to the beauty of eighteen-year-old girls.

"I haven't said anything that Eva doesn't want to hear," he says, glancing at Eva. "Have I, Eva?"

Eva's eyes dart between him and me a few times before she stands. "I need to get some air." She pushes past Dimitry, who tries to grab her hand.

"Do you want me to—"

Eva shakes her head. "No, I'll be back in a minute." She rushes off, her hips swaying from side to side, and she walks elegantly away on her mid-height heels.

My cock throbs at the sight of her from behind in that dress. An image that should be for my eyes and my eyes only. I notice Dimitry watching her in the same way, licking his lips like a hungry animal as she disappears out of sight.

I grip the edge of the table to stop myself from launching over it and knocking him out. He's a pupil, after all. I can't go around knocking out pupils because he touched another pupil. He has more right to touch her than I do—I'm her fucking teacher.

I glance over at the bar, noticing the round of drinks I ordered still hasn't arrived. "I ordered everyone drinks. I'm going to see what the holdup is." I stand and head toward the bar, clocking the server. "Where are we on those drinks?"

Her eyes widen. "Working on it. It's a big order." I nod in response. "I'm going out for some air. Deliver them anyway."

The server smirks. "Sure, I'm almost due my break if you'd like—"

"Not interested, sorry."

Her face falls, but she nods. "Of course, just the drinks, then?"

"Yes," I say.

I turn toward the exit of the club, feeling my heart pounding in my chest. It's reckless of me to go out there—to chase the girl who haunts my waking thought and my dreams. But there is no stopping my legs. Eva is like the center of my universe, pulling me right to her with such force I can't resist.

I march out of the club and onto the street, inhaling a deep gulp of the fresh air, as the club is sweaty, overcrowded, and stinks of booze. I glance around, searching for Eva, until I notice a small frame leaning against the wall of the club, head tilted upwards, her face gently basked in the moonlight.

Eva.

She looks like a vision standing there like that, making my stomach flip over at the thought of kissing those thick, pouty lips again.

I march toward her, hurrying as I get closer. Seeing Dimitry's hand on her was enough to make my resolve snap. I've had enough trying to keep away from her. It's about time I took what I want.

Eva's eyes snap to mine as I stand on a broken bottle, alerting her of my presence. Her eyes widen, and she folds her arms across her chest defensively, taking a few steps to the right as if scared of me.

A gentle growl vibrates through my chest as I move

toward her, closing the gap. There's fear in her eyes, as there should be. If Eva has any sense, she'd run far away from me and never look back, but there's a desire in her eyes too, which tells me she has no intention of moving.

Eva will be mine, so help me, God.

18

EVA

I made a big mistake coming out here alone.

Oak followed me. And now, he's staring at me like an angry, hungry predator ready to tear me to shreds. His beautiful blue eyes look almost silver in the dim streetlight and pale moonlight creeping through the clouds.

As he approaches, I take a few back steps, only to find myself caged in against the club's wall.

"Are you okay, principal Byrne?" I ask, not wanting to use his first name. It's too intimate for this setting, being that we're outside of school, and the way he's looking at me scares me.

He stops when he's merely a foot from me, tilting his head. "Am I okay?" His voice shakes with anger. "What the fuck are you doing here?"

The tone makes me wish I could disappear into the bricks behind me. "Natalya invited me," I murmur, wishing my voice didn't sound so insignificant compared to his. "I'm sorry for breaking the rules."

His eyes flash with something I can't quite discern at my apology as his gaze moves to my lips, then lower to my dress. "Why did you wear this dress?" He asks, running his finger slowly down the center of my body. "Were you hoping to attract male attention?" There's a lethal edge to his voice that makes me shudder.

I shake my head. "No, my friends insisted I wear it." I shrug. "I didn't even want to wear it."

The corner of Oak's mouth twitches upwards into an almost smile, but there's still danger sparking in his irises. "I never want to see you in a dress like this again," he orders, leaning down toward my ear, his lips softly caressing the shell. "Unless you are by my side." He grabs my hips with his large rough hands, digging his fingertips in enough to hurt.

His statement makes no sense, but my stomach flutters as I remember how good it felt when his lips descended on mine three days ago. "I don't understand, sir," I say, shaking my head and putting my hands on his chest to push him away from me. He doesn't move. "You're the principal of my school, which means I can't be by your side." I push harder.

He doesn't budge an inch. "You can and you will." One of his hands moves from my hip to the back of my neck, gripping me hard. "You're mine, Eva, and I never want to see Dimitry fucking Jakov near you again. Do you understand?"

Heat fires to life inside of me, roaring like the engine of a jumbo jet at the look of pure envy in Oak's eyes.

Is he seriously jealous of Dimitry?

A part of me wants to laugh, but I hold it in, knowing from the look on his face it would only anger him. "Why do you think you can order me around?" I lift my chin, meeting his intense gaze. "If I like Dimitry, then I'll speak to him. It's not—"

Oak's fierce, animalistic growl cuts me off as he wraps his fingers around my throat, glaring at me like a man possessed. "Careful, baby girl," he drawls, making my knees tremble as my palm remains flat against his hard chest.

"Oak," I breathe his name, my eyes fluttering shut at the warm, possessive grip of his hand around my throat. It's like he did in the corridor, only softer.

"If I say you're mine, then that's the end of it," he snaps, nostrils flaring. "You'll stay away from that boy, Eva. All he wants is to get into your pants."

"And you?" I ask, feeling my heart rate speed up as I watch the man holding me.

His eyes narrow. "What about me?"

"What do you want from me?" I ask, knowing that the question is dangerous.

His hand loosens from my neck and moves lower to my collarbone as he trails his rough skin across mine. "Everything," he murmurs, moving his hand even lower to cup my breast through the fabric of my dress. "All of you," he purrs, eyes hooded with desire.

"Oak," I breathe his name, blazing heat spreading through my veins. The possessiveness in his tone makes my body melt with need. My cheeks are on fire, and a deep ache ignites between my thighs at the hard length of his body against mine.

"I want to possess you," he continues, gazing into my eyes as his hand makes its way over every inch of my body. "I want every thought you have to be filled with me," he half-growls, looking a little feral as his grip on his control appears to slip. "I want you to want me as badly as I want you, Eva." His lips are now an inch from mine. "Do you understand?"

I swallow hard and nod. "Yes, sir," I breathe.

He groans and breathes the word, "Mine," before crashing his lips into mine in a dizzying and possessive kiss that steals the air from my lungs, my common sense, and any self-respect I still had as I moan into his mouth like a whore.

How does he have such power over me?

I've never cared about boys or men, focused solely on getting perfect grades so I can escape my parents. Boys were an unnecessary distraction I didn't need, and yet the moment I set eyes on this man, I could hardly focus on anything else.

My fingers dig into his hard, broad shoulders as I try to ground myself, feeling the strength of him forcing me harder into the wall of the club. I let them move from his shoulders into his dark, thick hair as he deepens the kiss, thrusting his tongue in and out of my mouth roughly, as though he has no control.

It's oddly empowering that a man like Oak can't control his urges for me, and it makes me feel more beautiful than I've ever felt, more wanted.

Oak breaks the kiss, only to continue the onslaught of his mouth lower down my neck. "So. Fucking. Beautiful," he says, grazing his lips over my collarbone. "And all mine," he breathes before pulling back to gaze into my eyes. "Tell me you're mine," he orders.

I lick my bottom lip, knowing this is utterly insane. He's my principal, for fuck's sake, but nothing has ever felt this right. Nothing in my life had ever felt right at all. "I'm yours, sir," I say.

"Good girl," he purrs before crashing his lips into mine again with a renewed vigor. This time, I let go of my insecurities, let go of my thoughts, and let him devour me from the inside out.

When we finally break free, I hear a grating laugh I recognize all too well. *Jeanie Doyle.*

"Shit," I breathe.

Oak turns stiff against me, shaking his head and bringing a finger to his lips. "Quiet."

"We need to get out of here," I whisper, noticing a group of three girls standing in the club's entryway. "They haven't seen us yet."

Oak searches my eyes before pushing away from me and grabbing my hand, pulling me down a dark alleyway. "I'm taking you home," he says, yanking me toward a road behind the club, where his SUV is parked.

"Haven't you had too much to drink?" I ask.

He walks past the SUV straight to a cab parked on the road. "The Syndicate Academy," he says to the driver before opening the back door for me.

"Get in," he says, glaring at me sternly.

I slide into the back seat, and he slams the door before getting into the passenger's seat next to the driver.

My stomach dips in disappointment that he didn't get in the back with me, but something tells me almost getting caught by Jeanie Doyle rattled him. The distance between us only makes me ache more.

It's a long, silent ride back to the Syndicate Academy campus, but once we're there and the cab starts its drive back down the long, winding driveway, Oak's hand lands on the small of my back. His body draws close, and the heat of him invades my space and makes my knees weak. "Come with me," he murmurs into my ear.

I clutch onto his arm as he leads me away from the main building, making my heart pound. "Where are we going?"

Oak tuts. "No questions, Eva."

I swallow hard and allow him to steer me down a small, dimly lit path that appears to wind toward the edge of the forest beneath an ornamental archway draped in an evergreen climber.

My stomach flips when I see a quaint, stone-built cottage at the end of the path. "Is this where you live?"

Oak squeezes my hip gently. "Yes," he murmurs, glancing around. "No one will walk in on us here."

My thighs squeeze together, and my heart races as I realize this is happening. Principal Oakley Byrne wants me. I don't know why, but he does, and it makes me crazy with need. As we walk closer to the beautiful little cottage, I know that I'm going to give him what he wants. Everything—all of me belongs to him.

It is wrong. It is forbidden. And yet, every moment I'm with Oak, life has never felt so right. It's as if I was born to be his. I shiver as an icy wind whisks through the grounds, forcing me to move closer to Oak's warmth.

He tightens his grip on my hip as we make the last one-hundred-yard walk to his front porch. He lets go of me, fishing his key out of his pocket.

I watch him as he unlocks the ornate wooden door and pushes it open before sliding his hand to the small of my back, steering me inside. His touch makes me shudder, but for all the right reasons. I'm so on edge, so needy for him.

And then the sound of the door clicking shut and him turning the lock snaps me right back into reality. My heart thumps incredibly hard in my ears. "Sir, what are we—"

Oak yanks me against him hard, cutting me off mid-sentence. "No questions," he breathes, his lips a mere inch from my own as he searches my eyes. It feels like he can see right through me, right into my soul.

I tremble, struggling to believe that Oakley Byrne, the most beautiful man I've ever met, actually wants me. "Are we going to do this?"

The smile that spreads onto his lips is wicked as he lifts a brow. "What exactly do you think we're going to do?"

I feel heat spread through my body, turning my cheeks into flame. "I-I…" Knowing that I've never been rendered speechless, I trail off. This man turns me mindless. I chew on my bottom lip, unable to meet his gaze.

Oak hooks a finger under my chin, lifting it, so my eyes meet his. "Tell me what you want me to do to you, Eva."

Shame coils through me as I'm too inexperienced, too ashamed to tell him what I want. Instead, I shake my head. "I don't know."

His grip turns forceful, almost painful. "Don't lie to me."

The dominance in his tone is addictive as I swallow hard, searching his hungry, aqua eyes. "I want you, sir."

A muscle in his jaw ticks as he lets go of my chin and grabs my hips instead, yanking me against his hard, powerful body. "What exactly do you want me to do to you?" He asks again, his lips moving to my neck as he kisses me softly, trailing them lower until they're over my collarbone.

I can hardly think with his lips on me. "Everything," I breathe, licking my lips, which have become too dry. "I want you to touch me."

"Hmm," he breathes, moving his hands from my hips to squeeze my ass cheeks in his palms. "Like this?"

I nod in reply, my eyes shutting at the sensation of his hands on me. "I want to touch you too, sir."

Oak pulls back, a smug smile tugging his lips upward. "Where?"

"Everywhere," I breathe softly.

His eyes flash with hunger. "Keep going, baby girl."

I squeeze my thighs together every time he uses that nickname. His lips return to my neck as he nibbles and licks and sucks at my flesh. It drives me wild with need.

"I want you to taste me," I say, feeling the courage blazing to life inside of me the more he touches me, heat elevating between us. "And I want to taste you."

He groans against my skin, which makes me feel oddly powerful. All I'm doing is talking, yet he seems incapable of keeping his hands off me. "Such a dirty little girl," He drawls. I'm surprised to detect a hint of a southern accent in his voice.

"I want you inside of me," I squeak as he nips my collarbone with his teeth harder than I expect, making me jolt. "I want you to be my first."

His body tenses at that, his hands tightening so hard

on my hips it feels like he's trying to break me. Perhaps that's what he wants, as there is a darkness inside this man, a darkness I could never comprehend. I have a feeling that tonight I'm going to see a glimpse of what lies beneath the beautiful, perfect exterior of this man.

19

OAK

"And last," I growl, feeling that sinister possession spreading through me like poison infecting my blood and corrupting my heart.

Eva raises a questioning brow, but I ignore it. She may not understand that remark, but once I've had her, there's no going back. She'll be mine forever.

It's reckless to bring her here, but I can't find it in myself to care. After discovering that bastard's hands on her, Dimitry, I need to stake my claim and make her mine.

"Once I take you, Eva. There's no going back." I pull her tight against my body, letting her feel how hard I am between us. "You will be mine."

Her nostrils flare slightly, and I see that defiant spark in her eyes, but she doesn't refute my claim. Instead, she tilts her head in an invitation, begging me to claim her lips.

I tease her at first, allowing my breath to fall against her soft, pillowy lips. The distance between us slowly grows smaller until I press my lips to hers in an agonizingly gentle kiss.

Eva trembles against me, and her body melts into me as she grasps onto my arms for support.

I groan as my tongue slips into her mouth, as all the dirty, sick things I want to do to her flash through my mind. There's a sickness inside of me—one that can't be soothed or cured.

I long to hurt the beautiful creature in my arms. To put her over a spanking bench and tan her hide red raw. My cock throbs at the mental picture. It's the reason I've been so brutal with her punishments. The reason I've had her bend over for me daily while I spanked her ass with a ruler.

Eva deserves a man who is gentle and kind—anyone but me. And yet, when that thought flashes through my mind, the demon inside of me growls in envious rage. No one can have her except me.

"Oak," she moans against my mouth as I break away, kissing her neck as I grasp her hips.

"Strip for me, Eva," I order.

Eva takes a step back, and I see the uncertainty in those unique hazel eyes. It melts away as she moves her hand to the zip at her back and pulls it down before yanking her arms out of the sleeves.

I'm so hard right now. All the blood in my body has rushed to my cock.

She slips it down so that her pretty black lace bra is showing, allowing the fabric to drift lower and lower until I can see the waistband of her thong peeking beneath.

At that point, I can't wait any longer. I move for Eva and grab the dress, yanking it down powerfully. "Too slow," I breathe, taking a step back once the dress pools at her ankles. "Beautiful." My eyes scan every inch of her, absorbing the sight of her like this for me, blushing and practically naked.

"Take the rest off."

She chews her lip before shaking her head. "You next."

I growl, irritated by her outright defiance of my order, but she has a point. It's only fair that I also take off some of my clothes. Quickly, I lose my pants and shirt, tossing them onto the floor.

Eva turns crimson the moment I'm standing there in a pair of tight boxer briefs that leave nothing to the imagination. My cock is hard and leaking, leaving a stain of wet precum on the front.

"Now, panties and bra off," I growl.

Eva licks her lips and nods. "Yes, sir."

Fuck.

My cock jumps when I hear her call me that, and she knows what it does to me.

She tilts her head as she unhooks her bra, allowing it to fall to the floor. "Is this why you hated me calling you sir all the time?" She asks, slipping a finger into the waistband of her thong and dragging it down and off her ankles. "Did it turn you on?"

I shock her by seizing her before she can stand, her eyes wide. "Yes," I reply gruffly, pulling her naked body hard against mine. She is so soft, so perfect against my skin, as if she was made for me. I let my hand move to her breasts and cup her right one first, stroking the pad of my thumb over her puckered nipple.

Eva gasps at the sensation, arching her back. Her eyes dip between us to the bulge visible through my boxer briefs. "Isn't it your turn, sir?"

"Soon," I purr, lifting Eva into my arms. "First, I need to taste you."

Eva moans as I carry her through my cottage to the bedroom at the back. I can feel her study me as I walk toward the bed and place her down on her back, admiring how perfect she is.

This past month of resistance has been painful, wanting her in a way I've never wanted another person before. I descend over her, my body pinning her down as I slide my knee between her thighs and kiss her.

Eva reaches for me, but I grab her wrists and pin them above her head.

"No touching, baby girl." I move my lips lower, trailing a path down her neck to her collarbone. All the while, I keep my hand wrapped around her wrists. "Keep your wrists above your head, okay?" I ask.

Eva nods. "Yes, sir."

I groan as I release her wrists and continue to kiss

lower, moving to her breasts, which are large and firm. Her nipples are already hard as I move my mouth over her right one and suck on it, causing Eva's hips to buck toward me.

"Oh, God," she shouts, squirming under my attention as I move my mouth to cover her left nipple.

My hands tighten around her hips as I move lower, trailing my tongue down the center of her navel, making her shiver. I've never felt so dominant as I watch Eva react to my touch, my kiss. It does something to me I can't quite explain. "Tell me what you want, Eva," I breathe, allowing my breath to tickle her inner thighs. My mouth is inches away from her center, which is dripping wet.

"Please, sir," she moans, peering down at me with those unique hazel eyes dilated so much I can only detect a small rim of color.

"Please, what?" I ask, clawing at her hips. "I want you to tell me what you want me to do."

Her eyes roll back in her head, and she licks her lips before meeting my gaze again. "I want you to taste me," she says, her voice hesitant.

I groan as I move my finger toward her center, grazing it through her sensitive flesh. "Is that right, baby girl?"

"Yes, sir," she moans, back arching as she offers herself to me. It's hard to believe that this beautiful, innocent creature wants me. I'm a man so corrupted by the darkness that I can barely see the light anymore.

My tongue delves through her soaking wet center, tasting her for the first time. It's fucking heaven. "You taste so sweet," I groan as I lavish slow attention on her pussy, first licking between her lips, before moving the tip of my tongue to her clit and teasing her with it.

"Fuck," Eva cries, hands moving to clutch onto my hair.

I grind my teeth, ignoring that she disobeyed me, moving them from above her head. If I want her not to move, I'd have to stop and get the restraints from my closet, and there is nothing worth stopping right now.

Instead, I enjoy the feel of her fingers rubbing against my scalp as she writhes underneath me. I slide one finger inside her, feeling how tight she is. "Fuck," I breathe as I curl my finger upward, striking the spot inside her that makes her moan.

And fuck, does she moan? A sound so torturously beautiful I don't think I'd tire of it if it were the sole sound I ever heard for the rest of my life. "That's it, baby girl. I want you to moan for me." I suck her clit into my mouth.

She arches her back, arousal gushing out of her as I play her body into a frenzy. "Sir, please," she breathes, eyes lulling back in her head as she rakes her nails over my scalp. "Please."

"Please, what?" I ask, teasing her wickedly as I know what she's begging for. She needs her release.

"Let me come," she groans, her hips pushing toward my lips hungrily, demanding.

I place a firm hand on her abdomen, holding her in place. "You will come when I deem it the right time and not a second before."

She huffs in irritation, fingers raking rougher into my scalp.

I enjoy the slight sting of pain as I continue to wind her up tighter than a coil, but never get her to the precipice. When she comes, I want it to shatter her world and make her forget her goddamned name.

Her taste is addictive as I thrust my tongue in and out of her, continuing to stroke a finger down the inner wall of her virginal entrance. Eva's body trembles with each touch as I bring her closer and closer to the edge, only to back off the moment I feel the tension tighten.

Eva growls in frustration as I stop again. "Please, Oak. I can't stand it any longer," she whines, her fingers tightening in my hair. "I need to come."

I raise a brow. "It will feel better the longer I make you wait," I say.

She shakes her head. "I don't care, please, sir." Her beautiful hazel eyes are full of fire as she begs me, making me so hard I can hardly think straight.

I focus all my attention on her body, thrusting my finger in and out of her vigorously. Her muscles practically clamp around me, pulling my finger deeper. I swirl the tip of my tongue around her sensitive nub before allowing my teeth to graze over her clit.

She jolts violently, screaming as the soft scrape of my teeth sends her tumbling over the edge. I lap up every drop of her sweet nectar, cleaning her beautiful virgin cunt hungrily.

I groan against her, tasting every drop of her orgasm as she continues to jolt and shudder, panting and moaning unintelligible words at the intensity of her climax.

By the time her orgasm fades, I'm ready to start all over again.

I move my lips to her center, only for Eva to yank my hair so hard it feels like she's trying to pull it from my scalp. "My turn," she growls, eyes alight with such intensity it drives me wild.

I tilt my head, not used to women making demands in bed. "Is that right?"

She nods, eyes narrowing. "Let me taste you, sir."

My cock throbs, agreeing with her. "Very well."

She lets go of my hair, allowing me to step off the bed and hook my fingers into the waistband of my boxer briefs. "On your hands and knees," I order.

Eva does as I say in a heartbeat, crawling to the edge of the bed.

I pull the waistband down and drop my boxer briefs to the floor.

Eva gasps, eyes widening as she takes in my size.

I move closer, letting the tip of my cock rest only an inch from her pretty little mouth. "Taste me, baby girl," I order.

Her eyes, which are so dilated, meet mine. "I'm not sure it will fit."

"Believe me. It will."

Eva reaches out for me, her small hand circling the girth of my cock.

I groan at the mere touch of her, longing to feel her hot, wet mouth encase me. "Open wide," I order.

She swallows hard before opening her mouth.

I thrust my hips forward, groaning as her mouth encases me. It feels better than I ever could have imagined as I lace my fingers in her hair and pull her closer, making her choke.

Her hands move to my thighs, and she tries to push away, but I don't relent. The monster lying beneath the surface is rising to the surface quicker than I'd like as I thrust my cock in and out of the back of her throat, taking what I want and not giving a shit about the consequences.

Eva's saliva spills down her face and all over my cock as tears spill from her eyes down her cheeks.

I give her a moment's reprieve. "Breath through your nose," I instruct before slamming right back into her throat again.

She groans in protest, but I can hardly hear anything beyond the roaring of my blood. I'm lost to the sensations, lost to the woman I was supposed to destroy. I no longer know anything beyond the fact that she is everything to me.

20

EVA

I collapse in a heap on the bed the moment he stops, gasping for oxygen. My heart pounds frantically against my rib cage, as I don't even know how to feel. I turn over and stare up at the man who so roughly fucked my throat.

"Were you trying to kill me?" I spit, clutching hold of my throat and glaring at him.

He chuckles softly. "Don't be so dramatic, Eva." He moves my hair back from my face and presses his lips to my mouth softly. "I'd never hurt you," he breathes.

The tension in my muscles eases as I let him kiss me, feeling at ease by his declaration that he'd never hurt me. Even though it makes no sense, since he already has inflicted pain on me repeatedly, I understand what he means. He'd never push it further than I'd enjoy. Despite his rough treatment, I believe him with all of my heart. "Fuck me," I breathe as his lips move to my neck.

He groans against my skin as he yanks me into his lap, forcing me to straddle his thick thighs. "Is that what you want?" He asks, allowing me to feel the immense length of him against my entrance.

I moan and writhe in his lap, finding friction against the velvety length of his cock. "More than you can know," I say, searching those stunning eyes of his.

"I assume your mother took care of the birth control for us?" He asks, making me tense at the mention of her.

I nod and tap the small implant under my skin. "As soon as she saw that photo, she hauled my ass to the doctor."

He smirks. "Good, I want to feel your pretty virgin cunt wrapped around my unsheathed cock," he growls, lifting me off his lap enough to free his hard length. "I want to fill your pussy with my cum." His eyes flash with hunger as he positions me above it, the head of his cock nudging against my dripping wet entrance. "Tell me, Eva. Have you ever had anything inside you other than your fingers and mine?"

I shake my head, swallowing hard. Although I own a vibrator, I'd never bought a dildo. The thought of it terrified me, and yet now I wish I had. At least I'd have some idea of what was about to happen and how it would feel. Fingers are far thinner than his cock.

He groans. "Then this will be a tight fit." His fingertips dig into my hips as he applies pressure.

I tense, which makes him stop. "You need to relax; otherwise, it'll be painful." He cups my cheeks in his hands and stares into my eyes. "Relax, and it will feel good before you know it. Trust me."

I nod as he captures my lips with his and kisses me tenderly. My body relaxes as his tongue plunges into my mouth, making me hotter and needier by the second.

He stops and trails his lips over my neck, collarbone, and lower.

I bite my bottom lip as he sucks my nipple into his mouth, applying more pressure on my hips as his cock sinks a little inside of me.

"Fuck," I breathe at the utter overwhelming sensation of being stretched by this man. The intimacy of the position he has me in is overwhelming as he stares into my eyes, watching me as he impales himself inside of me.

"So. Fucking. Tight," Oak growls, making my nipples harder than rocks.

I kiss him this time, letting him feel how badly I want him. My tongue thrusts clumsily into his mouth as the need for this man pierces through my heart and makes me desperate.

His fingers tangle in my hair, and he yanks my head back forcefully, staring into my eyes. "I want to watch your face as you take every inch of me inside of you, baby girl."

I moan, my eyes flickering shut involuntarily. "Look at me," Oak growls.

I meet his gaze and melt as he forces me further down on his cock, tearing me open. "Fuck," I pant, struggling to draw oxygen into my lungs. The sensation is both painful and pleasurable.

Oak's fingers move to my ass cheeks, and he spreads them wide apart, groaning. "That's it, take my cock like a good girl," he purrs, forcing me even harder down around his shaft.

"It's too much," I groan, struggling to get used to him stretching me so unnaturally, and yet everything about it feels natural. The deep burning ache inside of me that longs to be filled by him and yet can't take his immense size.

I tense as he teases the tight ring of muscles between my ass cheeks, sending a foreign sensation through me.

"Relax," he whispers before coating his fingers in my juices and moving his finger back to my asshole. He pushes the tip of his finger inside, making me moan at the utter filthiness of the act. And yet, while this unfamiliar sensation distracts my mind, he slides me over his cock.

"Fuck. You are so tight," He growls, glancing down between us where his cock has disappeared. "I'm all the way inside of you."

"Oh, God," I cry, glancing down at where we meet. "How is that even possible?"

He smirks and kisses me without moving at all,

giving me time to get used to being so full of him. The stinging pain of my muscles stretching to accommodate him morphs into a deep ache as he kisses me, making me rock back and forth in his lap in search of friction.

Oak's powerful arm wraps around my back as he lifts me halfway up his cock before thrusting his hips upwards and pulling me down all at the same time.

"Fuck," I cry, unable to organize the thousands of thoughts rushing through my mind all at once. I clutch onto Oak's powerful shoulders and move my hips, rising and falling to meet his thrust. What once felt like pain morphs into the most exquisite sensation of pleasure as he meets my movements, driving me higher and higher. "Oak," I moan his name, my head falling back as he drives me toward the cliff edge. "I need it harder, faster," I breathe.

Oak chuckles and viciously latches his mouth against my neck, sucking on the flesh until it hurts. "Is that right?" He tilts his head. "I thought you couldn't take it, and now you want it harder?"

I nod in response. "Please, sir."

He groans and lifts me from his cock, making me whimper at the sudden empty feeling where he had been. Oak places me down on my back, covering my body with his powerful frame.

His leg nudges my thighs wider, forcing me to remain open to him. "Be careful what you ask for, Eva," he murmurs before thrusting his hips forward and burying his cock deep inside of me.

My mouth falls open on a silent scream as he somehow gets even deeper.

Oak's aquamarine eyes are so dilated there's only a small rim around the pupil, making him look almost demonic as he stares at me. The hunger in the depths of them is both frightening and exciting.

"Fuck me," I breathe.

He smirks as he nips my bottom lip with his teeth. "Patience," he murmurs, teasing me as he plants soft kisses over my neck and down to my collarbone. "There's plenty of time to fuck like animals, but I want to explore everything that makes you tick, Eva." He bites my collarbone so hard I cry out, arching my back more. "How much pain you enjoy."

"A-And do you have an answer?" I ask.

The glint in his eyes is almost devilish. "It appears you enjoy pain as much as I enjoy giving it."

He bites me again, and I moan as he does, enjoying being devoured by him. It's an odd sensation, enjoying pain along with pleasure. The perfect blend of it he gives me feels addicting.

"Please fuck me," I beg, trying to roll my hips under his immense weight. The need for friction is so consuming, as he keeps me pinned and immobile beneath him.

Oak enjoys having me powerless. He enjoys having me begging him for it. I can see it in his eyes. "As you wish, baby girl." He draws his immense hips back and slams into me with force, knocking the air from my lungs.

His careful control slips as he fucks me mercilessly. Our bodies come together in a violent joining. Any sign of tenderness is obliterated, and I love it.

The roughness of his actions only makes me want more. He takes me like an animal, making me feel so wanted–more wanted than I've ever felt in my life.

I place my hand on his tight jaw, feeling his soft beard beneath my fingers as I let my hands dip lower to his inked chest, touching the hard muscle beneath soft skin.

"Eva," he groans my name, grabbing my wrists and forcing them harshly above my head. His eyes look unfocused as he moves above me, restraining me forcefully. "No touching."

I arch my back, enjoying the way he controls me completely. The powerless sensation of being dominated is more pleasurable than I could have imagined. I look up into my principal's dark eyes, knowing that we shouldn't be doing this, and yet that makes it more exciting. I've always stuck to the rules, and now it's time to fucking break them. After all, I've never got anywhere by sticking to the rules.

"Harder," I pant.

Oak growls, nostrils flaring. "Don't, Eva." A vein protrudes from his forehead as he glares down at me. "You can't understand what you're asking for." He's panting for breath as he holds back.

I tilt my head. "I want you to fuck me harder, sir."

He groans as if he's struggling to contain a part of

him that wants to unleash his wrath on me. "I could hurt you." His hands remain tight around my wrists.

"Perhaps I enjoy the pain," I say, knowing that I'm playing with fire.

His eyes flash as he growls, losing control as his hips move in sharp, violent bursts. "You're such a good girl, Eva." Each time he plows into me, it feels like he's trying to break me apart. The muscles in his neck strain as he continues to hold my wrists hard above my head with one hand, his other hand digging into my hips.

I moan as he thrusts into me with more violence and so much desire that it almost destroys me. "Fuck, I think I'm going to—"

Oak's hand moves from my wrists to my throat, and he squeezes, blocking off my airways partially, like he did in the hallway that time. "Come for me, baby girl," he snarls.

"Fuck, yes, Oak," I cry as the mere order from his lips has me tumbling over the edge.

My muscles spasm, and my vision blurs, either from the lack of oxygen or the breathtaking climax this God of a man brought me to. Perhaps a mixture of the two as I continue to writhe beneath him, taking every thrust of his hips as he becomes more uneven and uncontrolled, grunting and groaning above me.

He roars, sinking his teeth into my shoulder as he unleashes inside of me. Shot after shot of his cum floods my pussy, and it's the most overwhelming sensation as my vision returns, and Oak releases my throat, panting above me.

At that moment, I know that I've never felt so close, so connected to another human being before. As I look into his hazy, unfocused eyes, I feel my chest ache as I know this can't happen again.

Oak is the principal of this school and my teacher. And yet, I want it to happen daily. I never want to leave his bed, as I know this silly fantasy will be over.

Oak pulls his cock from me and lies down on his back, reaching for my hand. He squeezes it, making that ache in my chest deepen. We lay in silence, neither of us knowing what to say. Tonight was the best night of my life, but I fear it will have to remain a treasured and forbidden memory and nothing more.

21

OAK

As I walk toward leadership class with the seniors, each step I take is hesitant, knowing that Eva should be there. I haven't seen her since we had sex, as she didn't turn up for our class on Tuesday. It's now Friday, and I can only hope she turns up; otherwise, I'm going to hunt her down. I can't stand her avoiding me.

My stomach flips as I notice her instantly, sitting in her usual seat, doodling on her notepad as she so often does before class. I can't help the smile that twists onto my lips the moment I see her, which both irritates and confuses me.

I clear my throat and enter the room. "Morning, class," I say, keeping my eyes fixed on Eva, who, despite blushing a pretty crimson, doesn't meet my gaze. "Today, I want to discuss five different leadership styles." I turn to the board behind my desk and grab my marker pen, writing five words on the board.

Authoritarian
Participative
Delegative
Transactional
Transformational

I turn back to the class. "Which are the most common in the crime world?"

Natalya's hand shoots up, as always. "Authoritarian."

For once, Natalya isn't right. "Not exactly no. You would think so, but not the most common strategy." I search the faces watching me. "Does anyone else know the answer?"

To my surprise, Eva puts her hand up. "I believe delegative is the most common strategy since leaders don't do the work themselves. They delegate."

I clap my hands together once and nod. "Exactly right." I tilt my head and walk around the front of my desk, struggling to keep my eyes off of Eva. "Can anyone tell me the advantages and disadvantages of delegative leadership?"

Natalya puts her hand up. "Yes, Natalya."

"The advantages are that the leader can spend time on the important workings of the organization while his or her men handle the day-to-day running." She runs a hand through her hair. "However, it can lead to the people below believing they have more power than they do and may make it difficult for the leader to keep proper tabs on his or her soldiers." She shrugs. "In that case, it is a perfect breeding ground for disloyalty and betrayal."

"Thank you, Natalya. That's exactly right." I grab the textbook off my desk and hold it up. "All of you turn to page one-hundred and fifty-five and read the five pages on the different leadership strategies." I push off my desk and take my seat on the other side. "Then, I want a three-page essay on the leadership strategy you would choose and the reason behind your choice."

A few pupils grumble, but I ignore it as everyone begrudgingly pulls out their textbooks and finds the page. Eva, who is still a pretty shade of pink, won't look up at me as she focuses all her attention on the task at hand.

I lean back in my chair and watch her, utterly captivated by the girl who broke my resolve earlier this week. Eva has made me question everything I believed I knew for the past five years.

A knock at the classroom door draws my attention, and my brow furrows when I see my secretary, Melissa, standing there. I signal for her to come in. "What is it?" I ask.

She glances around nervously. "You should see for yourself."

I glance at my class, who focus on us rather than on their work. "Get back to work," I growl. "I'll be back shortly."

I stand, following my cryptic secretary into the hall.

"Melissa," I hiss, once we're out of earshot of my students. "Tell me what is going on."

Her brow furrows. "It's a student." She swallows. "He's dead, and there's no sign of who did it."

"Fuck," I growl, marching down the corridor. "Where?"

She nods toward the boys' bathroom. "In there."

I march in and hold my hand over my mouth the moment I do. The boy in question is, in fact, Henley Anderson, the son of Jackson Anderson from Oklahoma. We believe that they're currently embroiled in a rather heated war with the Russians on their turf, which means this was the Orlov Bratva. The leader's son is also in attendance here, Stepan Orlov. Henley was only fifteen years old. Stepan is seventeen years old.

My stomach churns at the sight in front of me. The blood and gore are indescribable. They have gouged his eyes out of his head and fixed his mouth open with a device. "Inform the family and get Ainsley here to clear it up."

This isn't the first death we've had to deal with here, but it's the first one we've had in two years. We have brutal fights that end with badly injured students, but death is luckily something we avoid more often than not. However, on this occasion, it's clear that nothing would stop the Orlov Bratva from having their revenge on the Anderson family.

"Of course," Michelle replies, looking rather green.

"I need to get out of here." She whirls around and heads out into the corridor. Her retching fills the air as I stand there, almost frozen by the scene in front of my eyes.

I sigh heavily, shaking my head. The craziest thing is that Stepan Orlov will get away with it. He's the heir of the Bratva in Oklahoma. He has every right to exercise his powers where the fuck he wants, and as the staff who are teaching him how to be the most brutal leader possible, how could we possibly punish him for being exactly that?

It is one thing I hate most about this academy. The darkness we nurture and inspire only sets them free to terrorize this country. Ironically, I fled this kind of world, unable to accept the immorality of the part I was due to play, only to end up teaching the exact people I despised.

I walk out into the corridor. "Is Ainsley on his way?" I ask.

Michelle nods, clearing up the sick off the floor. "Yes, he'll be here in five minutes."

"Good. In the meantime, don't allow anyone in there." I walk off.

"Where are you going?" Michelle calls after me.

"Back to class. Ainsley will handle it."

Ainsley is our fixer, who we call in during incidents like this. A man whose expertise is in clearing up and hiding messes so that it appears like they never happened, as well as handling the parents.

I return to the classroom, feeling chaotic.

Henley's parents will visit within the day, and they will not be happy. This means I'll have to pay a settlement, even though they signed the agreement, which detailed that SA and its staff have no responsibility for death or injury caused by classmates. However, there is no reasoning with grieving parents, even if they often are only grieving the loss of an heir rather than a child.

I run a school for the spawn of monsters, and money would assuage only a monster at the loss of a child.

I run a hand through my hair and slump behind my desk.

The class is quiet as they continue to work. Natalya stands after I return, placing the essay on my desk. "All done."

I nod and wave my hand. "You may leave."

The rest of the class isn't far behind until only Eva is left. She's a welcome distraction after the shit I just witnessed. She stands once we're alone and walks over to the desk, smiling hesitantly at me. "Here you go, sir."

I growl, knowing she's using the world to taunt me.

Eva turns to walk toward the door, but I cut her off before she gets to it, grabbing her hips and pulling her flush against me. "Where do you think you are going?"

"My next class, sir." She glances over her shoulder at me but arches her back, so her firm buttocks press into my straining erection. "I have physical education class next with Professor Daniels."

"Like hell you do," I growl, pushing her against the wall next to the door, ensuring no one can see us. My hand reaches for the blind over the window, and I pull it down. "I'll give you a better physical education, Eva," I murmur, letting my teeth tease at the shell of her ear. "What do you say to that?" I reach for the lock on the classroom door and turn it, making sure no one can come inside. This classroom is free this period, but I won't take any risks.

"I'll get in trouble for—"

"Not if I excuse you, you won't." I grab her wrist and force her to face me. "I need you right now, Miss Carmichael."

She wets her lips with her tongue. "Don't you have a class to teach?"

I shake my head. "Free period, baby girl." I let my hand gently skate over her thigh before squeezing it gently. "Stop overthinking and just feel." I kiss her lips, knowing that right now, all I need is to drown in her.

"The problem is, sir. I don't think I can be quiet enough." Her tone has turned flirty, which means she's into this.

I kiss her again before letting go and walking to my desk, pulling out a ball gag. "This should solve that issue."

Her eyes widen, and she inches toward the door,

fear sparking in her irises. "What are you planning to do with it?"

"Come here," I order.

She hesitates, but in the end, submits to my demand. Her steps are slow as she approaches me.

Once she's a foot from me, I say, "Turn around."

She does, spinning, so her back is facing me.

"Put the ball in your mouth," I say, passing it to her.

She does, and then I fasten the strap at the back of her head.

"If it gets too much for you, click your fingers. That will be our safe action."

Eva shudders as I move to stand in front of her, placing my hand on her shoulder.

"Bend over the desk," I order.

She does as I say, bending right over it, so her skirt hikes up halfway up her ass. My cock jumps in my pants at the sight of her wet and ready for me, wearing no panties.

"If I didn't know any better, I'd say you planned this," I murmur, reaching for her skirt and hiking it to her hips. I spank her right ass cheek, followed by her left. "Have you been thinking about my cock, baby girl?"

She groans behind the gag, nodding eagerly in response.

I unzip my pants, knowing that despite having this classroom free for a period, the quicker we get out of here, the safer. My cock leaks everywhere as I free it from my boxer briefs and line the head up with her dripping wet entrance. I grab her hip with one hand and keep the other wrapped around my cock as I thrust forward, impaling every inch to the hilt inside of her.

Eva screams around the gag, but it muffles the sound enough.

She obliterates any control over my actions or sense as I fuck her over my desk, my hips thrusting hard and fast as I take Eva mercilessly.

I grab both her hips and pull her toward me, fucking her hard and fast over my desk like the monster I truly am. Our skin slapping together is the only sound, along with Eva's muffled moans and my strangled grunts of pleasure.

It would be impossible to mistake the sounds coming from this room if anyone was standing outside. But I don't give a shit at that moment. All I care about is claiming the woman sprawled over my desk, clutching at the edge as I pound into her without mercy.

I lean over the length of her back and tease my lips over the shell of her ear. "You are such a good girl taking my cock so fucking well," I murmur, biting down on the sensitive flesh. "I want to feel your cunt come all over my cock, Eva. Right here in the middle of the classroom."

Eva moans behind the gag, driving me wild.

I stop suddenly, pulling out of her.

She whines in protest, but I flip her over onto her back and slide back in.

Her eyes roll back in her head as I fuck her with more force and speed, driving right toward the edge.

I wrap a hand around her throat and squeeze, making her eyes widen as I stop the airflow.

Initially, she is tense, but the tension eases as she looks into my eyes. She gives me a look of pure, untainted trust as she allows me to dominate her body, master it completely.

My cock swells inside of her as I get closer to the edge, but I can't let go until she comes for me. "I need you to come on my cock, baby girl," I murmur, my voice barely above a whisper, but the way her back arches tells me she heard me.

A muffled fuck comes from behind the ball gag as she comes undone. My fingers tighten around her throat as I slam into her twice more before exploding deep inside of her.

I roar against my free fist, knowing that we can't be too loud. Once I've spent every drop of seed inside of Eva, I release her throat. My cock twitches at the sight of the purple bruising already showing where I'd had my fingers.

I grab Eva's hand and lift her off the desk, pulling her against my chest. "Are you okay?" I ask as I undo the gag in her mouth.

Eva slumps against me, barely strong enough to

remain standing alone. "I think so," she says, shaking her head. "That was…"

"Intense?" I offer.

She nods, gazing at me adoringly.

I kiss her, searching every inch of her mouth as if we have all the time in the world.

Eva moans into my mouth, clutching hold of me as she straightens and searches for friction against my thickening cock. "Fuck," she breathes as we part. "I think I need more."

I smirk. "You are perfect, Eva." The bell rings, signaling that we just spent an entire period fucking and kissing in the classroom. My heart hammers as I realize another class will line up outside within minutes, and I force my semi-hard cock back into my pants. "You'd better get going. I'm teaching seventh grade in here."

Eva's eyes widen, and she nods. "Yes, sir. See you around."

I watch as she walks toward the door, flicks the lock, and struts out of the classroom boldly. Undeterred that we just fucked on school grounds like a couple of sex-crazed animals. As I watch her, I realize how royally fucked I am.

22

EVA

"Did I hear Elias is taking you to the winter formal?" Adrianna asks, eyes glued to Natalya.

Her cheeks flush as she nods. "Yeah, I'm not sure I have a choice."

"Asshole," I mutter, glaring over at the cocky, inked bastard who has his eyes fixed on our table. "Why do you let him push you around?" I ask.

Natalya just shrugs.

"Who are you going with, Eva?" Camilla asks.

I shake my head. "No one. I don't care about having a date." My stomach churns at the thought of attending the winter formal, when all I can think about is the man that runs this school. The man who fucked me in the classroom three days ago. It was so risky, especially after I had to lie through my teeth to my friends about where I disappeared on our night out. They were going crazy with concern and I was fucking the principal. "You?" I ask.

Camilla shakes her head. "Alek asked me as friends, so I said yes."

Alek is one of the few decent guys I've met here. He's from Indiana, and his family is not exactly powerful, but they have some sway.

"You should date him," Natalya says, shaking her head. "You'd make the cutest couple."

Camilla rolls her eyes, a slight smile on her lips. She says nothing, but I'm pretty sure that everyone knows Alek isn't into women. I see how he looks at Gavril, Archer, and Oak, and it's the same way the girls do.

"Have you got a date?" I ask Adrianna.

She shakes her head. "No, I don't want a date." She shudders. "The only guy to ask me yet is Hernandez."

Camilla and Natalya burst out laughing. "Seriously?" Natalya questions.

Adrianna's expression is grave as she nods.

I sit there, blankly watching as they struggle to contain their laughter. "Who is Hernandez?"

"Only the creepiest guy at this school." They look at a table on the other side of the cafeteria where a guy is sitting.

He has dark hair that is longer than Adriana's, and when he looks up, I can see he has a uni-brow that stretches right across his face. His eyes move to us, and he smiles the creepiest smile I've ever seen, making all of us look away sharply.

"Oh dear," I say.

Camilla and Natalya both burst out laughing again. "Trust you, Ad, to be asked to the winter formal by that freak," Camilla says.

Dimitry, the boy from leadership strategy class, approaches our table. He's good-looking with dark short-cropped hair and dark brown eyes and has a boyish appeal, but he pales compared to Oak.

"Good evening, ladies."

"What do you want, Dimitry?" Camilla asks.

His eyes land on me. "I was hoping to ask an exquisite woman if she would care to accompany me to the winter formal."

My stomach churns as I remember how Oak spoke to me *after* seeing Dimitry's hand on my thigh.

I never want to see Dimitry fucking Jakov near you again.

I chew my bottom lip, wondering how serious he was being. Dimitry can be forward, but I wouldn't do anything with him. He may be attractive, but I don't desire him. Oak can't tell me what to do with my life.

"So, what do you say, Eva?" Dimitry asks.

I swallow hard, realizing since I don't have a date, it would be weird to refuse, not to mention, other than Dimitry being a little forward, he seems like an alright guy. "Sure, why not?" I can't exactly take my hot as hell principal to the winter formal, anyway. The man I've fucked twice already, once after class last Friday in the classroom, and I haven't seen him since.

Dimitry's smirk widens. "Great, can't wait." He winks, which makes my stomach churn.

Once he's out of earshot, Natalya turns to me. "Dimitry?" She groans.

I turn to face her. "What? He seems alright."

She rolls her eyes. "Yeah, for an egotistical, misogynistic pig."

I laugh. "Don't worry. I can fend for myself."

At that moment, I feel *his* eyes on me. Oak stands in the cafeteria's corner, leaning against the wall with his arms crossed over his hard, muscled chest. His jaw is clenched, and his eyes are blazing with what I can only describe as rage, making my stomach churn.

Will he be jealous of me attending the winter formal with Dimitry?

I shake my head and draw my eyes away from Oak, listening as Adrianna rattles on about why she won't be attending the winter formal with anyone. She comes across as a girl who likes to shun society's expectations.

Oak can't be jealous, as he can't take me to the dance. It's not like I've agreed to sleep with him, attend a dance with him. It's been a week since we had sex in his cottage, a week since he took my innocence. Ever since, he's kept his distance from me, which hurts. All he does is stare at me hungrily from afar.

"I can't believe it's less than two weeks until winter break," Camilla says, shaking her head. "This semester has flown by."

"Right. What will I do without you three?" Natalya asks.

"Do we have to go home for the winter break?" it's crazy that I didn't even want to attend this school at first, but now the prospect of returning to my parents for two weeks makes me sick to my stomach. I can't think of anything worse than going home for winter break.

All three girls look at me like I'm crazy. "Why wouldn't you want to?" Natalya asks.

I shake my head. "I hate my parents."

She smiles. "I'm not exactly fond of my mother either, but I go home for my brother." Her eyes turn a little misty with emotion. "I love him like a father."

My throat closes up as I think about Karl. We were close, and when he died, it left a gaping hole in my world. It meant I was alone with them, the two people I despise most on this earth.

Camilla nods. "My father can be a bit of a nightmare, but my brothers would kill me if I didn't go home." Her brow furrows. "I'm sure they'd be happy for you to join us in Chicago this Christmas?"

I smile at her. "That's kind of you, but I'm shit with people I don't know."

"Wouldn't your parents wonder where you are, anyway?" Adrianna asks.

I shake my head. "One year, they forgot about me and drove down to my grandmother's two hours south of Atlanta. They only noticed when they got there, and she questioned them."

Natalya and Camilla gasp.

"What the fuck?" Adrianna asks.

"I know," I say, feeling my throat tighten as I remember. "My parents rang me and said I'd have to fend for myself for a week. It was the same year my brother died and my first Christmas without him."

"How old were you?" Camilla asks.

"Sixteen," I say.

"Shit. I mean, our world can be harsh, but it sounds like your parents are complete and utter assholes." Camilla shakes her head. "No offense."

"None taken," I say.

Natalya shakes her head. "If you wanted, you could join me in Boston. I'm sure my brother would make space."

Adrianna chimes in. "Or me."

I shake my head. "It's kind of you all, but I think I may stick around here if it's allowed." The last thing I want is to gatecrash someone else's family Christmas. My heart pounds as I turn my attention to the spot where Oak had been standing, but he's no longer there. I wonder what he is doing during the Christmas break.

Natalya shrugs. "I never heard of people staying behind."

"The problem is, you'd have to cook your own food," Adrianna adds, glancing at the cafeteria staff. "Pretty sure the staff doesn't stick around."

"You'll have to ask Principal Byrne for permission," Camilla says.

I nod in reply, glancing around the cafeteria again in search of him. "Yeah, I guess I best find him and ask if it's possible."

"Do you want me to come?" Natalya asks.

I shake my head. "No, I'll be fine. I'll catch up with you in class later."

They all nod as I head out of the cafeteria toward Oak's office. My heart is pounding frantically in my chest as I get closer, knowing that the only other time we've been alone since the night in the cottage, we ended up fucking.

I reach the door of his office and lift my hand to knock, fighting the nerves fluttering to life in the pit of my stomach. I rap my knuckles on the door three times and wait.

"Who is it?" His voice booms from the other side.

"Eva Carmichael, sir," I reply, twirling my thumbs together.

Footsteps follow a few moments of silence, and then he appears in the doorway, glaring at me. "Are you here to apologize?" He asks.

My brow furrows. "What?"

"I said, are you here to apologize?"

I shake my head. "What on earth for?"

Oak glances down the corridor as if checking it is clear, before grabbing my wrist hard and yanking me into his office. "For talking to Dimitry after I explicitly told you that I never want to see Dimitry Jakov near you again." The door slams shut as he leers over me.

"You can't tell me what to do," I say, holding my chin high. "You haven't spoken to me since the incident in the classroom." I gaze into his fierce blue eyes. "Dimitry asked me to the winter formal, and I said yes, since—"

Oak's animalistic growl cuts me off as he rushes toward me, grabbing my hips and pushing me face-first against the door. His body molded against mine. "You will not be attending the winter formal with that jerk," he says, his voice unusually calm.

"It's too late, I've agreed—"

"Rescind your agreement immediately," he barks.

I shake my head. "It's only a dance. I can't exactly take my principal, so you'd prefer I go alone?"

"Yes," he says. "I won't stand there and watch you dance with him."

I grit my teeth together. "You are being ridiculous. Nothing will happen. I don't like Dimitry."

"Good," he breathes, letting his lips gently brush against the shell of my ear. "Then it won't be hard to tell him you've changed your mind."

I try to wiggle free from Oak's iron-like grasp, but it's impossible.

"Will it?" He pushes.

"I will do no such thing. I'm going to the dance with Dimitry, and you can either act like the adult principal of this school and accept it or act like a pubescent, jealous idiot. I don't care which, but I'm going with Dimitry."

Oak growls softly. "You are such a feisty girl. Perhaps I need to put you over my knee to teach you a lesson," he purrs.

"I came here because I have a serious question to ask you."

"Is that right?" He asks, gently hitching the hem of my skirt until he can see my buck naked ass. "And do you often wear no panties when you want to ask serious questions?"

"Oak, please," I say, knowing that if I don't stop him now, I'll forget why the fuck I was here.

He lets go and takes a step away, allowing me to turn to face him as he pushes a hand through his thick, dark hair. "What is it, Eva?"

I bite the inside of my cheek. "Is it permitted for pupils to remain at the school during the winter break?"

His brow furrows. "Not usually, no."

My shoulders dip at his answer.

"Why do you ask?"

I sigh heavily. "I don't want to go home."

The corner of his lip twitches upward in an almost smile. "If I remember rightly, you didn't want to be left here six weeks ago." His head tilts. "What changed?"

I roll my eyes at him. "If you're expecting me to say it's because of you, then you will be disappointed." I fold my arms over my chest. "Being away from my parents made me realize how much I hate them."

"Hate is a strong word, Eva."

I shake my head. "Not for them, it's not." I bite my bottom lip. "I can't think of anything worse than returning home for Christmas."

Oak sits a little straighter. "Why is that?"

I feel my cheeks heat at the thought of admitting to Oak just how little my parents care about me. "Because they don't want me there, anyway."

His brow furrows. "I'm sure that's not—"

"You don't know what they're like." I shake my head. "The year my brother died, our first Christmas without him. They headed two hours down to my grandmother's for Christmas, forgetting one insignificant detail." I pause for effect. "Me." My throat closes up as I remember how much I cried that Christmas, how badly it hurt.

Oak's eyes flash with anger. "Did they return for you?"

I laugh at that, only to stop myself from crying. "No. They realized when my grandmother asked where I was, so they rang me and said I'd have to fend for myself for the holidays." I swallow hard. "I suggested I take a cab, but they said it wasn't worth it." A stray tear escapes my eyes, running down my cheek.

Oak looks at me with a strange look in his eyes that I can't quite determine. "Bastards," he growls, his fists clenching.

"So, I can't stay here for the holidays?" I ask, hating how pathetic my voice sounds.

Oak's jaw is tight as he watches me intently. "You could stay with me," he murmurs.

My stomach flips, and hope blazes in my heart. "Won't you be with family?" I ask.

A muscle in his jaw flexes at the mention of family, but he just shakes his head. "No." He stands from behind his desk and paces the floor. "I'll be in my cottage for the holidays if you want to join me." He stops pacing, a wicked look in his eyes. "I can't think of a better Christmas present than spending the entire break with you naked in my bed," he almost growls.

My cheeks heat, and my thighs clench at the thought. "Neither can I," I breathe.

He walks toward me, eyes alight with that dangerous spark. "Stand," he orders.

I do as he says, standing in front of him.

Oak's eyes search mine for a moment before he pulls me against him. His lips cover mine as he forces his tongue through my defenses, plundering my mouth with such need it makes my knees weak.

I clutch onto his powerful shoulders, wanting to melt into him.

He stops kissing me, our breathing ragged as he softly murmurs, "Come to mine for dinner tonight."

I raise a brow. "I've got a feeling my friends will notice if I'm not at dinner."

"Say you aren't hungry and eat a little." His grip tightens on my hips painfully. "Tell them you're going to bed early and be at my cottage by eight."

"Okay," I breathe.

Oak smiles and kisses me one more time before breaking away. "Now, get to class."

I nod and turn around.

Only for Oak to spank my ass playfully, making me yelp. "What was that for?"

He leans back against his desk, arms folded over his chest. "Because I felt like it."

I shake my head but can't stop the stupid grin that spreads onto my lips as I head toward his door. "See you later," I say, walking out into the corridor without a glance back.

The only response I get is a soft growl behind me. One that vibrates right to my core and makes me ache for the man behind me.

It's going to be a very long afternoon.

23

OAK

I'm not a skilled cook, but people have often complimented me on my lasagne, so that's what I've made for Eva, as well as a large helping of cheesy garlic bread.

It's crazy that I'm nervous.

This is the first time I'll be spending time with Eva, outside of a classroom setting or fucking her, even if that's where I want this night to end. I need to learn more about her, learn if she could want to ruin her parents as badly as I do.

It's quite clear that I can't keep my hands to myself when it comes to her. Instead of fighting it, it's about time I found out if we could become partners in crime and complete my quest for revenge with her by my side.

The only issue is that it means I need to reveal my true intent for her. Before I knew Eva, I had every intention of destroying her, along with her family. It's not a subject I wish to broach tonight, but over the two-week break with her, I'll have to come clean.

I glance at the clock, noticing that it's a quarter past eight. My jaw clenches. Either Eva's just running late, or they have caught her trying to sneak out of the school. Considering she was often late for discipline class, I'm going to assume it's the former.

There's a soft knock at my door sounds and the tension coils through my body. My hands are shaking as I reach for the door handle. I take a deep breath to calm my nerves, but it doesn't work.

I open the door, and there she is, wearing a beautiful, flowing pale blue dress that ends just below her knees. "You look stunning," I say before she can speak.

I glance around the vicinity, making sure no one is lurking around. "Come in." I stand to the side and allow her to sweep past me.

"Whatever you are cooking smells amazing," Eva says, smiling as she glances at me.

I clench my jaw as a stupid, fleeting notion enters my mind.

I could get used to this.

"I'm making lasagne." I tip my head toward the sofa. "Have a seat. What would you like to drink?"

She tilts her head slightly. "Whatever you are having."

I raise a brow. "I'm not sure you'd be too happy

with scotch." I walk to my fridge and pull out a bottle of white wine. "How about chardonnay?"

Eva smiles and then nods. "Sounds great."

I shouldn't be offering an underage pupil a drink, but then I shouldn't have her here in my cottage either. With Eva, I do everything I'm not supposed to do. I pour her a large glass and take it to her, placing it down on the coffee table.

"Food is in the oven. I'll join you in a moment," I say, heading to grab myself a glass of scotch.

When I return from my study, where I keep the scotch, Eva is standing by the bookcase in my living room, her fingers gently running over the spines of the first edition books. She startles when she hears me behind her. "I didn't hear you return," she says, looking a little sheepish. "You have a lot of ancient books."

I smile and nod. "Yes, I collect them." My brow furrows. "I have done since I was young."

She brings her glass up to her lips and takes a small sip before walking back to the sofa. "Do you like to read?"

I move toward her, struggling to keep the mental picture of her on her knees with my cock in her mouth out of the forefront of my mind. "Yes, but not as much as I like collecting rare books." I glance toward one painting on the wall. "As well as paintings, too." I tilt my glass to the wall, and Eva's eyes widen.

"Is it original?" She asks, gawking at the starry night painting by Van Gogh.

I nod and lift my glass to my lips, knocking back my whiskey. "Yes, although the museum of modern art believe they have the original."

She raises a brow. "I don't think I want to know how you got this painting."

I laugh. "No, I don't think you do."

She smiles as she lifts her glass of wine to her lips and takes a sip. "Where are your paintings?"

I grind my teeth, remembering that I told her I liked to paint. No one ever sees my paintings, and the thought of showing Eva them makes me anxious in ways I've never felt before. "Hidden in the attic somewhere," I say, waving my hand.

Her brow furrows. "Why? I'd like to see them."

I move toward her and sit next to her on the sofa. "I've never shown them to anyone."

"Oh," she says, twisting her fingers in her lap. "Perhaps you can paint me now, since you've already seen me in the nude."

I groan, shaking my head. "The chance of me ever finishing that painting would be slim." I set my whiskey tumbler down on the coffee table, moving her flowing golden hair away from her neck and pressing my lips to her skin. "I wouldn't be able to stop myself from fucking you."

Eva giggles, shaking her head. "You could try."

I can tell she's eager for me to paint her, but I know it won't work out. Instead, I change the subject. "Tell me, Eva. You know my passion. What is yours?"

"Animals," she says.

My brow furrows. "That's why you want to be a vet?" I run a hand across the back of my neck. "But what makes you so passionate about animals?"

"Taking care of them brings me joy." She smiles widely and reaches into her pocket, pulling out her phone. "Where we live in Atlanta, we're right by a woodland nature reserve." She flicks through photos that are mostly of animals. "These two squirrels were injured, and I nursed them back to health." Eva smiles proudly, handing me the phone. "There is no better feeling in this world than helping those less fortunate than you."

I swallow hard, a lump in my throat forming. Eva is right, and yet I do exactly the opposite. No doubt, word about Henley's murder has spread through the school. This is the behavior I facilitate. "I'm sure that's true, but I wouldn't know." I stand and walk toward the kitchen, grabbing the bottle of scotch and pouring another large glass. "Unfortunately, my job is anything but rewarding."

Eva tilts her head, watching me. "I don't know if that's true. You give these people a place to belong and teach them discipline, even if they go out into the world and do bad things. That's not your fault."

"Isn't it?" I ask, my voice harsher than I intended.

Eva doesn't cower, though. Instead, she shakes her head. "No, someone has to teach them. Perhaps the students that pass through here won't be as brutal as the ones who didn't."

I raise a brow. "Have you not heard what happened to Henley Anderson today?"

Her brow furrows, and she shakes her head. "I don't even know who that is."

"This morning, when I left the classroom." I run a hand through my hair as the horrific images flash to the front of my mind. "Another student had brutally murdered Henley Anderson."

Eva gasps, shaking her head. "Are you serious?"

"I'm surprised you hadn't heard the way gossip travels around the school." I walk back toward her and sit on the sofa. "He was collateral in a war his father was a part of." I meet Eva's wide-eyed gaze. "Make no mistake. This place is just as dark, fucked-up, and brutal as the world they belong to outside of these grounds."

Eva places her wineglass down on the coffee table and takes my hands, squeezing. "Why do you do it when it makes you miserable?"

"Do what?" I ask.

"Run this school."

My stomach flips as I look into her eyes. The answer to that question is not one I can dignify with an answer, not yet—not until I know I can trust Eva. "I don't know," I say, pulling my hands from hers. It's insane how well she knows me. Am I that easy to read? "I need to check on the food."

I glance back at Eva to see she is watching me with

disappointment in her eyes. The fact is, she can't yet know the truth. Not until I determine how far her hatred runs for her parents.

"It's ready," I say, smiling. "Have a seat at the table."

She does as I say, getting up and sitting in the chair next to mine. "Is here okay?"

"Perfect," I say as I place the dish of lasagne down on the heat mat in the center. "One moment. Can't forget the garlic bread."

Her stomach grumbles. "It all smells delicious."

When I get back to the table, I serve her a good portion and then help myself.

"Dig in," I say.

She does, making little moaning sounds as she eats. "Wow, this lasagne is amazing. What's your secret?"

"Italian blood," I say, laughing.

Her brow furrows. "Really? Oakley Byrne doesn't sound a very Italian name."

My heart hammers hard as I realize I've just made my first vital mistake. No one knows my Italian origins, not even my two best friends. Before I settled in Atlanta, the life I left was long gone, buried deep. "Yeah, on my mother's side. Half Italian," I lie.

"Oh, I see." She nods. "Is this her recipe?"

"Her mother's recipe. My grandma."

"Do they live here in Maine?" Eva asks.

I swallow hard, shaking my head. "No, my family is dead." At least, to me. I do not know what became of the family I abandoned so many years ago. A part of me misses my siblings and my parents, but I'm thankful I escaped the tyranny of the world I was born into most of the time.

"I'm so sorry, Oak," Eva says, placing a hand over mine. "I didn't mean to—"

"It's nothing," I say, waving my hand dismissively. "Eat."

Eva does as she's told, tucking into the food and making little satisfied sounds that make my cock hard and my heart skip a beat. We eat in amicable silence until we've eaten half the lasagne and all but one piece of garlic bread.

Eva leans back in the chair and places a hand on her stomach. "I've eaten way too much."

I raise a brow. "Does that mean you don't have room for dessert?"

Eva straightens and smiles. "I always have room for dessert."

I laugh, as it's the same line I use. "Good, because it is delicious." I stand and head into the kitchen to grab the pie I made earlier. "Pecan Pie."

"My favorite. Did you know it's really popular in Georgia?" Eva practically squeals.

I knew exactly that, hence the reason I made it for her. "Possibly," I say, smirking.

She tilts her head. "Were you trying to impress me, sir?" Her voice has turned a little flirty, making me forget all about the pie in my hands.

"Perhaps," I say, setting it down in the center of the table and cutting it into generous portions. I serve Eva a portion first before taking one for myself.

She tastes the pie, and her eyes flicker shut as she moans. "You are one hell of a cook."

I shake my head, laughing. "Not exactly. I have more or less exhausted all my skills tonight."

Eva watches me intently. "Hard to believe." She smiles. "It's all so delicious."

I swallow hard, hating the fluttering sensation I feel in my gut when she smiles at me. It's as if my world turns upside down every single time. Ignoring her compliments about my food, I eat the rest of my pie in silence, knowing that I might say something I'll regret.

I know I fear what my feelings for Eva mean, and if I'm feeling like this from one dinner, two weeks together over Christmas will be even more difficult.

"What are you thinking?" Eva asks, watching me as she spoons her last piece of pie into her mouth.

I raise a brow. "That I can't wait to get you in my bed," I lie.

Her hazel eyes flash with a heat that makes my cock hard as I adjust myself beneath the table. "Is that right, sir?" She lets her spoon drop to the bowl and stands, walking over to my side of the table. Gently, she places her hands on my shoulders and works the knots in them. "I can't wait either," she murmurs.

I growl and grab her hand, yanking her onto my lap.

Eva gasps as I position her with her back to me, allowing her to feel the heavy press of my cock between us. "Oak," she moans, arching her back.

"Perhaps I'll fuck you right here, in this position," I murmur, letting my tongue dart out over the shell of her ear. "Perhaps I'll fuck you in every place in my cottage except the bed."

Eva shudders, her head falling back against my throat.

"Would you like that?"

Eva arches her back in response. "Very much, sir."

I pull the skirt of her dress up to find her buck naked beneath before quickly freeing my cock from the confines of my boxer briefs and pants.

Eva moans the moment the head of my cock teases against her entrance. "Fuck me, sir, please."

I position the head of my cock up with her dripping wet entrance before sliding her over my cock in one swift movement.

The sound that comes from Eva's beautiful lips is one of unadulterated pleasure from the moment I'm inside her. I grab her hips forcefully and move her up and down, impaling her over and over on my cock. My grip is harsh on her hips, and I know it will bruise her, but a sick part of me wants to leave my mark on her skin, brand her, so no other man will ever touch what is mine.

I push her forward, forcing her to lean over the table and arch her back, giving me a teasing view of her perfect little asshole as I stretch open her cheeks. "Such a beautiful ass," I groan, still lifting her up and down my cock. "I can't wait to fuck it," I growl.

Eva stiffens before moaning softly. "There's no way it would fit," she protests.

"I would make it fit," I groan, watching her pussy devour my cock over and over. "I love watching my cock disappear inside of you." I spank her ass cheeks, making her groan.

"Oak, I think I'm going to—"

I hold her still, not ready for her to come yet. "Too soon, baby girl. If I let you come already, you won't be able to handle the number of times I intend to fuck you tonight." I reach around and cup her breasts in my hands, gently playing with her nipples. "I'm going to fuck you all night long," I murmur into her ear, pulling her back flush against me. "Do you understand?"

Eva nods in response. "Yes, sir." She squirms in my lap, seeking friction on her clit.

I hold her still, moving my fingers to her clit and massaging the bundles of nerves.

"If you don't want me to come yet, you aren't helping," she warns.

"Unfortunately, I'm torn," I say, stroking my fingers over her clit. "I love feeling that cunt come all over my cock, and yet I know if I let you come right now, you will be so exhausted by the time I'm through with you."

Eva whines, arching her back and trying to move up and down my shaft.

I hold steady, keeping control of the situation.

"Let me come. I don't care how tired I am when you finish with me, please," Eva begs.

"I can't deny you anything, baby girl." I quicken the caress of my fingers over her clit. "Ride me until you explode," I order.

She groans and moves her hips, grinding herself down over my cock with frantic movements. I use my other free hand to play with her puckered nipples one by one, making her moan as she drives herself toward the edge, using me for her pleasure.

"Oh fuck, Oak, yes," she screams, so fucking loud I'm thankful that I don't have any neighbors nearby.

Eva's hot pussy gushes around my cock, soaking me in her juice. Her muscles flutter around the thick, throbbing erection buried inside of her, drawing me ever closer to the edge.

I pull her off my cock and grab her ass cheeks, positioning my glistening cock between them and using her firm buttocks to rub my cock up and down.

"What are you doing?"

I spank her ass, enjoying the way her skin tinges red under my assault. "If I can't fuck that tight little asshole right now, I'll rub up against it instead."

Eva moans, pushing her ass closer. "I want you inside of me again," she whines.

I reach around and grab her throat, squeezing softly. "Such a greedy girl," I purr, licking a path up the side of her neck. "You'll have me inside of you all fucking night."

Eva shudders as I lift her off my lap and carry her in my arms, setting her down on her back on my sofa.

"Spread those thighs for me and hold your hands over your head," I instruct.

She does as I say as I lower myself between her thighs, nudging her open wider with my knee.

"Tonight has barely even started," I say before sinking inside of her in one quick thrust.

By the time I'm through with her, it will be a miracle if she can walk straight.

24

EVA

I wake the next morning and jerk upright when I see the light streaming through the drapes. "Shit."

Oak sits up, rubbing his eyes. "What is it?"

"I slept over, and it's…" I glance at the clock on the nightstand, jumping out of bed. "It's eight-thirty." I grab my clothes strewn across the bedroom floor, quickly dressing. "Natalya, Camilla, and Adrianna are going to wonder where they fuck I've been."

Oak watches me, looking unbelievably calm as I get dressed. "You're adorable when you panic." He waves his hand dismissively. "Tell them you're sick. Text them now." Oak sits on the edge of the bed, running a hand through his messy hair. "I'll make us pancakes, and then you can ride my cock like a good girl." He shrugs. "After all, I have a free period this morning."

My stomach flutters at the mere mention of having

sex with him again. This can't carry on. In the end, someone will catch us out. "Well, I don't have a free period."

He smirks. "I'll confirm that I've signed you off for one-on-one class this morning." Oak sighs. "I think it would be safer we wait to get together again until the winter break." The look on his face is pained. "Not that I want it that way, but we're being a little too risky." He tilts his head. "Especially when we fucked in the classroom, but I need you one more time." He stands and walks toward me, yanking my skirt out of my hands and chucking it on the floor. "And then, for two weeks, we can fuck day and night."

I groan as his hands move to my bruised and abused hips, and he gently tugs me against his powerful body.

"Pancakes and then sex, or sex and then pancakes?" He asks.

I feel the hard, demanding press of his cock against my thigh, and I can't consider eating. "How about sex and then sex?"

Oak smirks and nods. "I like how you think, baby girl." His lips cover mine, and his tongue hungrily plunders my mouth, stoking that blazing inferno inside of me as he lowers me to the bed and covers my body with his.

I groan as he nudges my thighs open and then pushes inside, stretching my already abused flesh around his thick length. "Oh God, you're too big," I whine.

He kisses me deeply, and his tongue thrusts in and out of my mouth urgently, stoking a greedy ache between my thighs. It's mind-blowing how one minute he can feel too large, and the next, I'm aching to feel him stretch me more and fuck me harder.

Oak doesn't hold back this time, plowing into me brutishly and taking everything he wants from me without mercy.

I arch my back, drawing him deeper. "Fuck," I pant, struggling to think straight. It doesn't matter how many times he has me. I can't get enough of this man. Our bodies entwine in a frantic clash of skin as Oak drives me right toward the edge with no teasing.

"Fuck," I scream as my climax claims me and I explode all over his cock as my pussy gushes around him, wetting the sheets.

"I'll never tire of making you come," he growls, ramming his cock inside of me three more times. He growls against my skin on the third thrust, coating my insides with his seed. I shake beneath him. The intensity of my emotions in that moment overwhelms me.

Oak has become my entire world, and that scares me. We're impossible for one on other, yet it's as if we were made for each other. "Are you okay?" Oak asks, brushing a hair out of my face.

I nod in response. "Yes."

His brow pinches together, but he doesn't question me. He gets off of me and slumps onto the bed by my side, grabbing my hand and yanking me against his chest.

I remain in his embrace, enjoying it for longer than I should have. When I glance over at the clock, I almost jump out of my skin. "Shit. It's nine-thirty. I need to get to my next class in half an hour."

Oak pulls me against him, kissing me lazily. "Go on then. I suppose I need to get ready, too."

I stand and get dressed in record time, heading out of the bedroom before he's even put his boxer briefs on.

Oak chases after me, buck naked. "Where are you going so fast?"

I gawk at him. "To my dorm to get ready for class."

"Without kissing me goodbye?" He pouts.

I narrow my eyes. "It's probably a good idea we remain a suitable distance apart, especially when you're so naked."

He laughs and closes the gap between us. "Kiss me, Eva."

I swallow hard and move toward him, rising on my tiptoes and pressing my lips against his in a chaste, quick kiss.

As I try to move away, he grabs a fistful of my hair and yanks my mouth back to his. Oak kisses me like a man possessed, his tongue delving filthily into my mouth as if he were fucking me with it.

I moan, clenching my thighs together. "Is that not going to happen again for almost two weeks?"

He smirks and tilts his head to the side. "I'm afraid not." He lets go of my hair and nods to the door.

I reach for the door and open it a crack when Oak grabs my wrist and pulls me back. "Give me your number," he demands.

I raise a brow. "Why?"

He grabs my cell phone from my hand. "If we can't fuck, we can at least sext."

I laugh at that as he puts his number into my phone and rings it so that he has mine, too. "I've never sexted before." I flutter my eyelashes at him. "You'll have to teach me."

"Gladly," he murmurs, pressing his lips to mine. "Now go," he says, spanking my ass as I turn around to slip out of his cottage. I'm walking on air as I sneak down the cottage path toward the overbearing school building, hoping I don't get seen.

FIVE DAYS LATER, I'm getting ready for the winter formal. It's been so damn hard to keep my distance from Oak, only sharing stolen glances in class and not speaking to him. The sexting we do every night has kept my spirits up.

My stomach flips as I hear my phone go off and rush to check it.

Oak: You better be a good girl tonight. If I

see Dimitry even try to touch you inappropriately, he will lose his fucking hand.

I swallow hard and type my reply.

I'm always a good girl. I can't be held responsible for that boy's actions. Just know I have no interest in being inappropriately touched by anyone but you.

I throw my phone down, knowing that Dimitry is likely to make a pass at me tonight. He's been flirty since the day I met him. He wouldn't keep his hands off me at the bar on the night Oak stole me away and fucked me for the first time.

My phone dings again, and I grab it.

Good. Send me a photo of you in your dress.

I type my response.

What do I get in return?

He fires back a one-word reply.

Now.

I twirl around, checking out my evening gown in the mirror. Natalya let me borrow it, and it's utterly stunning. It's pale blue with off-the-shoulder sleeves and has intricate lace applique detailing on the skirt.

Unfortunately, I didn't have any dresses suitable for the winter formal, and my parents wouldn't even talk to me to agree to buy a dress. I arrived here just over five weeks ago and they haven't spoken to me once.

I snap a photo in the mirror, sending it to him before placing my phone down on the dresser.

It quickly buzzes, and I pick it up.

Beautiful.

And then, a picture comes through, and my heart stills in my chest. It's Oak in front of the mirror dressed in a tux with his huge cock jutting out proudly from his black slacks. I clench my thighs together and groan, knowing I don't have time to get myself off right now. Camilla will be here any minute.

Cruel. I don't have time to come, and now I'm hot and needy.

I can see the bubbles as Oak types back.

Good. Exactly how I like you.

A knock sounds at my door, and I turn off my phone and place it in my silver clutch before opening the door to Camilla.

"Looking good," she says, smiling. "Are you ready?"

"Yes, you look beautiful," I say, trying to be polite. Ever since Natalya told me about what her family specializes in, I haven't been able to view Camilla in the light. I know it's not her trafficking the women, but she's a part of the family. It's hard to believe she doesn't speak out against such barbaric practices.

"Thanks," she chirps before looping her arm with mine and dragging me out of my room. "Come on. We don't want to be last to the party."

"Where's Natalya and Adrianna?" I ask.

Camilla nods up ahead to Adrianna, who lingers awkwardly in the corridor. "Adrianna is waiting for us, but Natalya went on ahead to meet Elias." Her brow furrows. "Where are you meeting with Dimitry?"

"At the dance, he said he'd find me there."

Camilla nods. "Alek too."

"Does Adrianna not have a date?" I ask.

Camilla shrugs. "No, she didn't want one, and Adrianna can be the most stubborn girl I know."

Adrianna waves when she notices us coming. "Hey, guys. Eva, you are stunning."

I smile at her. "Thanks, I love your dress," I say, admiring her beautiful emerald green evening gown that compliments her tanned skin. "You would have looked lovely on Hernandez's arm," I say.

Adrianna punches me hard.

"Ouch, what was that for?"

"For being an asshole," she says, laughing. "Hernandez is the last person I'd go to the dance with." Adrianna takes my other arm. "Let's get down to the hall before we're the last there."

I nod and allow my two friends to steer me to the winter formal. I'm not excited about this party. There's a buzz in the air, giving the often cold and serious school a thrilling atmosphere.

"How late does this party normally go on until?" I ask.

Camilla gives me an odd look. "This one we normally sneak away by about ten." A wide smirk spreads onto her lips. "That's when the real fun starts in the old ruins. The after-party away from the watchful eyes of the teachers."

I swallow hard, knowing that I have no intention of sneaking off to that. All I want is for this party to be over and the winter break to be here, so I can stop avoiding the man that makes me burn for him. The man I long to kiss again. It's only been five days, but it may as well have been weeks.

The moment I walk in through the grand mahogany doors into the events hall at the center of the school, I sense him. His eyes instantly on me from the corner of the room, drawing my attention to him.

Oak stands with Professor Daniels and Professor Jameson, looking magnificent in his dark tuxedo, but all I can think about is how he looked with his cock jutting out of the zipper. I never believed he could look more handsome than he already does, but in that tux, he's devastating.

His eyes dip down the length of my dress, and when they move back to my face, they're burning with desire.

"Did you hear me?" Adrianna asks, making me jump.

"Sorry, what did you say?" I ask, my attention snapping back to my two friends.

"I said that Dimitry's over there." She points. "Someone said he's been looking for you."

I sigh heavily. "Am I'm going to regret agreeing to be his date?"

"Probably," Adrianna says, laughing. "Isn't that what the formal is all about?"

I groan. "I don't know. He's coming over here."

Dimitry walks over, a cocky smirk plastered on his face. "You look gorgeous," he says, taking my hand and kissing the back of it.

"Thank you." I glance at his tuxedo, which is an impeccable fit. "You look smart," I say, trying not to be too forward. I can feel Oak's eyes on my back, burning holes into me.

"How about a dance?" Dimitry asks.

I swallow hard, knowing that despite wanting to put it off, I can't all night. "Maybe a drink first?"

He nods. "Sure, what do you want? I'll get you a drink."

"I'll have a glass of white wine, please," I say.

Adrianna clears her throat. "Make that two."

He smiles, despite looking put out at becoming a server for the both of us. "Coming right up."

"He wants to get into your pants. Otherwise, he wouldn't fetch you drinks," Adrianna says, shaking her head. "It's best to tell him you aren't interested in anything more than friendship sooner rather than later."

"You're probably right." I swallow hard. "God, I miss going to an all-girls school. We don't have this shit to deal with."

Adrianna raises a brow. "True, but then it wouldn't be as fun, would it?"

Dimitry returns swiftly with two drinks for us. "Here you are, ladies."

I smile and take the drink. "Thank you." I sip it, wishing his eyes weren't fixed on me. I haven't dared look in Oak's direction since we entered, knowing he's more than likely watching Dimitry's every move.

Something tells me tonight is going to be painfully long. I can't wait until it's over. I can't wait until it's winter break, and I can spend two blissful weeks wrapped up in the arms of my gorgeous principal.

25

OAK

I clench my fists by my side, watching as Dimitry's hand tightens around Eva's hip, pulling her closer to him. They've been dancing for a fucking hour nonstop, and I'm almost ready to deck him in front of everyone.

Eva's trying to wind me up, as she hasn't looked at me once. I saw her try to get out of dancing about twenty minutes ago, but that rat Dimitry won't let her out of his clutches.

She's insane if she thought I'd be okay watching him all over her like this. I'm a fucking loose cannon, ready to explode at any moment.

Archer claps a hand on my shoulder. "You look tense, Oak. What's up?" He squeezes my shoulder. "You feel tense too. Perhaps I should introduce you to my masseuse."

I narrow my eyes at him and nod toward Eva and Dimitry. "That's what is up," I growl.

He smirks at me. "Jealous, aye?"

Arch knows how to wind me up like no one else. "Careful, I'm on the edge of doing something I'll regret, and you taunting me will not help."

Archer laughs. "Chill. It's not like he has his tongue down her throat." He raises a brow. "They are dancing, and it's a dance."

I snarl, which makes Archer take a step back.

"Shit, Oak," he says, shaking his head. "I think you are in way too deep, buddy."

I narrow my eyes and glare at my friend. "If that weasel so much as tries to kiss her, he'll be dead. Do you hear me?"

Arch runs a hand through his hair. "I think you might need a timeout. We can't have you losing your shit over a student."

Gavril appears at that moment, brow furrowed. "Who is losing their shit over a student?"

"Oak, he's in over his head with the Carmichael girl." Arch nudges Gav. "Jealous of her date."

Gav stands in front of me. "Look at me, Oak."

I do as he says, meeting my friend's gaze. Gavril won't take any of my envious nonsense, but I fear that I'm impossible to reason with right now. Eva is deep under my skin.

"You won't do anything to fuck this." He crosses his

arms over his chest. "The boy is her date and nothing more. Get a grip."

I nod in response. "Fuck, I'm in the shit, aren't I?"

"It seems like you are head over fucking heels for the girl you want to destroy," Arch says, not skirting around the issue. "I would call that in the shit, yeah."

I keep my mouth shut, knowing that they have no idea. If I tell them the truth about Eva, that despite kissing her once, I ended up fucking her three times since they would probably call an intervention. I can't keep my fucking mind off of her, and even though we are keeping a distance from one another physically, we sext every night, sending filthy messages and pictures to each other.

I feel like I'm a teenage kid all over again, even though we didn't have mobile phones when I was younger. I'll spend the winter break with Eva, and these two clowns won't get in the way.

Gav nods, agreeing. "Yeah, you need to forget Eva."

Forget Eva? As if it is that fucking simple.

There's no forgetting her. She's embedded in my soul. A part of me I can't erase, and the past five days of staying away from her have been torture. The rest students leave in six days, meaning I'll go insane by the time I get my hands on her.

"Are you okay, Oak?" Gav asks, staring at me with concern. "You look a little pale."

"I'm fine," I say, snappier than I intended. "I need a

drink." I march away from my friends and head toward the bar, which is stocked with alcohol.

After all, the least of these students' crimes is drinking alcohol underage. We learned a few years ago that trying to keep alcohol out of the formal dances for seniors was futile, as someone always spikes the punch anyway, so it's safer to allow them to drink whatever they want.

"Hey Michelle," I say, greeting my secretary, who drew the short straw of having to man the bar tonight again. "Can I get a scotch?"

She smiles at me. "Sure, coming right up."

I drum my fingers on the makeshift bar, focusing my mind on anything but the girl on the dancefloor with Dimitry Jakov.

"Here you go." She places the drink down. "Enjoying yourself?"

I raise a brow. "Not particularly. Chaperoning a load of drunk students isn't my idea of enjoyment." I point my finger at her. "Try not to give anyone too much. I don't want to be cleaning vomit off the floor again."

She laughs, holding her hands up. "Of course not. I learned my lesson."

When I turn around, my heart stutters in my chest to see Eva is no longer on the dancefloor with Dimitry. I come up blank after a quick sweep. There's no sign of Eva anywhere in the hall. My thoughts race along with my heart pounding at a thousand miles an hour as I return to Archer. "Did you see where they went?"

His brow furrows as he turns to me. "Who?"

"Eva and Dimitry," I growl.

Archer shrugs. "How the fuck should I know?" He grabs my wrist as I'm about to walk away. "Are you intending to ruin her family, or do you intend to fucking marry her? As at the moment, you're acting like her crazed lover."

I snarl at him in response, and he lets go, reading the warning signs. I have to find Eva, not argue with him.

Gavril is talking to a student. I don't want to ask if he saw where they went. He's always more of a drag than Archer, so I know there's no use asking for his help. The students are supposed to remain in the hall during the event, but none of these fucking idiots follow the rules.

As I'm halfway down the corridor toward the library, my phone buzzes, and I reach into my pocket to find a message from Eva.

Dimitry has taken me to an after-party, and I don't like it. Can you come rescue me?

An inferno blazes to life inside of me as I march into the hallway, glancing down the corridor in search of them. I type a question back.

Where is this party?

The bubbles show up, suggesting she's texting back. And then they disappear.

"Fuck," I growl, shaking my head.

Where would the after-party be?

I'm going to need backup to break up a fucking party. The ruins are the only place for an after-party. I ring Archer's number, knowing I don't have time to go back and drag him out.

"Oak, what's up?"

"There's an after-party on campus. I'm going to break it up and might need backup."

He tuts on the other end. "Don't bother. There's one every year."

"What?" I growl.

"Get Eva out and leave it." He cancels the call.

How did he know about this after-party?

I rush toward the ruins, which, as I suspected, are booming with loud music. My heart pounds hard and fast in my chest as I shorten the distance.

When I get there, my stomach dips.

There're hundreds of students, not just seniors, gathered in the clearing. Most of them are too drunk to notice me as I push through the crowd, searching for Eva.

I pull my cell phone out of my pocket.

I'm in the ruins. Where are you?

I see her read it, but she doesn't reply. If Dimitry is stopping her from answering her phone, he'll be lucky to survive this night.

"Principal Byrne," two drunk girls approach me,

fluttering their eyelashes. One of them puts her hand on my arm. "Are you here to party with us?"

I shake her off. "No, out of my way." I push past them and search the crowd for any of Eva's friends. There's no sign of Natalya, Adrianna, or Camilla at this fucking party.

I can feel my patience wearing thin until suddenly my phone dings.

Sorry. I didn't have time to reply. I am by the fountain. Come quickly.

I push through the crowd toward the fountain, and my stomach churns when I see about a hundred students, most of them making out or worse.

Dimitry Jakov bought her back here to take advantage of her. I feel my body shake as I search for Eva and the Jakov boy, irritated that I still can't see them.

And then I hear her.

"No, Dimitry. Please stop," she cries, her voice coming from the further corner. I rush toward her, adrenaline pulsing through my veins.

"I said stop," she shouts, and they come into view just in time for me to see him forcefully hiking the skirt of her beautiful blue dress right up to her hips and reaching for her panties against her wishes.

I see red, and before I know what I'm doing, I plant my first firmly between his eyes, knocking him out cold before he even fucking sees me.

Eva's eyes widen, and then relief sags her shoulders

as she pulls the hem of her skirt down and sinks onto a rock, tears flooding her eyes.

I stand motionless, staring at my pupil knocked out cold on the floor. The principal of the school should not go around knocking out students. And yet I can't find it in myself to regret it one bit. Dimitry was assaulting her against her wishes, and I did what any sane, red-blooded man would do to protect his woman.

I groan internally the moment that thought enters my head. Eva can't be my woman. She's a fucking student, for God's sake.

When did everything become so complicated?

26

EVA

My heart skips a beat as I stare down at Dimitry, who Oak knocked out with a fierce right hook.

Everyone is so drunk and consumed by whatever they're doing that they didn't notice the principal of the school swoop in and save me. His aqua eyes blaze with barely contained rage, which scares me.

I reach for him, but he takes a step back. "Not here." He runs a hand through his hair. "Leave this party and meet me in the classroom where we have leadership strategy." He turns around and marches right out of the party, ignoring that students are drinking and doing drugs in his presence.

Once Oak is out of sight, I rush in a different direction toward the main school building, leaving Dimitry knocked out on the floor. I swallow hard and glance at Dimitriy, who's still out cold. Hopefully, no one noticed

Principal Byrne rush in like my knight in shining armor.

My heart hammers so hard it makes me feel sick as I rush down a pathway and take a side door back into the school. A faint sound of music is still coming from the main hall, but most of the students are down at the ruins.

I walk toward the classroom where Oak and I had sex. My palms are sweaty, and my stomach twists with anxiety as I reach the door, noticing a dim light coming from beneath it.

Oak's already there. I consider knocking but decide against it.

Instead, I reach for the door and push it open, finding him standing in the center with his back to me. His powerful shoulders rise and fall as he takes jagged breaths.

"Oak," I say his name, and he turns.

There's such a dangerous mix of emotions in his eyes that I don't dare utter another word. Instead, I shut the door behind me and turn the lock.

He rushes for me, crashing into me and pulling me against him. "Do you know how scared I was, baby girl?" He asks, his nostrils flaring. "You were in the hands of a fucking Bratva heir, and I couldn't find you. If he had—"

I reach up and cup his face in my hands, making him look me in the eye. "Don't talk of ifs and buts. He didn't, and that's all that matters because you saved me."

"Only just," he mutters, grabbing one of my hands and placing it on his chest. "Can you feel how fast my heart is racing?"

I nod in response, feeling the gallop of his heart drum against my fingers.

"I don't know what I would have done if I hadn't got to you in time." There's pure anguish in his eyes. "You're everything to me, Eva."

My heart aches hearing him say that. "Oak, I'm sorry."

"You should've listened to me when I told you not to attend with him." He pulls me tighter against him, wrapping his fingers in my hair and yanking my head back. "Do you know how it killed me to watch you in his arms?" His jaw clenches. "I wanted to walk over and choke the life out of him."

My eyes widen. "You wouldn't—"

"I'd do anything for you," he growls before kissing me.

It feels like I melt the moment his lips are on me. My knees wobble as I clutch onto his muscular shoulders, trying to find an anchor.

Oak lifts me off the floor, forcing me to wrap my legs around him. He takes me over to my desk at the front of the class and perches me on the edge, standing between my thighs. "I'm going to fuck you here on your desk like I've wanted to since the first class you attended."

His eyes blaze with power and purpose. "Do you know what I did that day when we were alone in here, and you were finishing your essay?" Oak asks, planting soft kisses down my neck.

I shake my head. "No, sir."

"I pulled my cock out under my desk and jerked off while I watched you work," he breathes, making my nipples harden at the filthy mental picture he's painting. "I came all over the underside of my desk thinking about fucking you."

"Are you serious?" I ask, my thighs clenching around him at the mere idea that he was so desperate for me even then that he couldn't control himself.

"Deadly." He bites my earlobe, making me jerk at the sensation. "I believe you walked over as I'd climaxed and asked if I was alright. My cum was coating the underside of my desk, and you stood over me with a furrowed brow. I knew then I was royally fucked." He licks a path right down my neck. "I knew you would be mine." He fumbles with the zip of my dress and drags it down, pulling the fabric below my breast. "So perfect," he breathes before closing his lips around my puckered nipples one by one.

I moan, allowing him to devour my skin like a wild animal. "I knew the moment I set eyes on you that I'd never met a man as beautiful as you."

Oak laughs. "There are many words you could use

to describe me, but beautiful isn't one of them." He grabs hold of the fabric of my thong under my dress and tears it apart, making me gasp. "I'm corrupt, dark, and dangerous, Eva," he murmurs into my ear, the zip of his slacks echoing. "The kind of man your mother warns you not to go near."

"Fuck my mother," I growl, angrier than I intended, grabbing his dress shirt and tearing it apart at the buttons. "She's never given two shits about me." I search Oak's eyes, which are full of surprise at my outburst. "You may be dark, corrupt, and all of those things you say, but to me, you're beautiful." I notice the gold medallion I've seen every time around his neck, knowing I'd meant to ask him about it, but never had the courage.

Oak groans, adjusting his position between my thighs. The head of his cock rests at my soaking wet entrance.

All I can think about is how he raced to my aid in those ruins. My knight in shining armor, despite the danger it posed to him if he were caught.

"I can never get enough of you," Oak says before thrusting deep inside of me.

I claw my fingertips into his back, trying to anchor myself on the edge of the small wooden desk. It's hard to believe that this man wants me.

Oak growls ferociously as he increases the tempo. His huge, powerful hands gripping my hips in a way I know will leave bruises. Every time this man takes me, he leaves marks on my skin that linger as a reminder of him, etched into my skin for days.

"I wish we could remain like this forever," I breathe, as Oak's body rams into mine repeatedly. "I want your cock in me all day, every day."

He groans, pressing his forehead to mine. "So do I, baby girl." He digs his fingertips into my hips, spreading a biting pain through my body. "These past five days have been fucking torture, even with all those sexy photos you sent me." He captures my lips, kissing me with a passion that robs me of oxygen. "I've jerked myself off more times than a pubescent fucking teenager."

I moan, arching my back. "How many times?"

Oak bites my lip. "Three or four times a day." He shakes his head. "Although, five today after you sent me the picture of you in that dress."

I moan, overcome by how badly he wants me. It's hard to believe I have the power to make a man like Oak that horny.

"I thought three times a day was a lot."

He grazes his teeth down the column of my neck. "Is that how many times a day you made yourself come for me?"

"Yes, sir," I pant, as he holds himself inside of me. "I can't stop thinking about your cock."

Oak pulls out almost completely, and then, when I think he's about to leave, thrusts every inch all the way back inside.

He groans. "My good little girl has got such a dirty fucking mouth."

"Fuck," I cry, clawing at him as he takes me over my desk.

"I've pictured fucking you in this exact spot so many times." His lips move to my collarbone, and he bites down hard, making me whimper. "Half the time when I'm teaching, all I'm doing is thinking about this tight little cunt wrapped around my cock," he rumbles.

His filthy words only drive me closer to the edge. "Harder, sir, please," I beg, arching my back.

Oak snaps, growling in such a fierce way that it almost tips me over the edge. He grabs my hips and lifts me onto my feet, bending me over my desk front first. "You're so fucking perfect." Oak's large palm lands on my left ass check with a harsh crack of skin against skin, followed by another on my right.

I feel the wetness dripping down my thighs as my arousal heightens.

He thrusts every inch inside of me and holds still, embedded so deep it feels like he's trying to break me apart.

I shudder as he grabs each of my butt cheeks and parts them.

"I'll never tire of watching your greedy little body take every inch." His finger teases at that forbidden back hole like he did the first time when he took my virginity. "But I can't deny I've thought about watching it disappear in this tight little ass hundreds of times."

I tense as it's not the first time he's mentioned it, and the mere idea of fitting such a huge object into such a tight space makes me wince.

"Relax, baby girl. I won't shove my dick in your ass."

I relax at his assurance.

"Yet, at least."

I glance over my shoulder at him. "What do you mean?"

"When I take your asshole, you'll beg me for it." He grabs hold of the back of my neck and forces me down hard against the wood. "You'll be so fucking desperate for it by the time I get your ass ready that you'll sit on my cock willingly and ride me until I shoot every drop of my cum deep inside of you." He spanks my ass cheeks and moves his cock painfully slowly out of my pussy before slamming inside. "You'll ride it until you come with my cock lodged deep in that pretty little hole." He spits on my asshole and rubs his saliva around my hole before gently edging the tip of his finger into my tight sphincter. "I want to own you, Eva. Every hole is mine to claim."

"Oak," I moan his name as he pushes me toward bliss. Despite my reservations about anal, it's so fucking filthy it makes me wetter. "I'm so close." The sensation of his finger in such a sensitive place only draws me closer.

"Good," he groans, slamming into me with the same irritatingly slow pace. "I want to feel that pussy come while my finger is in your ass." He pushes it a little deeper and then fucks me with it. "Prove that you love the feeling of something fucking your tight virgin asshole."

His dirty words are all it takes to send me over the edge. I scream, which forces him to jerk me toward him suddenly with his free hand as he clasps it over my mouth, muffling the sound. My entire body shudders and shakes in his powerful grasp as he keeps his finger lodged in my ass and his cock slowly thrusting in and out of me as he fucks me right through my climax. My vision blurs as I let go, a gush of hot liquid dripping down my legs.

"Fuck, baby girl," Oak pants, thrusting. "You squirted on my cock."

I groan, unsure what that means.

He bites my shoulder as he comes undone, grunting as he coats my insides with his hot cum.

I collapse on my desk, and Oak does too, covering my back.

"That was fucking insane," I murmur.

He gets off of me, lifting me with him. Oak sinks to the floor and holds me in his lap, his semi-hard cock pressed against my ass. "I don't think I'll ever get enough of you," he breathes, kissing me softly. "I need to be inside of you twenty-four-seven, and that isn't enough."

I moan as I feel him harden beneath me. There's no way we're getting out of this classroom anytime soon.

27

OAK

My eyes flicker open, and I find Eva in my arms, sleeping peacefully. I can't help but smile the moment I see her, wishing we could wake together like this every day. A stupid fantasy because Eva and I can't be together.

Ever since I've got to know her, it's become clear that she is nothing like her parents, which means I can't consider using her the way I intended.

Revenge seems unimportant for the first time in a long time as I stare at Eva. My desire to ruin the people that ruined me, as well as murdered an innocent woman I cared for, was all I had at one point.

My phone buzzes, and I grab it off the nightstand, finding a multimedia message from an unknown number. When I open it, my stomach dips.

It's a photo of me and Eva, half-naked and tearing

at each other's clothes in the classroom last night. "Shit," I mutter.

Eva stirs in my arms but doesn't wake. I remove my arm from under her and slip out of bed, pacing quietly out of the bedroom. I don't want to worry her about this, as she would panic.

I type my response to the number.

What do you want?

My heart pounds as I wait, expecting a swift reply. When I don't get it, I slam the phone down on the kitchen table and slump into one of my kitchen chairs, holding my head in my hands.

Perhaps it is fate. The Carmichaels wanted to destroy my world. Now, I've set out to destroy them, but I may have embroiled myself in a scandal I can't recover from. Not to mention, my feelings for Eva are anything but fake.

It's been clear that I've been in love with my pupil for a while. She reminds me of the boy who chose differently, like she wants to. Years ago, the boy escaped his parents' clutches to forsake his birthright to reign over a corrupt criminal empire.

I fled Italy at eighteen years old, took on my new identity as Brett Oakley Archer, and built Archer data corp from the ground up. All for Eva's parents to tear it down in less than two days.

The cell phone buzzes, and I grab it.

Money. A lot. Or, this picture goes to press.

I know threats like this never go away. If I pay this jerk money, they will soon ask for more.

I dial Ainsley's number, knowing he has a tech whizz on speed dial for this kind of shit. It will be a student behind it, so hopefully, his contact can trace the number and give me his or her identity.

"Oak, what can I do for you?"

"That whizz kid who helps out. Any chance he can help with a personal matter?" I ask.

"I'm sure he could. What exactly do you need help with?"

I run a hand through my hair. "I need you to trace a number to the owner. Some kid is trying to blackmail me, and I want to find out who."

There's some rustling at the other end of the phone. "Give me the number, and I'll get him to trace it."

"Can't I text you the number? I suggest.

He tuts. "Very unwise. Anyone could have tabs on your messages. Now, give me the number?"

I pull up the number and tell him the digits.

"Perfect. I'll have an answer for you within twenty-four hours." He cancels the call, and I stand and turn around to find Eva scowling at me.

"Who is blackmailing you?" She asks.

I sigh and sink into the chair. "Before I tell you, I don't want you to panic." I give her a pointed look. "I'm sorting it out." And then I beckon for her to approach.

She does, and I grab her hand, pulling her into my lap.

"This multimedia message came through this morning. I don't know who sent it." I place the phone in her hand, and Eva gasps, attempting to wriggle free of my grasp.

I grip her harder. "Eva, I told you not to panic. I'm handling it."

Her eyes are wide as she stares at me like I'm crazy. "Oak, someone at this school has witnessed us fucking in a classroom on campus." She shakes her head. "The only normal reaction is to panic."

I kiss her lips tenderly. "I can find out who is behind it. They won't get away with it."

Eva tenses against me. "What would you do if you discovered who was behind it?"

"I'd get the fucker to delete the photos and confiscate all of their media until I've checked there's no more incriminating evidence."

"And what if they talk?" Eva asks.

I shrug. "It would be a stupid rumor, with no evidence to back it."

Eva doesn't look very convinced. She folds her arms over her chest. "Rumors have power." She shakes her head. "And it would be a rumor with truth to it." She sighs heavily. "My parents would be here in a heartbeat."

"If that happens, then I will handle it." Even though that was my original plan, I will have to deal with it if that happens. "Once we know who it is, perhaps I can find some dirt they don't want out."

Eva sighs heavily and rests her forehead on my shoulder. "Maybe me staying with you for winter break is a bad idea."

I growl softly and tighten my arms around her. "You are not getting out of that. There will be no one around to catch us," I murmur, pressing my lips to hers.

Eva's eyes move to the small window over the cottage kitchen sink. "What if the person is watching us?"

"This is the exact reason I should have stayed away from you until the winter break." My arms tighten around her. "But if I'd stayed a way, who knows what Dimitry would have done last night? I hate to think about it."

Eva shudders against me. "So do I."

"The guy I know reckons he'll have an answer for me in twenty-four hours." I release Eva from my arms. "I guess in the meantime, we should keep away from each other."

Eva's shoulders dip, but she nods in agreement. "Five more days, right?"

I nod and stand, closing the gap between us. "First, I'm going to make you pancakes." I press a kiss on her forehead. "And then we'll take a shower."

Eva shivers in my arms, eyes dilating. "I assume it won't just be washing we'll be doing in there?"

I kiss her pillowy lips softly, enjoying the feel of

them against my own. "Of course not." I claw myself away from her and grab the ingredients I need for pancakes. "But first, we need food. We have to refuel after last night."

Eva's cheeks go pink, obviously remembering how crazy we were last night. I took her on every surface in this cottage after fucking her three times in the classroom. I fucked her over her desk, a second time over mine and a third over Dimitry's as a fuck you to the bastard who tried to touch my woman.

I groan softly as that word resurfaces again. Eva isn't mine, yet just thinking that makes my whole body recoil in disagreement.

The pancakes are easy to make.

Eva watches me, looking exhausted, as if she could spend the rest of the day sleeping. We didn't get anywhere near enough sleep last night.

Once the pancakes are ready, I plate them up on two plates along with a good helping of blueberries and maple syrup, passing one plate to Eva.

"I am so hungry," she says, eagerly trucking in.

I smile. "You'll need your strength, as I'm going to make the most of our last few hours together."

That makes her smile as she continues to eat. Eva's phone buzzes and she picks it up. "Shit. Natalya is asking where I am."

"Tell her you went for a walk in the woods," I suggest.

She swallows hard. "I can't be too long, though.

She'll wonder why I'm walking alone in the cold." She types her response and sends it to Natalya. "I've finished my pancakes. Shall we get in the shower?"

I raise a brow. "I don't know whether to be offended or pleased." I stand and approach Eva, towering over her. "I'm glad you are eager to have me inside of you, but I'm pretty sure it's because you can't wait to get back before your friends wonder where you are."

"You should be both," she says, standing in front of me, pressing her firm breasts against my bare chest.

All that lies between our skin is my shirt from last night, loosely buttoned up to her breastbone. "Lead the way, sir," she says.

I groan and grab her hand, dragging her through the bedroom to the en-suite bathroom. "Strip," I order.

She slowly unbuttons the shirt, giving me such a dirty look I can feel my cock tenting my boxer briefs.

I don't take my eyes off of her as I step toward the shower and turn on the faucet. And then I drop my boxers to the floor.

I'll never tire of seeing the utter delight in Eva's eyes each time she sees me naked. "Come here," I say as she drops the shirt to the floor.

She walks over to me and stands obediently in front of me, gazing up at me with those bright hazel eyes. "What is your command, sir?"

I groan and grab a fistful of her hair, pushing her forcefully onto her knees. "Suck it, baby girl."

Her eyes dilate as she reaches for it with her hand, which I swat away. "Mouth only."

"Yes, sir," she says before opening her mouth and eagerly swallowing the entire length of my cock right down her throat.

"Fuck," I gasp, shocked at how good she has gotten since the first time when she told me I almost killed her by fucking her throat. "That's it, baby, take it all the way in."

She gags slightly but controls her breathing, softly bobbing her head so my cock rocks in and out of her throat. Hot pre-cum spills down her throat as she works on me like a fucking pro.

I lose control and tighten my first in her hair.

Eva looks at me with a naughty glint in her eye, as if egging me on to take control. And that's what I do. I move my hips back and forth as I plunge in and out of her tight throat, groaning as more precum spills from my cock.

The desire to spill my seed is hard to resist. I pull my cock out of Eva's mouth and yank her to her feet, grabbing her chin. "Open your mouth," I order.

She does, and I spit in it, which makes her moan.

And then I lick at her tongue. "You're such a dirty girl. My perfect little cocksucker," I murmur, sliding my tongue against hers in filthy caresses. "Now it's time for me to feel that pretty little pussy wrapped around my cock." I push her under the spray of the shower, and she places her hands on the wall to brace herself, arching her back.

Before I enter, I open the cabinet in my bathroom and grab a small buttplug out of it, along with a bottle of lube. I move under the water, grabbing her firm ass cheeks in my hands and parting them. The sight of her glistening and wet for me drives me wild, as does the beautiful ring of muscles I intend to one day plow my cock into. I need to stretch it and train it to take something bigger.

I position my cock between her cheeks and rub against her sensitive back hole, making her shake. I squirt the lube on her ass, making her tense. "What are you—"

I spank her ass cheek. "No questions."

Eva whimpers as I slide my finger into her asshole gently, feeling the muscles give way. After sliding my finger in and out a few times, I put lube onto the plug, positioning the tip at her entrance.

"Relax, it's only a small toy," I murmur, stroking her back with my hands as she remains bent over for me.

Eva does as I tell her, remaining relaxed as I gently apply pressure to the plug, easing it into her tight, virginal ass. She groans, wiggling a bit as it goes half the way inside of her. "It feels weird," she whines.

"Give it a chance," I murmur, reaching with my other hand to play with her swollen clit.

She moans as I work her into a frenzy before applying more pressure.

Suddenly, the plug disappears into her ass, and Eva gasps, straightening a little. "Oh," she says, adjusting to the sensation.

"How does it feel, baby girl?" I ask.

She arches her back. "It feels good," she says, glancing over her shoulder at me. "I think it would feel better if your cock was in my pussy, though."

I growl and grab her hips harshly, position the tip of my cock with her glistening wet entrance. "As you wish."

My hips thrust forward hard as I bury myself inside of her, groaning at the tight fit with the plug embedded in her ass. It's not exactly a large plug, but it's always tight inside of her.

"Oh fuck," Eva moans, head rolling back as I fuck her. "That feels so…" she trails off, seemingly unable to find the words as she claws at the glass panel in front of her.

I groan as I watch the steamy image of her in the mirror opposite the shower. Her blonde hair splayed over her face, and her eyes unfocused as I fuck her. I've never felt so utterly in awe of another human before. As I watch Eva, I find it hard to believe she's not a fucking angel who has fallen from heaven.

"Oh, Oak," she screams, her body spasming around mine with more force than I've ever felt. A gush of hot liquid squirts onto my dick, making my cock swell as my release comes, too. Every time Eva has anything in her ass, she squirts, and it's the sexiest thing I've ever fucking seen.

"That's it, baby, squirt on my cock," I growl as I release my cum deep inside of her.

Eva shudders as I fuck her through it, ensuring every drop of my seed is deep inside of her. "What do you mean, squirt?" she asks, her voice so innocent it makes me crazy.

I force her to straighten and pull my cock out of her, making her whimper. She turns to face me.

"Every time you have something in your ass when you come, you squirt," I say, my brow furrowing. "It's a bit like when a man comes, you shoot a liquid out of your tight little pussy." I kiss her lips. "It's so fucking hot."

Eva moans into my mouth as we kiss as if we've all the time in the world.

I wish we did, as every time we part, it kills me. Five days until the students fuck off for winter break, and then I will have her all the damn time.

28

EVA

"Where have you been?" Natalya asks the moment I enter the cafeteria that evening.

Heat floods my cheeks as I sit in my usual spot. "Studying in the library. I have a lot of work to do."

Her brow furrows, but I'm thankful when she doesn't press me any further. "Fair enough."

Camilla clears her throat. "We were thinking of having a movie night in Adrianna's room since she has a TV. You in?"

I nod in reply. "Sounds good." I need to keep my mind off the fact that someone sitting in this cafeteria has images of Oak and me fucking last night.

"You alright?" Adrianna asks, nudging me.

"Yeah, why wouldn't I be?"

She shrugs. "You look a little vacant."

I spoon a fork full of macaroni and cheese into my

mouth and ignore her comment. I wish I could discuss the crazy shit that's happened with my friends, but I know I could never tell them about Oak.

Once I'm finished eating, Camilla heads to the counter to grab some snacks for the movie.

"What movie are we going to watch?" I ask.

Natalya shrugs. "We'll pick something on Netflix."

Adrianna nods. "A chick flick, of course."

I groan inwardly, as I wouldn't say I like those kinds of shallow movies, but I say nothing. My preferred genre is a psychological thriller or drama, something I have to think about.

Camilla returns with a large bag. "Let us get out of here."

I stand and follow my friends, only for Jeanie Doyle to step into my path.

She glares at me, crossing her arms over her chest.

I try to side-step, but she matches my movements. "Get out of my way."

"Or what?" She asks, her eyes dipping to the leg they stabbed, fully healed now.

I move toward her and straighten, so I'm standing taller than her. "Or I'll make sure this time you're the one that gets stabbed." Not that I'd stab her, but she pales at the threat.

"I'd like to see you try," she says.

At this point, my friends realize Jeanie has stopped me, returning with furious looks on their faces.

Natalya speaks first. "Get out of her way, Jeanie."

She glances at the three girls now ganging up on her and then returns her attention to me. "Whatever. You aren't worth it, anyway." She steps out of the way, glaring at me.

"No, not worth the risk of being sent to Nitkin again, hey?" I ask, smirking as her face pales. I walk toward my friends, thankful that it didn't escalate further.

Camilla loops her arms with mine, smiling. "You tell her. She's a pathetic, jealous bully."

"That's what we should watch," Adrianna says, drawing our attention to her.

"What?" Nat asks.

"Mean girls," she says, looking pleased with herself.

The other two laugh, nodding in agreement. "Deal," Camilla says.

It sounds like a terrible idea, but I can't say that since I've never watched the movie. "Have you seen it before?"

Adrianna raises a brow. "Of course, who hasn't?"

I hold my hand up. "Me."

"No freaking way," Camilla says, dropping my arm and gawking at me.

"How have you not seen it?" Natalya asks.

"I've never been into chick flicks."

You'd think I'd just offended all of their families by the look on each of their faces.

"Challenge accepted," Camilla says, taking my arm again. "We'll convert you tonight, I guarantee it."

I laugh as we head into the dormitory wing and down the corridor to Adrianna's room. Her room is the largest of the four of us and decorated extravagantly with a huge sixty-inch television on the wall.

"Why is it that your room is so big?" I ask.

Adrianna looks a little sheepish, shrugging. "I guess because my parents paid more."

Natalya sighs. "Yeah, she's got the richest family out of all of us. After all, she's cartel."

I swallow hard at the word, wondering how vicious her family is. The cartel is renowned for being a step above the rest for violence.

Adrianna waves her hands in the air. "Enough about that. It's time to convert Eva into a chick flick lover."

"I don't think that will ever happen," I say as the girls flop down on Adrianna's huge couch. Curling my legs beneath me, I sit on the end and get comfy while Adrianna finds the movie on Netflix.

"Buckle up. You're in for one hell of a ride," Camilla says, winking at me.

I shake my head and get comfortable, smiling to myself. When my parents sent me here, I was sure I'd be friendless because I didn't belong in these girls' world. They know I don't have any interest in life in the mafia, but they accept me. It's more than I can say for most of the girls at my last school.

I've never felt I belonged anywhere, and the last place I expected to belong was at a school for criminal heirs. Perhaps the saying, *don't judge a book by its cover,* relates to this school.

I'M thankful that the next five days pass by without incident, even though Oak's contact hasn't been able to unmask the mystery blackmailer. He apparently will need longer to find the culprit since they used a burner phone. It was silly to think they didn't know what they were doing. This school is full of criminals.

We've kept our distance from each other, even if it felt impossible at times. As I stand in the school's main hall, waiting to see off my three friends for the winter break, my heart is pounding frantically. Oak and I will be alone here in his cottage for two weeks within hours.

Natalya appears and rushes over to me. "I am going to miss you," she says, hugging me tightly.

I laugh, shaking my head. "It is only two weeks."

"Still, we must text every day," she says, squeezing my hand. "I can't believe you are staying here on your own for Christmas."

I shrug. "I've got a lot of studying to catch up on for the SATs next year."

"Boring." She rolls her eyes. "If you get bored, grab a cab down to Boston and call me."

"I won't get bored," I say, knowing that with more certainty than she could understand. I can't think of anything better than spending two weeks with Oak alone in his cottage.

Camilla appears through the doorway and approaches us. "Thank God I didn't miss you, Nat. I thought you'd already be gone." She gives me a sad look. "Are you sure you'll be okay?"

I nod. "Certain."

Adrianna approaches from behind, startling all of us. "She's as sure as the ten other times you asked her."

I laugh at that. "Indeed. You all ready?"

Adrianna nods. "Yeah, my driver's waiting outside to take me to the airport. I envy you two being able to drive home."

Adrianna lives over the border in Mexico, so she has to fly home. She gives me a hug and then the other two. "See you all in two weeks." She turns and leaves, dragging two enormous suitcases behind her.

There is no way I thought I'd find three wonderful friends in this place, even if they're nothing like me. I've had to push the fact that they belong to powerful criminal families out of my mind. Perhaps that's why we get on so well because we're all very different.

Camilla sighs. "My driver is here too. I best be going." She smiles at Natalya and me. "See you two bitches in two weeks." She grabs a large holdall and drags a suitcase behind her as she heads out of the hall.

"Is your driver here yet?" I ask Natalya.

She shakes her head. "He texted and said he was running a bit behind schedule."

My stomach churns as I notice Elias approaching us, eyes fixed on Natalya. "Here comes trouble," I warn.

Natalya glances behind her and groans, her shoulders tensing.

"So I guess I should wish you two a lovely winter break." He places his hand on Natalya's back, drawing her close to him. "I hear Boston is lovely at this time of year." He leans down to whisper something in her ear.

I clench my fists when I see her tense, knowing he's just threatened her. After Elias' rather brutal warning in the corridor, I've tried to stay out of it, but I hate seeing him torment her.

"Fuck off, Elias," I say, glaring at him.

He smirks and stands straighter, squaring up to me. "Did you forget my warning, Carmichael?"

I narrow my eyes at him. "You told me to stay out of the way of you and Natalya. It doesn't mean I can't tell you to fuck off when you are in my way." I lift my chin high, despite knowing this psychopath could squeeze the life out of me with his bare hands if he decided to.

He chuckles and shakes his head. "I like you, Carmichael." With that, he walks past me and heads out of the hallway.

Natalya's shoulders relax, and she sighs in relief.

"What did that asshole say to you?" I ask.

Natalya shakes her head. "Nothing. It doesn't

matter." She folds her arms over her chest and slumps down on a chair. "I hate him so much."

I sit down next to her. "You should stand up to him." I meet her gaze. "Why are you letting him push you around?"

"It's complicated," Natalya says, glancing down at the floor. "I don't want to talk about it."

It seems Camilla and Adrianna are right. Every time the subject of Elias comes up, she closes off. I nod in response, and we fall into silence together, waiting for Natalya's driver to arrive. The hall empties as students leave, mainly with drivers, although I've seen a few parents come to collect their kids. Someone in this school is blackmailing Oak over our relationship, and the fact I'm staying here at the Academy for the winter break will only compound the issue.

Oak assures me he can fix it, but I'm not certain. It seems a little foolish that I'm staying here. Perhaps I should have accepted Natalya's invitation to spend Christmas in Boston. It's too late now, though.

Natalya's phone dings, and she stands. "He's here. See me out?" She asks.

I smile and nod. "Of course, I should expect you need help with your bags." Out of the three girls, she has the most luggage for a two-week break. "I've never seen someone pack so much for two weeks."

She shrugs. "I don't know what events I'll be attending while I'm home, so I had to pack for all possibilities."

I laugh, shouldering a backpack and grabbing the handle of one of her heavy suitcases, leaving her to grab the other two. "Lead the way."

I follow Natalya out to her car as the last few students get into cars. The driver swiftly takes the bags from us and places them in the trunk.

Natalya turns to me. "I mean it. If you get bored, you call me and come down to Boston."

I nod. "I promise," I say, despite knowing it's never going to happen.

"Good, now one more hug." She wraps her arms around me and squeezes the life out of me before turning and slipping into the back of the black town car. I stand and wave her off, feeling a prickle of excitement race down my spine at the thought of heading over to Oak's cottage later.

We both agree it's safer to wait until night to ensure all the students are gone. I turn to go back into the building to find Dimitry standing in my way. His nose still looks a mess after Oak practically broke it.

"Dimitry, what are you—"

"I hear you're staying here for the break. Is that true?" He asks, raising a brow.

I nod in response. "Yeah, my parents don't want me home."

He moves close to me, smirking. "Why don't you come home with me?"

I shudder at the thought, remembering the way he

touched me without my permission at the party in the ruins. "Over my dead body."

His eyes flash, but he smirks at me. "You can deny it all you want, but I've seen the way you look at me." His voice lowers, and he steps close. "I know deep down you're a dirty little whore."

I straighten and slap him across the face, which stuns him.

A car pulls up behind us, and the driver gets out. "Are these your bags, Dimitry?"

Dimitry looks irritated at the interruption, his fists clenched by his side as if we were going to hit me.

I step away from him. "Have a great break, asshole," I say, walking back into school.

He mutters something in response, but I don't care what. It's winter break, and I'm going to spend two blissful weeks with Oak, and not even Dimitry Jakov can bring me down.

29

OAK

*E*va sits in my living room, her legs curled under her as she reads a book. It's Christmas Eve, and I'm surprised to say that her parents haven't once inquired where she is. She's received no text or phone call from them.

My instincts were right from the start. Eva is as much a victim of her parents' cruelty as I was, which is why I can only hope she will understand when I tell her the truth, but that can wait until after Christmas.

I swallow hard, realizing that I've never felt so at ease with another person before. With Eva, every interaction is so natural, so effortless.

She notices me and places a bookmark in the book she was reading, setting it down on the coffee table and looking at me. "Any news?"

I swallow hard, knowing that the mystery of the

blackmailer is eating away at her. Unfortunately, whoever sent the message isn't an idiot. They used a burner phone, and Ainsley's contact is still trying to track down the owner. He assures me it's possible but that it'll take a couple of weeks. "Not yet. It's Christmas, and I don't expect to hear from him until the New Year."

Eva sighs. "How about from the person blackmailing you?"

I shake my head. "No, I made an initial payment. I'm sure they will remain quiet until the start of next semester."

Eva relaxes slightly but shakes her head. "This is all my fault. If I'd listened to you and refused Dimitry, maybe—"

"This isn't your fault." I sit down next to her on the sofa, wrapping an arm around her shoulders. "It's the asshole who took pictures of us who is at fault."

She rests her head against my chest, wrapping her arms around my neck and squeezing. "I'm so glad I'm here with you for the winter break."

I smile as I've been thinking the same thing. "What do you want to do tonight?" I ask.

She sits up straighter and searches my eyes. "I don't know. What do you normally do on Christmas Eve?"

"Honestly, nothing," I say, shrugging. "Never been big on Christmas."

Her brow furrows. "What happened to your family?"

I swallow hard, knowing that I can't answer that. Nothing happened to my family, and when I told her they were dead, it was a lie. As far as I'm aware, they're all happily living their lives across the Atlantic in Naples, maiming, killing, and growing an empire from blood and heartache.

I worked hard to rid myself of my Italian accent and blend into American society as well as I could. "I don't wish to dwell on that right now." I smile at her and squeeze her thigh. "How about I cook us a pizza, and we can watch a movie?"

Eva tilts her head to the side. "You're going to make pizza from scratch?"

I smile. "I got some dough I'd made out of the freezer earlier. So yeah."

"Another one of your mother's recipes?" She asks.

I nod and silently stand, walking toward the kitchen. It was my grandmother's recipe on my father's side, as he was originally from Naples, the home of the best pizza in the world.

Despite erasing practically every link I have with my homeland, the food is something I still enjoy. I haven't uttered a word of Italian in fifteen years, yet sometimes I still have phrases rattling around in my mind.

"Did your mother teach you Italian?" Eva asks, surprising me as I hadn't realized she had followed me to the kitchen.

I turn around and lean against the counter. "Yes, I'm fluent."

Eva's brows hitch up. "Really, say something."

I swallow hard as I realize I'm letting this girl know parts of me I've kept hidden for a long time. "Da quando ti conosco la mia vita è un paradiso. Dammi un bacio."

Eva walks toward me and sets her hand on my chest. "What does it mean?"

I lean close to her ear and whisper, "Since I met you, my life is a paradise. Kiss me."

Eva's chest heaves as she pulls back to look into my eyes. "I like you speaking Italian." She rises on her tiptoes and presses her lips to mine, pulling me down to meet her.

The kiss quickly deepens as I lift her onto the kitchen island, parting her thighs. My cock is hard and throbbing between us as I lift the hem of her skirt. "I don't think I can stop myself from devouring you." I kiss her lips. "But the pizza won't make itself."

Eva groans, pulling me closer as I thrust my tongue into her mouth like a sex-starved, ravenous monster. It doesn't matter how many times I take Eva; the desire, the need, only heightens the next time around. She makes me insatiable, and that's a dangerous feeling.

I force myself to stop kissing her and set her back down on her feet. "Go back into the living room and read. I need to focus on dinner." I smile at the pouty look of disappointment on her face. "We have plenty of time to fool around afterward." I kiss her lips softly, brushing my nose against hers. "Now do as I say."

She sighs heavily and turns around. "Yes, sir."

I groan, knowing she used that word just to wind me up. Instead of rising to the taunt, I turn my attention to the pizza dough on the counter. I already heated my oven to the highest temperature possible along with the pizza stone, so I get to work stretching the dough.

Once stretched, I layer it with toppings and place it on my pizza peel. I then transfer the pizza into the oven. While I wait for it to cook, I open a bottle of Catalanesca white wine from the region of Italy I grew up in, pouring two glasses.

I carry them into the living room and clear my throat. "Wine?" I ask.

She smiles and nods, sitting up straighter. "Yes, thank you."

I pass the glass into her hand and sit down next to her. "Pizza will be ready in a few minutes." I grab the remote for the TV and turn it on, switching straight to Netflix. "What kind of movie shall we watch?"

Eva shrugs. "Anything but a chick flick."

My brow furrows. "Why's that?"

She rolls her eyes. "Natalya, Camilla, and Adrianna attempted to convert me by forcing me to watch Mean girls." The look she gives me suggests she wasn't converted. "And it was torture. I'm not into those kinds of films."

"What films do you like?" I ask.

"Thrillers mainly." Eva tilts her head. "What about you?"

The timer on the oven dings at that moment. "Hold that thought, or we'll have burned pizza." I push off the sofa and return to the kitchen, quickly removing the pizza with the peel from the stone. I put it on a large pizza platter and cut it into ten slices. I grab two napkins and then head through with the pizza, placing it on the coffee table.

Eva's eyes widen. "Wow, that looks delicious."

"You haven't tasted it yet." I pass her a napkin. "Tuck in."

She grabs a slice and sits back on the sofa, holding it over the napkin.

I can't help but watch as she takes a slow bite, eyes shutting as she tastes it. "It tastes as good as it looks."

I laugh. "You are just being polite."

She shakes her head. "No, it's one of the best pizzas I've ever tasted."

"You should go to Naples, then. The pizza there is to die for."

Her brow raises. "You've been to Italy?"

I nod in reply but say nothing else. I was born there, but I can't tell her that. Not yet, perhaps never. It's too dangerous for anyone to know my true identity.

Eva sighs. "I'd love to go there. Maybe we can go together sometime?" she suggests.

I swallow hard, knowing that I shouldn't return to my homeland. Fifteen years may have passed since I left, and the likelihood is no one would recognize me, but it would be risky. "Perhaps," I murmur mindlessly.

Eva looks a little disappointed by my half-hearted reply.

"So, what movie shall we watch?" I ask, changing the subject.

Eva shrugs. "You never answered what movies you like to watch."

I smile at that. "No, I didn't." I give her a pointed look. "I love chick flicks."

Her brow furrows, and she glares at me. "Are you messing with me?"

I laugh. "Yes, I fucking hate them."

She sighs in relief, sagging back on the sofa. "Thank God. I've had enough of them with my friends."

"I like thriller and action movies," I reply.

"Let's pick a thriller, then. Have you seen Gone Girl?"

I shake my head. "No, is it good?"

"Amazing." She grabs the remote from me and finds it on Netflix. "Let's watch it."

"Okay," I say, grabbing another piece of pizza. "Don't forget the pizza, or it will go cold."

Eva smiles and grabs another piece, sitting back as the movie starts.

I can't help but watch her as she eats. She's exquisite. Somehow, she makes everything that she does so elegant.

"What are you looking at?" she asks.

I smirk. "You."

She shoves me. "You're supposed to be watching the movie," she scolds.

I laugh. "Sorry, I just find you infinitely more interesting."

She glares at me. "Pack it in. You need to concentrate, or you won't know what is going on."

I hold my hands up in mock surrender. "Alright, don't get your panties in a twist."

She narrows her eyes at me. "You know I'm not wearing any."

I grab her thigh and drag her toward me. "Is that right? Shall I check—"

"Oak," she growls, pushing me from her. "Are we watching the movie or not?"

I sigh heavily and let go of her. "Yes, sorry."

Eva grabs another slice of pizza and passes me the last one.

I pull her against my side, getting comfortable with her in my arms. No matter how hard I try to focus on this movie she loves so much, it's almost impossible with her in the room. I want her every second she's near.

Gently, I rub my fingers in circles over her thigh, enjoying the way her skin feels beneath my calloused fingers. She fidgets a little, getting restless the more I touch her. After about twenty minutes, she sighs in defeat. "You aren't watching it, are you?"

I press my lips against her neck and breathe deeply. "It's so hard when you are anywhere near me to focus on anything."

She sighs and grabs the remote, switching off the movie. "Any dessert?"

I tilt my head. "I have Ben and Jerry's ice cream in the freezer."

"What kind?" She gives me a stern look. "Your answer might change my opinion of you."

"It's salted caramel core." I laugh. "Do I pass your test?"

Her face lights up. "Yes, because that is my favorite." She jumps up and rushes out toward the kitchen.

I stand and follow her, leaning on the doorframe into the kitchen and watching as she rifles through my freezer. Her nightgown rides up her legs, giving me a teasing view of my favorite part of her body. "What do you think you're doing?" I ask.

She glances over her shoulder and smirks. "Finding the ice cream."

"Did I give you permission?" I ask, feeling a need to discipline rise to the surface. Ever since she's got here, I've tried to keep a handle on my darker urges, but the desire to inflict pain on her is overwhelming.

Eva pouts at me. "Am I not allowed to go in the freezer?"

"You didn't ask before looking." I crack my neck. "I'd say you need punishing for that."

She finds the pot of ice cream and stands, walking toward me. "I thought you had finished punishing me." There's a hint of excitement in her eyes.

I clench my jaw. "Do you like being punished, baby girl?"

Eva's throat bobs, and she looks a little torn. "Would it be weird if I said yes?"

I shake my head and pull her toward me, inhaling her floral scent. "No, it's not unusual to take pleasure from pain." I grab her hips forcefully, digging my fingertips into her flesh. "Bend over the table for me," I murmur.

She shudders in anticipation, glancing at the tub in her hand. "What about the ice cream?"

I take it from her hand and set it on the table. "Let me worry about that."

Eva turns and bends over the table for me, hiking her nightgown up to her hips.

My cock thickens in my pants at the sight as I step toward her, grabbing her cheeks and parting them to get a good view of how wet she is between her thighs. I get the sense she was as needy as I was while watching the movie.

I bring my hand down in a forceful yet erotic slap, instantly tinging her skin pink with the impact.

Eva moans, arching her back in an invitation for more pain.

In the past, women only allowed me to inflict pain on them because I was rich and successful. Half of them never enjoyed it at all, and none of them craved it how Eva does.

I slap each cheek twice and then caress the stinging skin before starting again, repeatedly, until she's panting and moaning. "You're such a good girl, Eva," I say, reaching between her thighs to feel how wet she is. "So good." I grab the pot of ice cream and spoon some of it onto her red skin, making her jump in shock. And before she can question me, I lick it off of her, making her moan.

"Oh God, that feels amazing," she cries.

I place some of the ice cream between her ass cheeks, right on her asshole.

Eva's muscles strain, but she relaxes when I lick it all off, dipping my tongue inside her.

"Oak," she pants, clawing at the table.

I put more on her ass cheeks and ass hole and then lick it all off in one go, savoring the taste and the way my woman shudders and jolts. I walk around, standing in front of her. "Open your mouth," I order.

She does as I say.

I spoon some into her mouth, making her moan. She swallows it like a good girl. "You're making me so fucking horny," she murmurs.

I grab her chin between my finger and thumb. "Such a dirty mouth," I muse, leaning down to slide my tongue into her mouth, sliding it against her own in desperate strokes. "Lean back," I order.

She does as I say, and I put some ice cream on her hard nipples, making her groan.

I lick it off before it melts off her and onto the table.

"Fuck, I need you," she breathes. "Please, fuck me, sir."

"Do you think you've been punished enough?" I ask.

Eva nods, eyes hazy, as she watches me disappear behind her. "Yes, please, sir, please fuck me."

Her begging is fucking delicious as I return behind her, pull my throbbing cock from the confines of my pants and slam it between her thighs in one hard stroke.

Eva screams in surprise, since I gave her no warning. Her back arches out of instinct as I begin my violent assault on her greedy pussy. My nails dig hard into her hips as I claw her onto me with each thrust, fucking her so hard it feels like I might break her if I'm not careful.

All my sense is gone as I take her like a man possessed, like a beast let out of its cage. The more I try to suppress my dark, sadistic side with Eva, the harder it pushes back, forcing me to lose control.

Eva moans, screams, and whimpers as I take what I want unapologetically.

My mind repeats one word over and over like a tribal chant; Mine. That's what she is.

Mine to break. Mine to hurt. Mine to fuck.

Darkness clouds my mind, and in that moment of clarity, I realize that even if she hates me when I tell her the truth, I won't be able to let her go. I'll never let her go, even if she thinks that somehow this thing between us has an expiration date. The beast inside of me would never allow her to escape.

The thought makes me fuck her with more brutal strokes.

Eva's nails dig into the wooden table as she cries out my name in a plea. I can't tell if she's begging me to stop or begging me to send her over the edge. All I know is there is no stopping right now.

I spank her ass as I rut into her, my balls slapping against her inner thighs as I do. My voice sounds foreign to my ears as I speak. "I want you to come for me." I spank her again. "I want to feel your pussy grasp hold of my cock like it never wants me to fucking leave," I snarl.

Eva whimpers, and then I feel her muscles twitch around my cock, clamping down hard as if they're trying to break it in two. "Oh my God," she screams, thrashing around on the kitchen table as her orgasm breaks her apart.

I grab hold of her neck and pull her against me, flattening my chest against her back as I remain buried deep. Eva shudders as I slide my arm around her throat, blocking her airways as I fuck her through her climax. My release is powerful as it hits me, and I groan, sinking my teeth into her shoulder to leave marks.

Eva whimpers at the pain, but she doesn't pull away. She allows me to claim her like a fucking feral beast.

Both of us collapse on the table, panting for oxygen as our mutual pleasure wraps around us. I keep my hands tight around Eva's hips, my cock deep inside of her, wishing we could remain wrapped up in our bubble for the rest of our lives.

30

EVA

I grasp onto the gift I purchased in town for Oak, hating the way my stomach twists with nerves. I've only known him for a short time, so I'm not sure he'll like it. Last Saturday, before the winter formal, I went into town and found a quaint antique shop tucked down an alleyway. This little painting caught my eye immediately, and I knew I had to get it for him, but after seeing the amazing artwork he has on the walls of his home, I'm not sure it's up to standard.

Christmas music plays softly in the background as I walk into the living room, finding Oak standing by an already lit fireplace. The Christmas tree is alight with flickering candle effect lights, and a couple of gifts lay beneath it.

"Happy Christmas," I say.

He turns around, smiling at me. "Happy Christmas." He walks toward me and leans down to kiss my cheek. "I didn't want to wake you, as you looked so peaceful."

My stomach flutters as I hold out my gift, which cost me more than I could afford, but I wanted to get him something meaningful. "I got you a gift, but if you don't like it, I won't be offended."

Oak takes the package and grabs my hand, forcing me to sit next to him on the sofa. "I'm sure I'll love it."

I watch as he frees the painting from the wrapping paper to reveal a beautiful watercolor of a stream running through a pretty forest in summer framed in an ornate gilt frame.

"It is beautiful, Eva." The smile he gives me is the most stunning thing I've ever seen. "I love it." He stands and walks over to the far wall, which is rather bare. "How would it look here?" he asks, holding it against a bare nail on the wall.

"Perfect," I say, despite feeling it's a little out of place with the Van Gogh on the opposite wall. "Although it's not as rare as your other pieces." My brow furrows. "I don't recognize the artist."

He shakes his head. "It is perfect because you bought it for me."

My cheeks heat at his heated gaze as he hangs the painting on the nail, taking a step back to admire it. He looks contemplative when he faces me. "I was thinking maybe I could start a painting tomorrow." There's a devilish glint in his eyes. "I don't think it's so inappropriate anymore if I paint you nude."

I laugh. "As long as I can read, otherwise I might get bored sitting still."

"Deal," he says, walking toward the Christmas tree and grabbing a gift. "I got you something, too." He walks toward me and sits on the sofa, placing it in my hand.

I carefully free the paper to reveal an ancient-looking book. My heart skips a beat as I let my fingers trace over the beautifully bound cover, tracing the title. *Jane Eyre.* "Is this a first edition copy of Jane Eyre?" I ask.

"Yes, I remembered it was your favorite."

I swallow hard and shake my head. "This would have cost a fortune." I glance at the painting on the wall. "Now, my gift feels utterly pathetic."

Oak kneels in front of me and cups my face in his hands, staring into my eyes. "Don't be ridiculous. I love the painting." He rises and presses his forehead against mine. "I stumbled across this in the rare bookstore in town and decided I wanted to get it for you." He brushes his lips over mine softly. "It doesn't matter how much it cost me because you're worth everything I own."

I feel a tightness in my throat and fight the tears pooling in my eyes. Oak's gift is the most thoughtful gift anyone has ever purchased for me. Thinking about how much it would have cost him, though, makes me a little sick. The first edition copy of Jane Eyre has to be worth tens of thousands of dollars.

I return his kiss, wishing I wasn't falling deeper and deeper into this fantasy with him. When we break apart, I look into his beautiful eyes and feel a stray tear trickle down my cheek.

He wipes it away. "Why are you crying?"

I shake my head. "What are we doing, Oak?"

"What do you mean?"

"This fantasy we're living. It can't continue forever." More tears fall down my cheeks. "We can't carry on like this."

Oak kisses away my tears, making my chest ache more. "Let's enjoy today together and not think about anything else. Alright?" He stands. "It's Christmas Day, and I've got the turkey basted and ready to cook. We should go for a walk in the snow."

"Okay," I say, wiping the rest of my tears away. "I'll get dressed."

He smiles, but it doesn't quite reach his eyes as I disappear back into the bedroom to get ready. It's freezing outside, so I opt for a thick pair of pants and a shirt and jumper, followed by my coziest winter coat and a thick matching scarf, hat, and gloves.

Oak appears, leaning against the doorframe. He's already dressed in his winter gear. "Ready?"

"Yes," I say, smiling and trying to ignore the tugging in my gut. I know what we have right now has an expiration date. After the winter break, if we continue, we'll only get caught by someone, eventually. When I'm with Oak, I'm happier than I've ever been in my life, and yet there's always this doubt hanging over my head.

Oak takes my gloved hand in his and leads me out of the front door, keeping me close against his side. Even with all the layers, his heat penetrates through them and helps stave off the icy cold.

"Where shall we walk?" I ask.

Oak smiles. "I've got a place in mind I want to show you. It'll be magical at this time of year." He tugs me toward a snow-covered path into the forest, and we walk for about fifteen minutes through the snow-kissed landscape, admiring how white everything is. It's utterly beautiful. We get snow often in Atlanta, but it's not as thick or as blanketing as the snow here.

"We're almost there," Oak says, nodding up ahead.

"Almost where?" I ask.

He smiles and it is one of the most beautiful scenes I've ever seen. "You'll see."

"Wow," I gasp as we come to the edge of a stream with a waterfall that is entirely encased in ice. It's one of the most breathtaking things I've ever seen, frozen in time as it was flowing over the rocks.

Oak nods. "It's beautiful, isn't it?"

I nod and then look at him. "I thought you said you don't have time to venture into the woods. So, how did you find it?"

"I may have told a little white lie." There's a glint in his eyes. "To be honest, you drove me so crazy I just wanted you to stop talking."

I punch him in the arm. "That's not very nice."

He grabs my wrist and yanks me against him. "Not because I didn't want to hear you speak, but I was hard around you from the day we fucking met." His warm breath falls on my face as he closes the gap between us. "Everything you did made me want you more, Eva, especially after I'd had to help you get dressed in that fucking hospital."

I whimper at the strength and warmth of his body against me. "I wanted you so badly that day," I admit.

Oak's eyes move to my lips, and then he covers them with his own. His mouth is hard and demanding as his tongue probes at my lips, forcing them open.

I groan as I feel his cock hard between our bodies. It's crazy how our desire for each other seems impossible to quench. "We are supposed to be admiring the beautiful natural wonder," I murmur against his lips.

"I am," he breathes, pressing kisses to just below my ear.

"Oak," I moan his name, feeling the icy wind chill my skin as his warmth sinks into my flesh. "Is it possible to be cold and hot at the same time?"

He chuckles and removes his lips from my skin. "We probably shouldn't stay here too long."

I grab his hand as he turns to look at the frozen waterfall again. "We should come back here when it's thawed out," I say.

Oak nods. "Yeah, spring break, I guess." There's a sad edge to his tone, but I know after he cut me off earlier, not to mention the dilemma we're in. "Unless you're bored with me by then," he jests.

I shake my head. "I think it is the other way around."

The serious look on his face surprises me. "That could never happen, Eva." He cups my face in his gloved hand and rubs his nose against mine. "Never, do you understand?"

I swallow hard, wishing I wasn't falling for this man so fast. We're star-crossed, forbidden, yet my heart yearns for this to be permanent. "Let's walk back," I say, my throat aching as it feels like every day I fall deeper in love with him.

He squeezes my hand and nods, leading me back the way we came. A branch snaps up ahead, making both of us freeze as we search for the source of the noise. My heart skips a beat as I notice a large black flash of fur between two trees tugging gently on Oak's arm.

"What is it?" he asks.

I nod up ahead. "A black bear."

His brow furrows. "They don't normally venture this close to the school." He tries to push me behind him, but I stop him.

"It hasn't seen us," I whisper, shaking my head. "We're not in danger, as long as we don't startle it."

Oak tenses beside me as the bear walks away from us, but it's an utterly breathtaking sight to behold. I've wanted to see bears in the wild, and there one is, happily going about its own business in the forest.

"Let's go that way slowly," I whisper, nodding in the opposite direction to the bear.

Oak leads the way, and we slowly back toward the second path away from the bear, thankful when it disappears. "Shit, that was close," he says, shoulders slumping in relief.

I tilt my head. "Don't tell me you were scared," I say, nudging him.

He raises a brow. "Weren't you?"

"No, it had no reason to harm us unless we threatened it."

We walk the rest of the path in silence back to the cottage. I shudder when I see the smoke rising out of the chimney, longing for the warmth of the fire. "It's so cold," I say, hastening my steps toward the cottage.

He hastens them too, shoving the key into the door and opening it for me.

I shudder the moment the warm air hits me. "I'll tell you what I need right now."

"What's that?"

"Hot cocoa. Would you like some?" I walk toward the kitchen.

He nods in reply.

I get out the milk and heat it over the stove before adding the cocoa and sugar. Oak stares at me with a strange look.

"Could you find me two mugs?" I ask as I grab the pan off the stove.

Oak stands and grabs two mugs, setting them down on the counter. "Let me," he says, taking the pan out of my hand and tipping the contents into the two mugs.

He also turns on the oven and grabs the huge turkey off the counter, placing it into the center. "I might have got a too big turkey for two people." He shrugs. "They didn't have anything smaller."

I pass him his mug, which I've now added cream on top and chocolate sprinkles.

"Thank you," he says, sitting down on a stool and yanking me to perch on his lap. He nuzzles the back of my neck with his nose, inhaling deeply. "I think this is already the best Christmas I've had in years."

"Me too," I say. I feel the ache return deep in the center of my chest as I sip my hot chocolate and enjoy the warmth of his body against mine.

This feeling of being protected, but importantly, the sense of belonging he makes me feel, is what I've longed for my entire life. Oak gives me everything. I wish the rest of the world would fade away, leaving us alone in this fantasy forever.

"I'm stuffed," I say as I set down my knife and fork, leaning back in the chair.

Oak chuckles. "We're going to be eating a lot of turkey for the next week."

I scrunch up my nose. "I'm not sure I can stomach anymore for a year," I say, looking at the food we've just eaten.

He shakes his head and stands, clearing the dishes off the table to put them in the washer.

I help, grabbing the leftovers and taking them to the far counter. "Where do you keep your Tupperware?" I ask.

He signals to a drawer on my right, and I pull it out, fishing out and boxing up the leftovers to put in the fridge. Once we've cleared everything away, he looks at me with that all too familiar hungry expression.

"What are you thinking?" I ask.

He walks toward me, closing the gap between us. "I'm thinking that this day has been perfect, but there's one way to make it better."

The air escapes my lungs as he yanks me against his hard, muscled chest. "How?" I ask.

He leans down and whispers in my ear, "If you let me stretch your little ass out with my cock."

My thighs clench at the thought, forcing me to grasp onto his arms for support. "You would tear me apart," I breathe, confused why my nipples harden the moment I say that.

"I'd never hurt you." He runs his hands down the length of my back, sending need right to my core. "But if you're not ready, I understand."

"No, I am," I say, surprising myself. "I want you to."

Oak growls, grabbing a fistful of my hair and yanking my neck back. His lips fall on my exposed throat as he nips at my pulse, sending it spiking higher. "Go into the bedroom and strip for me," he murmurs, biting my collarbone enough to sting. "Wait on the bed on all fours."

I look into his eyes. "Yes, sir," I reply, turning to do as he says.

He spanks my ass as I do, sending a stinging need right to my core. "Such a good girl," he purrs behind me, making an odd sense of pride well up inside of me. Every time he praises me, it drives me crazy, and he knows it.

I head into the bedroom and quickly strip out of my pants and blouse, throwing my clothes onto a nearby chair. Once I'm entirely naked, I glance at the bed. An idea strikes me, but I don't know how much time I have. Quickly, I rush into the bathroom and grab the buttplug Oak used on me before and lube before returning to the bedroom.

I get in position, working the buttplug into my ass. Once done, I throw the lube on the nightstand and wait, feeling needier than ever with the buttplug in my ass, unsure when he'll walk through that door.

His soft footsteps echo through the cottage as he approaches, making my heart race. When he gets to the door, I hear a feral growl tear from his chest. "Did I tell you to put that buttplug in?" he asks, his voice deep and husky.

I glance over my shoulder. "No, sir, but I thought it might help as a start."

His eyes flash, and he walks toward me, grabbing my butt checks and spreading them wide.

I gasp as he drops to his knees and sucks my clit into his mouth, making my hips jolt. "Oak," I breathe his name.

He groans as he slides his tongue between my legs, tasting me as he does. "So fucking sweet."

I push myself harder toward him, which forces him to grab hold of me and hold me in place.

"No moving." His dominant tone makes me shake with desire.

I can't believe I'm about to let him fuck my ass. It's so dirty, so forbidden, and yet it makes me hornier than I could ever have imagined.

Oak grabs my hips and then pulls at the buttplug in my ass, gently yanking it out.

I groan at the sudden empty sensation.

Oak slides three fingers inside of me, filling the hole in seconds. The stretch stings as they're bigger than the buttplug, but I feel a deep ache ignite in my stomach as he thrusts them in and out, adding more lube as he does.

"This greedy little hole is practically sucking my fingers inside," he growls, squirting more lube onto it and adding a fourth finger.

"Fuck," I cry, wiggling my hips to get used to the sensation of being stretched so wide. Arousal and lube dripping down my inner thighs onto the bed, making a mess.

Oak works his four fingers in and out until I'm moaning and clawing at the bedsheets. And then he removes them, making me whimper. "I think you're ready, baby girl."

I swallow hard, understanding what he means. "Are you sure?"

He spanks my ass cheeks. "Don't question me."

"Sorry, sir," I reply.

I feel the cold, wet sensation as he pours more lube onto my stretched and abused hole, using his fingers to push it inside of me. And then I feel him position the head of his cock at my entrance, tensing instantly.

"Relax, Eva. If you tense, it will hurt."

I nod and focus on relaxing rather than the image of such a huge object being stuffed into such a tight space.

"You're already suitably stretched. You had my four fingers up to the knuckle inside of you."

I moan at the mental picture, arching my back as he increases the pressure. The head of his cock slips through the tight ring of muscles, and he stops, allowing me to get used to the sensation. After a few moments, he bears down again, pushing forward. I allow him inside, relaxing as best I can.

At first, it hurts like hell, as his cock is so hard it feels like he has shoved an iron rod inside of me. "Fuck," he breathes, his voice so husky my thighs tremble. "That feels so damn good." He moves forward another inch and groans. "Looks so damn good."

I glance at him over my shoulder, and he smirks. "You've taken every fucking inch."

It's hard to believe as I enjoy the unbelievably full sensation deep inside of me. "It feels… good," I say.

He growls and grabs my hips. "Tell me if it hurts too much," he grinds out behind closed teeth before pulling his cock back so slowly. "Fuck, I love watching your tight little hole cling to my cock like that, baby girl."

I moan as he thrusts back inside of my ass, opening my eyes to a whole new meaning of pleasure. "Fuck me," I beg, glancing at him over my shoulder.

Oak's jaw is tight, and a vein protrudes from his left temple as he claws onto the control he so desperately tries to wield. I don't want him to keep control. The dark, dirty side of him wants to take everything, own everything, and inflict pain. I want the beast to come out to play.

"Stop trying to hold back and give me everything," I taunt.

Oak's aqua eyes snap to mine and narrow. "Don't tempt me," I grind out.

I smile at him. "Fuck me so damn hard I can't sit for a week," I beg.

He roars and digs his nails hard into my already

bruised hips, pulling them so hard against him so that he sinks even deeper. Every thrust of his cock slides all the way as his balls slap against my throbbing clit. And then he releases the beast as his hips pull back all the way, only to slam into me with such force I can hardly breathe.

"Fuck, sir," I cry as he tightens his grasp, brutally abusing my ass with his cock. I love it more than I can explain. It's so rough and so fucking dirty. "Yes, just like that," I say, as I feel myself nearing the edge of no return. The sensations of anal sex are so different, so thrilling, that I know my orgasm is going to be mind-shattering.

"That's it," he grunts, fucking me even harder. "I want you to come while my cock is deep in your ass." He reaches down and grabs the back of my neck, pulling me up so my back is in line with his chest. And then he wraps his arm around my throat, partially cutting off my airways. "I want you to squirt all over this bed like a good girl."

A flush of hot liquid shoots from my pussy, soaking the bed beneath us as he continues to fuck me through it. I scream, but it's silent as I can't make a sound with his arm tight around my throat. All I see are stars behind my eyes as my climax hits me like a freight train, knocking me right off the tracks as I freefall into oblivion.

I tremble so violently that I wonder if there's something wrong with me. Oak groans, and I can tell he's about to come too. "Fuck, you're practically milking me cock," he growls, as he spills every drop of his cum deep in my ass.

He releases my throat, and I gasp for air, falling flat on my face on the bed. Oak pulls his cock out of me gently, but then I feel something else replace it.

"What is that?"

He smirks. "The buttplug. I want you to keep my cum inside of you all night," he breathes, collapsing next to me.

I shake my head. "That was fucking amazing."

His nostrils flare as he pulls me against his chest. "I don't know what I did to deserve you, Eva Carmichael." He presses a kiss to my forehead as I press my head tight against his chest, allowing his heartbeat to lull me to sleep.

31

OAK

*E*va isn't in bed when I wake, so I search for her. My heart pounds harder when I don't find her in the kitchen or the little library. The light in the glasshouse is on, where I keep my laptop and journal.

"Eva," I say her name as I walk in.

"What is this?" Eva asks, signaling to my laptop open on the photoshopped image of her kissing the janitor.

I must have left my laptop on without locking it. Either that or she guessed my password. The look in her eyes is one of pure anguish, and it makes my chest ache. "You were the one who sent the photograph to my parents." She shakes her head. "Y-you." Her voice breaks, and a stray tear escapes her eyes, trickling down her cheek. She nods at the open diary on the table too. "I know everything."

"Eva, listen." I move toward her, but she takes a step back.

"No," she barks, louder than I've ever heard her speak. "Don't come near me. Natalya warned me someone wanted me here." She clenches her fists by her side. "She said that someone doctored the images, so my parents sent me here. I should have listened to her."

I stop moving toward her, holding my hands up in surrender. "Please, Eva, just listen to me."

She shakes her head. "This entire time, you've lied to me." Her eyes narrow as she glares at me with a look of hatred. "You punished me for not telling you the truth about the janitor and all along…" Her voice cracks as more tears flow down her cheek. "You are sick," she spits, grabbing the diary off my desk and throwing it at me.

I catch it and place it down on the side table next to me. "I guess you didn't read from the beginning. The reason I'm doing this."

"I don't give a shit why you are doing it, Oak." She clenches her fists by her side. "You used me. You…" She turns away from me, rushing out of the glasshouse into

I follow her, knowing that this is the last thing I want. My intention to explain everything to her and test the water has backfired.

Eva is in the bedroom, packing her bag.

I lean against the bedroom door. "What are you doing?"

"Getting as far away from you as possible." The look in her eyes is one of hatred, fear, and utter anguish that cuts me to the core.

I move toward her and set my hands on her hips gently, forcing her to stop. "Please, Eva. Let me explain."

"Don't touch me," she growls, trying to escape.

I can't let her go, not this easily. She needs to calm down and listen. "You can leave as soon as you've let me explain."

Her body turns rigid beneath my fingers. "You don't deserve the chance to explain anything."

I let go of her, shutting the door to the bedroom and locking it. "I'm not letting you go until you listen to me."

Eva gawks at me, glancing between her half-packed bag and the locked door. "You're holding me captive?"

"No, I'm forcing you to hear me out." I take a step toward her, but she steps away.

"You don't need to be anywhere near me for me to hear you out." Eva crosses her arms over her chest and glares at me. "You sit over there." She points at a chair in the corner. "I'll sit right here." She points to the edge of the bed.

I sigh and do as she says, moving to sit in the chair far from her. All I want to do is hold her, melt her resolve, and tell her I never wanted to hurt her, not since I got to know her.

"What part of my journal did you read?" I ask.

Eva's jaw clenches. "The part about you getting me here under false pretenses."

I run a hand through my hair. "I have a sordid history with your parents."

Her fists clench at the mention of her parents. "What does that have to do with me?"

"Five years ago, your mother and father destroyed my multi-billion-dollar corporation all because I refused to pay them protection money and do work for their crooked enterprise in Atlanta." I lean forward and rest my elbows on my legs, steepling my fingers together. "They left me an ominous message two nights after I'd refused them, and I got to my data corporation building to find the entire place on fire." I clench my jaw, memories of that night flooding back. "They didn't only destroy my company that night." I meet Eva's gaze, feeling a little weird telling her about Jane. "They killed my recruitment officer in the fire. A woman who loved me, and I'd loved her, even though we'd never acted on our feelings. After all, I was the CEO." I swallow hard, trying to gauge Eva's reaction to my story.

She is just sitting there, blankly taking in each detail.

"That night, I died right along with my corporation. I changed my name and fled Atlanta, knowing that staying would be foolish." I give Eva a pointed glance. "You can't recover from being on the wrong side of your parents."

I swallow hard. "So, I got my insurance money from

the company being destroyed and bought the Syndicate Academy, with the view of getting my revenge through one of the Carmichael children." I clench my jaw, knowing she won't like my initial target was her brother. "Initially, I targeted your brother, but your father wanted him involved in the family business from a young age rather than studying."

"And what exactly did you intend to do with him?" She asks, her voice calm considering what I'm telling her.

"Embroil him in a scandal, force your parents to come rushing back to the Syndicate Academy and…" I rub my face, knowing that uttering the next two words might destroy everything with Eva. "Kill them."

Eva gasps, eyes widening. "You want to murder my parents?"

I stand, feeling fresh panic coil through me. "Eva, you must understand that they crushed my dreams and killed the only woman I had ever loved, all because I didn't want to work for them." I pace the floor of the room. "It only felt right that I take everything from them." I sigh heavily. "Until I met you."

"And you would have been able to murder them?" Eva asks as if trying to work out whether I'm capable of such violence.

"Eva, we have more in common than you'd ever know." I meet her gaze. "I told you of my Italian roots. My birth name was Luca Moretti, and I came from

Naples." My heart is pounding so hard and fast as I've told no one about my true origins, not even my two closest friends. After all, my family will never give up their search for me. "I was their first-born son, set to inherit and rule a criminal empire, but I never wanted that life." I pace the floor, not looking at Eva as I tell her my deepest, darkest secrets. "So I ran away to America when I was eighteen and took on a new identity, building Archer Data Corp from scratch by the time I was twenty-eight years old."

I look at Eva now and see the shock in her eyes as she listens. "They brought me up the same way your brother was, taught to be ruthless, but I was never cut out for a life of crime. My younger brother was far more suited to the job, and so I got out of the way, but when your parents killed Jane..." I shake my head. "It unearthed something dark inside of me. What you must understand is that I was raised to be a killer, Eva."

I notice her shudder. "So you were going to murder them?" Her brow furrows. "Have you killed before?"

I cast my mind back to the horror of my childhood. My father was a monster, perhaps worse than her parents. "My father forced me to kill from the age of thirteen."

"Thirteen?" Eva echoes, her face pale.

"Yes." I nod and meet her shocked gaze. "I had every intention of using you to get to your parents until I met you."

Eva sits a little straighter, her eyes giving nothing away. "What do you mean?"

"You were everything I didn't expect. Good and pure and innocent. The fucking opposite of your parents, and I knew I couldn't use you the way I'd intended."

"How did you intend to use me?" Eva asks, her voice cracking with emotion.

I move toward her, and this time she doesn't shy away. "I'd intended to embroil you into a scandal." I shrug. "I intended to throw you into the arms of Professor Daniels." I sit down next to her. "But I couldn't let him near you. I couldn't let anyone near you." I take her hand, and she stiffens, but she allows me to hold it. "You made me realize that there is more to life than revenge, and then I realized you hated your parents as well."

She pulls her hand away. "I hate them, but I'd never harm them in the way you want to."

It's amazing how a girl nurtured all her life by such evil is untouched by it. Unfortunately, I can't say the same about myself. I may have run from the darkness, but a part of it lives inside of me. "I know." I place a hand on her thigh and squeeze. "That's why I concocted a new plan. One that doesn't involve killing, but it will hurt your parents just as bad."

Her brow furrows. "How could it?"

I hold a finger up. "Wait here a moment." I head into my adjoining closet and search for the ring my grandmother gave me before escaping their clutches. I miss her the most among my family.

She understood why I didn't want to be a part of it. A few days before I made my escape, she practically told me to go and gave me her engagement ring as a gift to remember her. I reach for the box and open it, gazing down at the simple yet beautiful ring. A flawless one and a half-carat diamond sits at the center of a floral crown white gold band.

Eva is going to think I'm insane. After all, she's eighteen years old. She has her entire life ahead of her, and yet I want to lay claim to her. I want my ring on her finger and my name after hers before her life has started.

I shut the box, returning to the bedroom to find Eva gone.

"Fuck," I growl when I see the door open. I rush out of the room, not finding her in the kitchen or living room. My heart pounds as I open the door to the cottage, the icy air whipping around me and making me shiver as I rush into the snow without a coat on.

Instantly, the panic eases when I see her sitting on a bench near the archway into my cottage, kicking her booted foot through the thick snow. She's wrapped up in her thick winter coat, gazing longingly at the wintery, magical scenes surrounding her.

"Eva," I call her name.

Her gaze snaps to me, and the look of pure anguish in her eyes cuts me right to my core.

"I'm sorry." Eva's brow furrows as she gazes at the snow. "I needed some air."

I march toward her, feeling the blood rush harder through my veins at the prospect of proposing to this woman. I've only known her for two months, but I know without a doubt that I can't live without her. The question is whether she feels the same way I do.

I stop in front of her, kneeling at her eyes level. As I gaze at her, I know with surety that I love her, and I can't let her go without a fight. I believed I'd loved Jane, but it never felt like this. I kept my hands to myself with Jane and could resist the pull, but it was impossible to resist Eva.

Eva's eyes widen when I pull out the black velvet box. "What are you—"

"Let me speak," I say, flipping open the lid to reveal the ring. "Eva Carmichael, over the past two months, I have gotten to know you, and you are the kindest, most beautiful person I've ever known."

Her mouth gapes open, and she glances between me and the ring.

"I love you, and I'm not willing to let you go." I search her hazel eyes, trying to find the answer behind the unshed tears now forming in them. "Will you marry me?"

She shakes her head, and my heart sinks into my stomach. "Oak, my parents will murder you."

I tilt my head to the side. "No, they won't. I was expendable before, but I've got a lot of power as the principal of this school. Many powerful families owe me countless favors, and even your parents can't go after a man like me." I reach for her hand and squeeze. "This is your way out. A chance for you to go to college and get your qualifications to become a vet." I can feel my chest ache. "I'll protect you and keep you safe for the rest of our lives."

A tear slides down her cheek. "Oak."

"Yes, baby girl?"

"Are you serious? Won't it ruin your reputation as principal?"

I shake my head. "It will cause a bit of a stir, but nothing I can't handle. After all, if we're married, it's not like I pose a threat to any other girls attending." I don't even know if that's true, but I have to make it work.

Eva sobs then, the tears coming fast down her face.

"I didn't mean to upset you," I say, sitting next to her on the bench and pulling her against me. "I want you to know I love you, Eva." My chest aches as I've never loved another person before in my life. Not like this.

"I'm not upset, I'm so…" Eva pulls away from me and wipes her face. "So happy. Yes, I'll marry you." She cups my face in her hands. "I love you, too." Her lips crash into mine as she pours every ounce of feeling into the kiss, making my heart sing.

I don't know how lucky I got to find my soul mate. It seems fate has a way of screwing with you, but somehow, everything will work out better than I planned. Revenge is for people who have nothing, but my quest for revenge brought me everything and more.

Eva is my world, and I can't wait to spend the rest of my life with her.

32

EVA

I pace the floor of Oak's cottage, waiting for him to get off the phone with his contact.

Although our new arrangement means that the blackmailer has nothing, not once we announce that we're married. Oak intends for me to move in with him at the cottage for the rest of the year, as we will be husband and wife.

The priest has already been called to wed us before school starts again. If we are going to pull the wool over my parents' eyes, we have to act fast. They haven't even contacted me over the Christmas period, which isn't surprising. Half the time, they seem to forget I exist, even though they believe I'm important for the future of their clan.

Oak's betrayal hurt me more than I can explain. I'm still angry at him about what he did to me and his intention to use me as collateral in his quest for vengeance. It all made sense, though, once he explained everything. My parents tore apart his world, so I guess it's only natural to want to make them pay.

He appears from the study, a grave look on his face.

"What's wrong?" I ask.

"It's Dimitry."

My stomach dips as that means he must have followed us after Oak knocked him out. "So he was faking being knocked out?"

He nods. "It's the only explanation how he knew where we were." Oak runs a hand through his tussled hair. "He wants to sue me for assault."

"How do you know that?" I ask.

"My contact put tabs on his phone, and he's been talking to lawyers about his *case*."

I roll my eyes. "Dimitry doesn't have a case, as he was sexually assaulting me." I cross my arms over my chest. "I could take him to court."

Oak nods, but he still looks concerned. "True, but once we marry, who will believe you? It will appear like you are trying to cover for your husband."

I sigh. "Can't we find some dirt on Dimitry?"

"My man is on it, but he hasn't found anything yet." Oak bites his bottom lip.

"What is it?" I ask.

"Would getting married tomorrow be too soon?"

Too soon.

I don't think I can marry this man soon enough, no

matter how irritated I am that he kept the truth from me for so long. "No."

An easy smile spreads onto his lips. "Good, because Archer is back tomorrow from his break, and he's agreed to be my best man and our witness."

I raise a brow. "Professor Daniels?" I confirm.

"Yes, he's my closest friend." He pauses, chewing on the inside of his cheek. "He knows everything about my quest for revenge, as does Gavril. They know I kissed you, but I never told them it went any further until I rang Archer earlier and asked him to be my best man." He tilts his head. "Do you want Natalya to come?"

I shake my head. "No, I would prefer it just to be us."

"You are a rare gem, you know? Most girls wouldn't stand for anything but the biggest wedding possible."

"Well, I'm not most girls."

"No, you are not." He kisses the back of my hand, sending a shiver down my spine. "What time will we get married tomorrow?"

"The priest has agreed to a noon wedding in the school chapel."

I swallow hard, as the last time I was in that chapel, he forced me to scrub blood from the floor. "I'm still angry at you, though, for forcing all those punishments on me when you knew I was telling the truth." I narrow my eyes at him. "Why did you do it?"

Oak pushes his hand through his messy hair, sighing. "Honestly, it was a good excuse to put my hands on you. That's the only reason." He grabs my hand and squeezes. "I'm no saint, Eva. Darkness is a part of me, and I struggle with it every single day." His eyes search mine. "It's why I enjoy punishing you." He cracks his neck. "I enjoy inflicting pain on you, even though I want to protect you from everyone else."

I grab his hand and squeeze. "You're lucky I seem to enjoy pain, aren't you?" I ask, understanding that his punishment was a way to quench his desire for me.

Although I hated that he wouldn't listen to me when I told him the truth, deep down, I wanted him to punish me and touch me, as I felt closer to him that way.

I notice the medallion he wears around his neck hanging outside of his shirt, and I drag my fingers over the metal. "Is this a family heirloom?"

He glances at the medallion, a sad look in his eyes. "It belonged to my grandfather, the man who gave my grandmother that ring." He signals to the engagement ring on my finger. "He left it to me in his will, and it's the only possession other than the ring, which I kept with me after I escaped from Naples."

"It's beautiful." I look at it closer, noticing there are words engraved in it. "What does it say?"

"It's a family slogan, and it says blood binds us, blood forges us." He looks pained as he recites the words. "I broke that bond the moment I fled Italy, but I'd do it all over again if I had to."

I can sense that his emotions about his family are

about as messed up as mine. "Did you have any siblings?"

He nods. "Two siblings, a brother, and a sister. Benito and Adria."

"Do you miss them?"

His jaw clenches. "Of course, but I did what I had to when I left." He swallows hard. "I don't want to talk about my family anymore."

"Of course, why don't we watch that movie we tried to watch on Christmas Day?" I ask.

He chuckles. "Sure, I promise I'll pay attention this time."

I grab the remote, and I settle down, wrapped in his arms, and put it on, feeling lucky that in one day I'll be able to call this man my husband.

I TWIRL my fingers through my hair, gazing at my reflection in the mirror, struggling to believe I'm going to walk down the aisle today and marry the principal of my school.

Professor Daniels will attend the ceremony, which seems a little weird, but apparently, he's Oak's closest friend.

It's insane. I can't even imagine what Natalya, Camilla, and Adrianna will say when I tell them the news at the start of next semester.

A woman clears her throat behind me, forcing me to

turn. "Are you ready?" she asks. I think she's the florist as she's clutching a bouquet of white roses.

I nod in reply, and she enters the small changing room next to the school chapel. "These are for you."

I smile. "Thank you."

She nods, and then her brow furrows. "Where are your parents?"

I narrow my eyes at her. "They couldn't make it," I lie.

"I'm sorry to hear that." She turns to leave. "Good luck."

I don't reply, glancing at myself again in the mirror. Marriage isn't something I ever thought about, and now I'm getting married. Many girls dream of their wedding as some grand and magical event, but I can't think of anything worse. A small wedding with only the man I love and one witness in attendance sounds like heaven.

I turn around and exit the changing rooms, heading toward the half-open doors into the chapel.

The priest is waiting outside, and he smiles when he sees me. "Miss Carmichael, I assume?"

"Yes, father."

He signals for the music to play. "I shall go inside now. Wait one minute, and then you can enter." He nods his head toward the clock on the wall.

"Of course," I say in response, watching as he disappears into the chapel. My heart is pounding hard as I glance into the chapel, spotting Oak standing to one side with Professor Daniels next to him.

My palms feel sweaty as I watch the man I'm about to marry. There is no way I'd ever have believed it if someone told me I'd get married at eighteen years old. I glance at the clock, noticing it's been one minute since the priest stepped through those doors.

I slide through the doors, and the single violinist switches to the wedding march, drawing Oak's attention to the end of the aisle.

He smiles the moment he sees me, and any pre-wedding jitters disappear. The moment he looks at me, everything feels right. I quicken my footsteps, rushing to get to his side as the priest waits by the altar.

Once he's in reaching distance, he holds out his hand to me, and I take it, feeling all of my nerves disappear from the moment his skin is against mine.

"Dearly beloved, we are gathered here today to join this man, Oakley Byrne, and this woman, Eva Carmichael, in holy matrimony." He glances at the empty pews, brow furrowing. "If anyone has any objections to this union, speak now or forever hold your peace."

Of course, silence follows, and the priest clears his throat. "Now, Oakley, please say your vows, and Archer, please bring the rings forward."

Oak pulls a card out of his pocket, and my stomach twists. "Eva, since the first day I met you, I knew my life had changed as I knew it. You're the epitome of all that is good in this world, a girl so untouched by the darkness of this world I wondered if you were an angel."

My cheeks heat at his words.

"I fell in love with you the moment I saw you, and I vow to love, protect, and cherish you for the rest of my life. As long as I have breath in my lungs and a beat in my chest, I will be by your side until I die." He grabs the ring off Archer and slides it onto my ring finger.

A tear trickles down my cheek as the emotion in his voice overwhelms me.

"And, Eva. You may say your vows now."

I nod and speak the words I recited in my head. "Oak, I was never interested in romance. It all seemed a little trivial until I met you. The moment our eyes met, something inside of me shifted." I smile at him. "You made me feel safe for the first time in my life and gave somewhere to belong." I shake my head. "You listened to my dreams and understand how much they mean to me. I love you so much it hurts, and I know I will spend the rest of my life loving you." I slide his ring over his finger, struggling to believe that this isn't all one crazy dream.

The priest nods in satisfaction and then says. "I now pronounce you man and wife." He glances at Oak. "You may kiss the bride."

Oak grabs my waist and kisses me deeply, his tongue sliding through my lips.

I don't mind, as there aren't many people around. If it was a big wedding, I might have been embarrassed.

However, Professor Daniels quickly breaks us apart before we get too carried away. "Easy, you two." He claps Oak on the shoulder and gives him a wink. "Save it for the wedding night."

Oak glares at him, but nods. "You going to join us for a celebratory drink at the cottage?"

Archer nods. "Sure, just give me twenty minutes to change out of this fucking thing." He signals to the tux, which he looks rather handsome in. I'm so used to seeing him in gym gear since he teaches Physical Education and Combat Training.

"Okay, see you then," Oak steers me the opposite way toward the external exit of the chapel. "Let's get back to the cottage."

I smile at him, clasping his hand. "I don't think I've ever been so happy before."

"Neither have I."

We walk back to the cottage in comfortable silence, but something feels off as we approach the archway.

I know Oak feels it, too, as the smile on his face disappears. "Someone has broken in," he murmurs, eyes fixed on the busted lock on the front door.

My stomach swirls with unease as I clutch tighter to my husband, wondering who would have broken into Oak's home. And then I notice the car parked two hundred yards up the road. "My parents," I mutter, nodding to it.

It's their car. A black range rover with black wheels and a Georgian state registration plate.

"Shit," Oak breathes, muscles tensing. "How did they find out?"

"No idea." I shake my head. "They haven't even called me over the Christmas break."

He grabs my hand and squeezes. "Stay behind me, alright?"

I swallow hard, knowing that I don't want Oak to have to face my parents, not after everything they did to him. They are monsters and won't listen to reason. "We shouldn't go in there. It's too dangerous."

"Everything will be okay, I promise." He drops my hand. "Now, stay behind me."

I watch him as he walks toward the busted door of the cottage, his powerful shoulders full of tension. My heart is racing like galloping horses charging across a field as I stay close to him, lacing my fingers in the fabric of his dress shirt.

Oak leads the way into the cottage, but we're met by my father glaring at us hatefully as he aims his gun right at my husband's heart.

I swallow hard, knowing my father is an excellent shot. He never misses. Suddenly, I'm staring my worst nightmare right in the face, knowing that the appearance of my parents has ruined the blissful happiness of marrying my soul mate. The fantasy has been shattered by the two people who should support me no matter what.

33

OAK

I stare down the barrel of Jamie Carmichaels' gun, knowing I can't let him win this time, not when I have so much more to lose. Eva means more to me than anything I've ever possessed.

"Put the gun down, Jamie." I cross my arms over my chest and glare at him. "If you kill me, you might as well kiss goodbye to the clan for good."

Eva inches closer to my back, fisting my shirt.

"Hand over my daughter, and then I'll leave." He signals at Eva, who cowers behind me. "Eva, stop this at once and come here," he barks.

"I'm afraid you are too late, Jamie. Eva is already my lawfully wedded wife, and therefore she's no longer your concern as of about half an hour ago."

"I won't stand for it." Jamie snarls, cocking the gun. "Eva is our heir, and she will marry a suitable husband who can rule our empire."

Eva steps out from behind my back with her chin held high. "I'll never do that because Oak is my husband, and as I've told you since the day that Karl died, I have no intention of having anything to do with the clan." She glares at her father. "You just never listened to me." She tilts her head. "How did you find out?"

I was thinking the same thing, and there's only one possible explanation.

Dimitry.

"A picture," he says, nose wrinkling in disgust. "I always knew you were a dirty whore after seeing the photo of you and the janitor, but—"

"Watch your mouth," I growl, clenching my fists by my side. "You're talking about my wife."

Jamie glares at me as the door to the living room opens, and Angela Carmichael walks in. "Eva, get in the car at once," she calls, nodding toward the door we came through.

"I'll never go anywhere with you," she spits, glaring at them with as much hatred as I feel. "You sent me here, so it's your fault that I fell in love with Oak and married him."

"Married him?" Her mom splutters, eyes widening. "What are you..." she trails off when she sees Eva's white wedding gown and the ring on her finger. "You bastard." She glares at me. "Why the fuck would you do this?"

"I have my reasons," I say, keeping cool despite

Jamie holding a gun and pointing it right at me. "You ruined my life once. It seems only fair I return the favor."

Angela's nose wrinkles. "What are you talking about?"

I harden my glare, knowing that these two self-centered, arrogant pricks still don't know who I am. "Five years ago, I left my life behind and changed my name."

Jamie's eyes narrow as he regards me more carefully, trying to work out who I am.

"Brett Archer ring any bells?" I ask.

His eyes flash with fury. "You fucking bastard."

"You call me a bastard?" I growl, shocking myself at the viciousness in my voice. "You tore my world apart, and all I've done is marry your daughter. It doesn't come close to what you did to me." My attention moves to my wife. "I didn't marry her to spite you, anyway. Although I did doctor that image as Eva tried to tell you over and over, she never touched the janitor." I swallow hard, knowing that uttering the next words could backfire. "Eva is my world, and I will cherish and protect her if that means anything to you at all."

Eva steps closer to me, crossing her arms over her chest. "You're both dead to me. You might as well adopt some kid who wants to be a part of your plans."

Her mother gasps, looking scandalized by her daughter's words.

What did she expect?

She can barely be called a mother the way she treats Eva. It's a fucking disgrace.

I clear my throat. "If you shoot me, you will have to deal with a catastrophic fallout."

Jamie's eyes narrow. "If you don't give me back my daughter, I'll have no choice." He takes a step forward, making me tense. "You have a lot of power, Oak, but so do I."

Archer walks through the door at that moment, startling Jamie and Angela, as he points the gun at him instead of me.

"What the fuck is going on here?" He asks.

He holds his hands up when he notices Jamie aiming the gun at him.

His distraction couldn't have come at a better time as I lunge forward and snatch the gun right out of Jamie's hand. The impact forces him to the floor as I point the gun right in his face. "Don't fucking move," I growl.

A gun cocks behind me, and I freeze, glancing over my shoulder.

Angela is holding a tiny gun and pointing it at my back. "Put the gun down, Oak," she orders.

I shake my head. "We're at an impasse. I can shoot your husband in the face and not miss. The question is, will your shot kill me?"

Eva gasps. "No, Oak, don't stoop to their level."

I hate that she's right. My father may have forced me to murder at a young age, but I've done nothing like that since I left Italy. I back up to see her better. If I pull the trigger, then I'm no better than her parents.

"Angela, put down your gun, and I will put down this one." I signal to the gun.

"Mom, do as he says," Eva pushes, which only seems to enrage her mother.

"You worthless little brat." She slaps Eva across the face with her free hand, setting my blood on fire.

"Don't touch my wife," I growl, glaring at her. "Do you want me to shoot your husband?"

Eva backs away from her mother, hatred sparking in her eyes. "You're a pathetic excuse for a mother," she murmurs.

Angela glares at her. "You're the worst daughter I could have asked for." She points her finger at her. "I wish you had died in place of your brother."

Eva's face twists in anguish. She may hate her parents, but they can still hurt her, still twist the knife in her gut. Tears form in her eyes.

"Angela, I said put the gun down," I repeat, keeping my voice calm. "Let's talk about this like grown adults."

"Grown adults!" she shrieks, clearly hysterical. "You're thirty-two years old, and you just married an eighteen-year-old." Her eyes narrow. "You're a sick fucking pervert who needs to be stopped in his tracks."

"Shut up, mother," Eva snarls, stepping toward her. "Put the gun down and stop being a fucking bitch."

"How dare you speak to me like that?" She turns and aims the gun at Eva instead of me, making me see red. "I brought you into this fucking world, so I'll be damned if I can't take you out of it." Her finger hovers over the trigger, the entire gun shaking in her hand.

"Angela, don't be so foolish," Jamie says, genuine fear in his eyes.

I can spot a loose cannon from a mile away, and Angela has it in her to kill her daughter, I'm sure of it. Before she has a chance, I rush for her, drawing her attention back to me. "I'll die before you shoot my wife," I growl.

A gunshot echoes as she pulls the trigger, aiming it back at me. Pain tears through my left shoulder as I fall to the floor in agony.

Two rounds go off a moment later, but I don't know who shot them.

"Oak," Eva calls, rushing to my side.

I sit up. "I'm okay." I glance to see Angela is lying in a pool of her blood, a shot right through the center of her forehead. "Who shot your mom?"

"Archer," she says, nodding toward my best friend, who's holding his gun.

His eyes widen when he sees us staring at him, and he rushes over to help. "Oak, I'm sorry, I just—" He shakes. "I reacted on instinct."

My brow furrows. "What are you apologizing for?"

He glances at Angela's dead body. "I've never killed someone before."

"You have got an excellent shot, though," Eva says.

He nods. "I attend target practice."

"She shot me, Arch. I would expect nothing less from you, but maybe you should apologize to Eva. It was her mom you shot dead."

Arch's eyes widen. "Angela Carmichael?" he confirms, turning as white as a sheet.

"Don't apologize to me," Eva says. "I was ready to shoot her myself after she shot you." Tears still well in her eyes. "I'm pretty certain she would have shot me if you hadn't…" She squeezes my hand. "Are you sure you're okay?" Her eyes move to the gunshot wound again, leaning over me.

"Yes, I'm fine." I squeeze her hand back. "It's a flesh wound."

Eva glares at her father, who is crying over her body, but I doubt his tears are genuine.

Archer rips open my shirt and checks the wound, making me wince. "Is Elaine back from break yet?"

I shrug, regretting it the moment I do. "I don't know. Call her."

Archer digs his cell phone out of his pocket and rings her number. "Hey, Elaine. Are you back at the academy, by any chance?" He nods. "Perfect, well, Oak has had a bit of an accident. Can you meet us at his cottage?" There's a few moments of silence on his end. "Excellent, see you in a moment."

He meets my gaze. "She's on her way. Five minutes."

I grunt and move to glance at Eva's dad. "Get security to remove him from the premises."

Jamie jumps to his feet, fisting his hands by his side. "Have some respect. Your monkey murdered my wife."

Archer growls and squares up to him. "Who are you calling a monkey?"

"Dad, just leave," Eva says, glaring at him. "Take mom's body but just go."

He looks into her eyes, and I can see a hint of regret in them as he looks at her. "Fine, know that I wanted none of this, Eva. I wanted you to be successful, married to a man that could run our empire." He swallows hard. "And I don't share your mother's sentiments for what it's worth."

Eva's throat works as she swallows, unshed tears gleaming in her eyes. "I never wanted to be a part of your empire, and you know it. That's all that matters since it's my life."

He sighs and pulls out his cell phone, no doubt ringing his driver to come and help him move Eva's mother's body from my living room floor. One of his guys appears a moment later, eyes wide as he takes in the chaotic scene in front of him.

"Help me move her," Jamie orders.

He does as he says, getting her legs as Jamie gets her arms and then ungracefully carries her out of the cottage toward the car.

Nurse Jasper appears a few moments later, a little out of breath. "Oh dear, what happened here?"

"Oak's been shot in the shoulder," Archer says, shaking his head. "I don't think it's too serious."

Archer and Eva get out of her way so she can check my wound. Elaine pokes at it, moving my arm around painfully.

"You'll be fine," Nurse Jasper announces. "We'll get you to the infirmary for some stitches, but the bullet exited, so you'll just need some aspirin and a sling to rest it." She gives me a pointed look. "You're very lucky, though." Her brow furrows. "What are you doing here, Eva?"

I clear my throat. "Eva and I were married this afternoon."

Elaine's eyes widen, and she scoffs. "Excuse me?"

"Yes, we got married," Eva reiterates. "That's not important right now." She walks over and helps me to my feet, supporting me. "We need to get my husband patched up." She gives Elaine a pointed look.

Elaine looks a little disgusted. "Of course, follow me."

I clutch onto Eva for support, and Archer offers me his arm, too, as we make our way to the main school building.

This isn't how I pictured our wedding day ending, but all I can say is that I'm thankful that we're both alive and Jamie has conceded. The fact he left with his wife's body suggests he has no intention of fighting this.

Eva is finally free, and I can protect her from the world she wants no part in.

34

EVA

My heart pounds so hard I can hardly hear the students on the other side of the curtain.

Oak intends to announce our marriage to the entire school during the welcome back meeting in the hall today in exactly five minutes.

He told me I didn't have to be here, but it didn't feel right to leave him to tell everyone alone. Natalya, Camilla, and Adrianna all arrived back here yesterday at my request to break the news to them personally.

I rendered all three speechless at first, but once they finally started talking, I explained all the crazy, sordid things that happened over winter break. They were happy for me once they got over the shock.

Oak has told all the staff, who, other than Gavril and, of course, Archer, were very shocked. A few protested against it, saying it was immoral. However,

Oak argued the entire school construct was immoral, so he doesn't feel their argument stood up.

I'm prepared for the funny looks and the jokes at my expense once it becomes public knowledge, but I don't care. I am married to my soul mate and I have three great friends to support me.

Oak clears his throat into the microphone, and I know it's time.

Fuck.

This is crazy.

We expect a bit of backlash from the students' parents, too, once it becomes common knowledge, but Oak believes it won't be as bad as I'd expect.

"Welcome back to the Syndicate Academy. I hope you all had a good winter break."

There are a few shouts in the crowd, but Oak ignores them.

"I have a rather controversial announcement to make, one that may shock a lot of you." Archer nods to me as it's my cue, and I walk out onto the stage with Oak, spotting Natalya beaming at the front of the crowd encouragingly. "Eva Carmichael became Eva Byrne, my wife, over the winter break. She now lives with me in my cottage on the grounds. If any of you wonder why you see your teacher kissing his student or sneaking her into his home." I notice him pointedly glaring at Dimitry, who looks furious at our sudden announcement.

Many students whisper to each other, and everyone looks confused or disgusted.

"I understand that this is very unusual, but Eva and I fell in love, and we got married. It's that simple. If you have questions, I will accept them now."

Elias smirks and lifts his hand. "Yes, Elias."

"Did you fuck her in the classroom, professor?"

Oak's temple bulges as he clenches his jaw. "Anyone who has anything stupid to say will be spending the morning with professor Nitkin. I'll only accept respectful questions." He nods at Gavril, who walks forward, grabs Elias by the elbow, and drags him out of the room.

The entire hall of students falls silent, making me wonder what Gavril Nitkin does to people.

How does he inspire such fear in students born to be killers?

"Any other questions?" I ask.

A young boy, who I don't recognize, raises his hand. "Yes, Jaden."

"Does that mean you will no longer be teaching her, as surely there may be a question of unfair treatment when it comes to grades?"

His question gets a few snickers, but I suppose it's a fair one. "Eva will remain in my classes that I teach, but professor Nitkin will grade her papers and exams to avoid any potential issue of favoritism."

Oak glances around the rest of the pupils. "Anyone else."

My stomach sinks when I see Dimitry lift his hand.

"What, Dimitry?" Oak snaps, tension coiling through him.

"Is that why you assaulted me in the after-party at the ruins, professor?" he asks.

We were expecting him not to drop this stupid claim of assault. It may be true that he hit Dimitry, but Dimitry tried to touch me.

"Do you mean the time I defended Eva when you tried to tear her panties off of her while she screamed at you not to?" Oak asks, calm as I've ever seen him.

Dimitry's cheeks redden, and he can't meet Oak's gaze. "Whatever," he says, waving his hand.

A lot of the students laugh at him. Hopefully, that should put the matter to bed, but if he pursues it, we'll fight him.

"Any more useless questions?" Oak asks. He's met with silence, and he nods. "Good, everyone, go to breakfast."

All the students chatter as they rise from their seats, heading out of the hall toward the cafeteria. Natalya, Adrianna, and Camilla linger, beckoning me over.

I turn to Oak. "I'll see you later. I'm going to attend breakfast with my friends."

He smiles and slides his hand behind my neck, pulling me close for a quick kiss. "Okay, don't be late home tonight."

I swallow hard as my cheeks heat, turning around to find quite a few students gawking at me. I rush to Natalya's side.

"I can't believe you are married to that God of a man," she says, shaking her head.

I tilt my head. "Are you saying he's out of my league?"

"No, God no. You are gorgeous, but he's our fucking principal."

Camilla laughs. "Perhaps I'll try to bag Nitkin."

All of us look at her like she's insane.

"What? He's hot."

"Yeah, and fucking crazy," Adrianna says, rolling her eyes. "No one would voluntarily get with that man. He's a sadist."

Camilla's cheeks redden, but she shrugs. "Doesn't take away from how gorgeous he is, and now I know it's possible…" she laughs. "I'm joking, though."

"Right," Natalya says. "It's your funeral."

I shake my head. "We'd best get to breakfast before everyone eats all the good food."

Natalya hooks her arm with mine. "I can see now why you were so eager to spend winter break here, alone," she stresses the last word, and I can't help but smile.

"Yeah, sorry I didn't tell you, but it was too soon." I shake my head. "I never expected we'd get married."

"I do have a bone to pick with you." Natalya pouts at me. "Why the fuck wasn't I your maid of honor?"

I laugh, shaking my head. "Because no one was invited."

As we enter the cafeteria, Jeanie Doyle steps into our path.

"What the fuck do you want now, Doyle?" Camilla asks.

She holds her hands up. "I merely want to say fair play to Eva for bagging the hottest teacher in school." She gives me a genuinely impressed look. "I underestimated you, Carmichael. Or should I say, Byrne?"

"Eva would do," I deadpan.

"Fair enough." She holds her hand out to me, and I regard it warily. I take it and shake, knowing if I show fear, it will boost her ego. "Congrats, Eva." She winks and then walks away to sit back down with Anita and Kerry, the two girls who attacked me on my first night here.

Being stabbed was horrible, but in a way, I think they bought Oak and me together faster. The tension between us started from that night and only elevated from there.

"What was that all about?" Adrianna asks as we take our seats at our usual table.

"No idea," I say.

"You've probably won the admiration or envy of every girl in the school," Natalya says, glancing around at the looks we're getting. "Practically every girl had a crush on the brooding, grumpy Principal Byrne, and you've put a ring on it."

Adrianna laughs. "I still can't quite believe it. I mean, it's crazy, right?"

"Yeah," I say, grinning. "Oak's expecting a bit of fallout from parents when the words get out, though."

Camilla waves her hand. "Most of the parents won't give a shit about the principal marrying a pupil. After all, he's off the market. My dad wouldn't even bat an eyelid hearing the news."

"Mine either," Adrianna agrees. "It's not like this is a normal school."

I relax at their reassurance, but Oak is sure some parents will kick up a storm. We'll have to deal with it when it happens. For now, I'm going to enjoy being newlywed and ignore the haters.

I ADJUST my backpack as I walk down the path toward the cottage. A sense of someone watching me makes the hair on the back of my neck stand on end.

"Eva," Elias calls.

My stomach dips as I turn to face him. "Elias, what do you want?"

He smirks and crosses his arms over his chest, leaning against a nearby wall. "Why don't you come and sit?" He signals to the wall.

I shake my head. "I'm alright here, thanks."

His eyes narrow. "Just because you're now the principal's little pet, don't get any ideas about Natalya and me." He stalks toward me. "You may think it gives you power, but with Natalya, you stay the fuck out of it."

I glare at him. "Why don't you stop messing with Nat and admit that you have feelings for her already?"

His jaw clenches, and he stops moving toward me. "I don't know what you're talking about."

I tilt my head. "I think you know what I mean. Why else would you be so obsessed with her?"

"Obsessed?" he asks, his brow furrowing. "I'm not…" He trails off as if only now realizing that he's obsessed with my friend.

"Did the penny just drop?" I ask, teasing.

Elias glares at me, fists clenching as he moves forward. "Just stay out of my way, understand?"

"I understood you the first time, Elias. And have I gotten in your way since?"

Elias smirks and leans back. "No, but I'm saying don't get *Oakley* involved."

"I had no intention of doing so." I glare at him. "Now, if you don't mind. I'm going home."

The crunch of gravel as someone approaches draws our attention as Oak marches toward us. His eyes are on Elias, and his fists are clenched. "Elias, what the fuck are you doing here?" he growls.

I set my hand on Oak's chest. "It's okay. We were talking."

Elias' grin is so cocky it makes me want to punch him. "Yeah, are you getting so jealous Eva can't even talk to guys anymore?"

"Not boys that fucking throttle her in empty corridors," Oak growls.

Elias holds his hand up in surrender. "Alright, calm down. I'm leaving." He turns away and strolls down the path back toward the school.

"What did he want?" Oak asks.

"Just asking about Natalya. I think he has a thing for her."

"I doubt it, Eva. The boy has spent his time here tormenting Natalya."

I shake my head. "Why can't anyone else see it?"

"See what?"

"Nothing," I mutter, wondering if I've imagined it. I see the way Elias looks at her from across a room. It reminds me of how Oak looks at me. Hungry, possessive. It's as if he wants to own her in every way possible, both physically and emotionally. Clearly, he doesn't have the emotional maturity to go about it like a man and has to torment her instead.

"How was your day?" Oak asks as we enter the cottage.

I throw my bag down and slump onto the sofa. "Weird."

"Weird?" he asks.

I nod. "Yeah, to start, Jeanie congratulated me."

Oak raises a brow.

"She was being genuine and told me she admired me for bagging the hottest teacher in school."

He laughs. "Is that right?"

I nudge him in the ribs for being cocky. "And then,

everyone was giving me high-fives or giving me filthy looks, but it was better than I expected."

"Good." He sits next to me. "I must admit, my day was tough."

"Parents?" I ask.

He shakes his head. "Not yet, but I had to sack Alice Jameson today."

"Oh no, she was my favorite teacher. Why?"

He rubs a hand across the back of his neck. "She had a lot to say about us, and tried to make a pass at me, which I refused and dismissed her."

I clench my fists. "What did she try to do?"

"She tried to kiss me, but she didn't get close." Oak leans toward me and presses his lips to mine. "No other woman will ever come within an inch of these lips," he breathes.

"Good," I reply, pressing my lips to his. "Because they're mine."

He smiles. "Yes, they are." He yanks me onto his lap. "I'm yours, and you're mine." He wraps his fingers around the back of my neck and pulls my lips to his. "I missed you today."

I smile against his lips. "That's silly."

"It's not. I miss you whenever we're not together." He kisses me, deepening it. "Before I go past the point of stopping, I need to make us dinner."

I groan as he slides me off his lap and escapes toward the kitchen. "And then I'll devour you." He winks and disappears into the kitchen.

After insisting he's not the best cook, it appears he's pretty skilled in the kitchen. I love his food. I love him. I flop back against the back of the sofa and rest my head, smiling to myself.

The next few months may be turbulent after the unveiling of our relationship, but we can get through anything together.

35

EPILOGUE

EVA

"Class dismissed," Oak announces, eyes fixed on me. "Mrs. Byrne, stay behind."

A few students snicker, and Natalya gives me a knowing glance. "I'll catch up with you later."

I nod in response and remain seated at my desk, staring at my husband. The look in his eyes is one of pure lust as the last student leaves the room, shutting the door behind him.

"How can I help you, sir?" I ask, twirling a strand of hair around my finger.

He stands, approaching me as I remain seated behind my desk. "I wished to discuss Spring Break since it starts tomorrow."

I raise a brow. "And what exactly did you want to discuss Spring Break for?" I ask.

He grabs hold of the collar of my blouse and yanks me up to stand in front of him, eyes blazing with a mix of desire and irritation. "We didn't have a honeymoon. I'm going to take you to Naples."

My eyes widen, and I shake my head. "Isn't it dangerous considering—"

"My past?" he finishes for me.

I nod in response.

"It's been fifteen years since I saw my family. None of them would recognize me now, and my passport is in my new name." I shrug. "I think we can risk it so you can taste the best pizza in the world."

I tilt my head. "I'm not sure any pizza is worth risking your life over." I shake my head. "Why don't we go somewhere nearer?" I suggest.

There's a strange flash in Oak's eyes. "I just heard my grandmother passed away, and her funeral is in three days." His eyes flick to the ring on my finger. "The same woman who gave me that ring."

"I'm sorry," I say, placing a hand on his chest. "Surely you can't safely attend the funeral?"

"No, but I can watch from afar. There are old ruins about seven hundred yards away, and I want to be there while they bury her."

It all sounds risky, and after doing a little research on his family, they are just as dangerous as my parents were. "Okay, but we have to be very careful, Oak. When you got shot by my mother—"

He cuts me off. "It was nothing more than a superficial flesh wound."

"I know, but it didn't mean I wasn't scared." I cling onto the front of his shirt. "I can't lose you."

"You won't." He presses his lips to mine, and I kiss him back. It quickly turns heated as I glance at the glass door into the classroom, clutching onto his shoulders. "I should get going."

He yanks me harder against his body. "No chance. I have a free period, and so do you."

"The door," I warn.

He grunts and then goes to pull the blind down over the window. "Now, bend over for me, wife."

I do as he says, a thrill spreading through me at the tone of his voice.

Ever since we announced our marriage to the rest of the students, we've been a little reckless, but then we have no one to answer to. After all, Oak runs this school. There were a few complaints from parents, but Oak assured them that their students were in safe hands now that he was bound to one woman only.

Oak pulls open the drawer in his desk and grabs a bottle of lube, making me shake with anticipation.

"Not here," I murmur, shaking my head.

He smirks and pulls out the ball gag, holding it up. "Yes, I want to fuck your ass over my desk."

I clench my thighs together at the thought. It's as if he has to push it one step further each time. Thankfully, we only have a couple of months until I graduate, and then I will enroll in a veterinary school nearby in the fall.

He gently slides his hand over my bottom, dipping a finger into my soaking wet arousal.

I cry out as he circles my clit with the pad of his thumb, driving me crazy.

"Quiet, baby girl, or the entire school will hear." He slides the ball gag into my mouth and secures it. "That should help."

He drops to his knees and buries his tongue deep inside of me, tasting me like a man starving for pussy.

Our desire for each other knows no bounds. It just builds the more time we spend together, making functioning like a normal person difficult. All I can think about is him.

Oak dips two fingers deep inside of me, stroking them expertly and hitting the spot that makes me cry into the ball gag. I find it impossible to understand how he can know my body even better than I do.

I watch as he reaches for the lube, and then I feel him squirt the cold liquid onto my sensitive hole. Slowly, he eases his fingers inside, stretching me, forcing me to moan around the gag in my mouth.

Within moments, he has me stretched out enough and squirts lube onto his thick cock, lining himself up with my tight ring of muscles. His rough hands tighten around my hips, and I hold my breath, waiting for him to impale me with his cock.

He jerks me back against him with force and slams forward, taking me like a savage. Once inside me, he moves his hips with slow, deliberate movements. He knows I want it hard and fast and can't even beg him for it. Instead, all I can do is squirm and make strangled noises behind the gag.

"That's it, baby girl, take my cock in that ass." He spanks my right ass cheek and then my left, rutting into me harder as I feel his resolve to tease me slipping. "You are mine," he growls, leaning down to press kisses against my still-clothed back. "You belong to me."

"Harder," I cry behind the gag, but it just comes out muffled.

He grabs the back of my neck and forces me upward, sending a thrilling heat right to my core. "What was that?" He grazes his teeth over the back of my neck. "I'm afraid I can't hear you, and neither can the school."

He groans and pulls out of my ass, flipping me onto my back as if I weigh nothing. And then, without giving me a second to get used to the new position, he buries himself back inside of my ass.

I cry against the gag, the pleasure and the pain blending into one mind-blowing sensation that turns me into putty in his hands.

"Take it, baby girl," he grunts, gazing down at me with such desire it makes me feel like the most beautiful girl in the world. "I want to watch my wife as she comes on my cock." He leans down and chokes me a little with his hand, making sure he squeezes hard enough to leave a bruise. "I want you to squirt all over my shirt, so I have to change it before my next class. Do you understand?"

My eyes roll back in my head as his hips move faster, harder, driving me to the edge of the cliff so hard it feels like he might break me in half before I make it.

"Come for me," he orders.

I can't deny him anything as my body shakes. Every muscle contracts as I squirt all over his shirt, making a mess. Stars burst behind my eyelids as I clamp them shut, moaning shamelessly into the ball gag.

Oak squeezes my throat harder. "Look at me while I come in your ass," he orders.

I force my eyes open and watch my husband as he thrusts two more times before climaxing, too. The look on his face is so utterly addictive as he fills me with his cum. He releases my throat and gazes into my eyes adoringly for a few moments, watching me, utterly submitting to his every want and need. And then he slides his cock out of me and replaces it with a large buttplug. "I want it there for the rest of the day. Don't remove it." He unfastens the gag and chucks it on his desk. "Do you understand?"

"Yes, sir," I say as he captures my lips and kisses me deeply.

"Be a good girl and get to your next lesson."

I jump off the desk and walk away from him, squealing as he spanks my ass as I go.

"Quickly, or I might throw you over my desk again," he warns.

I walk away, finding it impossible to believe that a man like him could want me that much. He may have darkness deep inside of him, but it only makes me love him more, perhaps because deep down under my desperation to remain untouched by the darkness of my parent's world, a part of it did infect me.

Oak watches the proceedings through a pair of binoculars, while I remain seated on a deck chair, keeping out of sight as he instructed.

I can see the anguish as he watches her funeral from afar, and it pains me not to comfort him. So, I stand, ignoring his order, and wrap my arms around his waist.

"Are you okay?" I ask.

He shakes his head. "No, my father, brother and sister aren't here." His brow furrows. "My uncle is acting like he's calling all the shots." He pulls out his phone, typing something in Italian into google. And then, he drops his phone to the floor, sinking down along with it.

"Oak, what is it?"

He shakes his head and I pick up the phone, scrolling through an Italian news article. It's about his two siblings and father. Apparently, they died last year in a car accident in Sicily.

"They're all dead," he mutters.

I run a hand through his hair and kneel in front of him. "I'm so sorry."

His Adam's apple bobs as he swallows. "I don't know how I didn't know." His brow furrows. "My grandma's death was all over the papers, but their death wasn't. At least not here in Naples."

A tear trickles down his cheek as he stares blankly at me.

"You didn't know," I say, pressing my lips to his cheek to wipe away the tear. "It's not your fault."

Oak nods. "I know, I just…" He shakes his head. "It was a tough decision, leaving everyone I loved behind, but I knew I couldn't be a part of the bloodshed. I guess I always knew it would come to this. My family slaughtered."

"It says they were in a car accident."

Oak laughs humorlessly. "Don't be so naïve, Eva. My father had a long-standing feud with the mafia boss of Sicily. His death was no accident."

I swallow hard and ignore the uneasiness in the pit of my stomach. "At least you escaped this world." I run a hand through my hair. "You might have been dead otherwise."

He meets my gaze and sighs. "You're right." He stands and grabs his binoculars, glancing over at his grandmother's funeral. "My mother is still alive and my grandmother died of very uneventful old age. At least I can be thankful for that."

I wrap my arm around his waist and hug him, and

we remain there long after the funeral is over and everyone has disappeared. Oak finally stands when the sun dips below the horizon in the distance. "We should get going if we're going to make our reservation at Sorbillo."

I shake my head. "We can cancel if you'd like."

His brow furrows. "Why would we do that? It's the best pizza in Naples."

"Because you just witnessed your grandmother's funeral from afar and found out your brother, sister and father are dead."

His chest heaves. "I want to eat pizza where I used to visit as a child. It's a good way to remember them, isn't it?"

I nod. "Yes, of course." I can't imagine what he's feeling right now. "Let's get going."

He leads me to the rental car and we head down the windy roads back toward Naples from Ercolano. It's about a twenty-minute drive back to the city, where Oak parks near to the restaurant. We walk in and it's busy; I notice a glimmer of tears in Oak's eyes as he glances around the little pizzeria, so I squeeze his hand.

He smiles, but it doesn't quite reach his eyes.

All I want is to take away his pain, but I know it's impossible. I can only be there for him. The server seats us after a fifteen minute wait at a small table at the back.

Oak clutches onto my hand over the table. "It's just as I remember."

"Did you come here a lot when you were a child?"

He nods. "Special occasions mostly, but because we were such a large family, there were lots of those." He laughs. "We'd use any excuse for a Sorbillo pizza."

"It smells delicious in here." I lick my lips. "Can't wait to try them."

Oak links his fingers with mine and squeezes. "I love you, Eva." His expression turns serious. "So much." I notice he looks a little hesitant, as if he wants to say something, but isn't sure how.

"What is it?" I ask.

"We got married so fast, I never asked if you wanted kids in the future?"

I'm surprised by his question, but nod in response. "Yes, once I've finished school and I'm secure in a job, I'd love to start a family with you."

He smiles and his shoulders sag in relief. "That's good. I've always wanted a family, even though I never believed it would be possible for me."

"Why not?"

"I believed I was too broken and dark to find love."

I squeeze his hand on the table. "That's ridiculous. I love every part of you, even the darkness."

He smiles. "I know. That's why I'm pretty sure I won the damn lottery by finding my way to you."

A server approaches with our pizzas. "A margarita?" he asks.

I hold my hand up and he places it in front of me.

"And diavolo for you," he says, setting it down in front of Oak.

I know it's eating away at him not being able to speak Italian here, but we both agreed it was safer, so we didn't raise questions about his background.

"Thank you," I say, smiling at him.

He nods. "Buon appetito." He walks away, leaving us to enjoy our food.

I tilt my head. "Is this pizza better than yours?"

"For certain," he says, laughing. "Mine isn't a patch on proper wood fired Neapolitan pizza."

"I'll be the judge of that." I cut a piece with my knife and fork and lift it to my mouth, tasting it. "Oh my God," I say, still chewing. "It's the best pizza in the world."

He smiles smugly. "I told you."

"You're right, it's better than yours, but yours was very good for homemade."

He shakes his head and tucks into his own pizza. "Always so diplomatic, my wife. One of the many reasons I love you so much."

"I love you, too," I say, feeling a little overwhelmed as I stare into his eyes.

Ironically, the one place I knew I wouldn't fit in was the place I found my soul mate. It's crazy to think that the principal of a school that stands for everything I despise about our world turned out to be the love of my life.

THANK you for reading the first book in the Syndicate Academy, I hope you enjoyed reading Eva's & Oak's story as much as I enjoyed writing it!

If you are interested in following the students at the academy, then the next book in the series follows Natalya Gurin, who featured in Wicked Daddy, also as Mikhail's sister, and Elias Morales, in Cruel Bully.

Cruel Bully: A Dark Mafia Academy Romance

He's spent years tormenting me, but now he wants to own me.

I've spent my life at SA trying to avoid Elias Morales, King of the syndicate academy. He hated me on first sight, and I learned to hate him. A hatred that never had any cause, but defined us both. Elias may be the most devastatingly handsome boy, but he's cruel to the core.

Senior year is finally here, and my escape is in sight. I'll never have to see my tormentor again once I graduate. But, Elias doesn't intend to let me go that easily. He wants to make sure I'll never forget him, no matter how hard I try.

He blackmails me when he finds dirt on my family. Information that could tear our world apart. I will not let him destroy the one thing I care about. Which means I have to be his pet for the rest of the year.

He intends to own me and claim my innocence on his terms. And leave me broken and destroyed in ways I never imagined were possible. I thought I knew what this sick and twisted hatred was between us. They say there is a fine line between love and hate.

I can already feel the line blurring as my tormentor lays his claim. The question is, will I walk out of the academy free or will Elias finally break me?

Cruel Bully is the second book in the Syndicate Academy Series. This book can be read as a standalone and has a happily ever after ending. This is a dark bully romance story and has dark themes, hot scenes, violence, content some readers may find upsetting, and bad language.

ALSO BY BIANCA COLE

The Syndicate Academy

Cruel Bully: A Dark Mafia Academy Romance

Chicago Mafia Dons

Merciless Defender: A Dark Forbidden Mafia Romance

Violent Leader: A Dark Enemies to Lovers Captive Mafia Romance

Evil Prince: A Dark Arranged Marriage Romance

Boston Mafia Dons Series

Cruel Daddy: A Dark Mafia Arranged Marriage Romance

Savage Daddy: A Dark Captive Mafia Roamnce

Ruthless Daddy: A Dark Forbidden Mafia Romance

Vicious Daddy: A Dark Brother's Best Friend Mafia Romance

Wicked Daddy: A Dark Captive Mafia Romance

New York Mafia Doms Series

Her Irish Daddy: A Dark Mafia Romance

Her Russian Daddy: A Dark Mafia Romance

Her Italian Daddy: A Dark Mafia Romance

Her Cartel Daddy: A Dark Mafia Romance

Romano Mafia Brother's Series

Her Mafia Daddy: A Dark Daddy Romance

Her Mafia Boss: A Dark Romance

Her Mafia King: A Dark Romance

Bratva Brotherhood Series

Bought by the Bratva: A Dark Mafia Romance

Captured by the Bratva: A Dark Mafia Romance

Claimed by the Bratva: A Dark Mafia Romance

Bound by the Bratva: A Dark Mafia Romance

Taken by the Bratva: A Dark Mafia Romance

Wynton Series

Filthy Boss: A Forbidden Office Romance

Filthy Professor: A First Time Professor And Student Romance

Filthy Lawyer: A Forbidden Hate to Love Romance

Filthy Doctor: A Fordbidden Romance

Royally Mated Series

Her Faerie King: A Faerie Royalty Paranormal Romance

Her Alpha King: A Royal Wolf Shifter Paranormal Romance

Her Dragon King: A Dragon Shifter Paranormal Romance

Her Vampire King: A Dark Vampire Romance

ABOUT THE AUTHOR

I love to write stories about over the top alpha bad boys who have heart beneath it all, fiery heroines, and happily-ever-after endings with heart and heat. My stories have twists and turns that will keep you flipping the pages and heat to set your kindle on fire.

For as long as I can remember, I've been a sucker for a good romance story. I've always loved to read. Suddenly, I realized why not combine my love of two things, books and romance?

My love of writing has grown over the past four years and I now publish on Amazon exclusively, weaving stories about dirty mafia bad boys and the women they fall head over heels in love with.

If you enjoyed this book please follow me on Amazon, Bookbub or any of the below social media platforms for alerts when more books are released.

Printed in Great Britain
by Amazon